MAIN CHANCE

Dear Charlotte,

Merry Christmas.

please read my book in good health — I hope that one day you can find it in yourself to forgive me.

Love,

Colin Forbes

By the same author

BLOOD STORM
NO MERCY
THE CELL
THE VORPAL BLADE
RHINOCEROS
SINISTER TIDE
THIS UNITED STATE
THE SISTERHOOD
THE CAULDRON
PRECIPICE
FURY
THE POWER
BY STEALTH
CROSS OF FIRE
WHIRLPOOL
SHOCKWAVE
THE GREEK KEY
DEADLOCK
THE JANUS MAN
COVER STORY
TERMINAL
THE LEADER AND THE DAMNED
DOUBLE JEOPARDY
THE STOCKHOLM SYNDICATE
AVALANCHE EXPRESS
THE STONE LEOPARD
YEAR OF THE GOLDEN APE
TARGET FIVE
THE PALERMO AMBUSH
THE HEIGHTS OF ZERVOS
TRAMP IN ARMOUR

THE MAIN CHANCE

COLIN FORBES

POCKET BOOKS

LONDON • SYDNEY • NEW YORK • TORONTO

First published in Great Britain by Simon & Schuster UK Ltd, 2005
This edition first published by Pocket Books, 2006
An imprint of Simon & Schuster UK Ltd
A CBS COMPANY

1 3 5 7 9 10 8 6 4 2

Simon & Schuster UK Ltd
Africa House
64–78 Kingsway
London WC2B 6AH

www.simonsays.co.uk

Simon & Schuster Australia
Sydney

A CIP catalogue record for this book is available
from the British Library

ISBN 978-1-8473-9287-9

Typeset in Plantin by M Rules
Printed and bound in Denmark by
Nørhaven Paperback A/S

Author's Note

All characters portrayed are creatures of the author's imagination and bear no relationship to any living person.

The same principle of pure invention also applies to all residences, villages, towns, districts, apartments, their occupants, institutions, organizations and mountains both in Great Britain and abroad.

THE MAIN CHANCE

Prologue

There was nothing to warn Tweed he was setting out on the strangest case of his career, as Deputy Director of the SIS and, earlier, as Scotland Yard's ace detective.

It was a glorious March day as he drove well south of London with his second-in-command, Paula Grey, seated beside him. She studied a map, navigating for him; they had left the motorway on her instructions, were now driving south-west along a wide country road. On either side rose steep banks topped with hedges, green leaf-shoots already showing. The sun shone down out of a clear blue sky. Occasionally they passed an isolated house, its front garden covered with crocuses and sheaves of daffodils.

'This is the life,' Paula remarked, glancing out of the window. Attractive, slim, thirty-something, jet black hair reaching her neck framed a well-shaped face.

'Any idea where we're going?' Tweed asked.

'Of course I have. Hengistbury Manor is buried

deep inside what they call The Forest, which is vast. A weird area to site the headquarters of the Main Chance Bank.'

'Richest private bank in the world, so Buchanan said.'

It had started early that morning, when Tweed arrived at SIS headquarters, at Park Crescent in London. All his key staff were assembled in his spacious first-floor office. The tall ex-reporter Bob Newman sprawled in an armchair. Typically, Harry Butler, the Cockney, perched on the floor, Paula sat at her desk in a corner near the windows. Marler, ace marksman, stood next to Pete Nield.

Tweed had hardly settled behind his antique desk, a present from his staff, when the phone rang. He raised his eyebrows. 8 a.m. Who was calling at this hour?

Monica, his secretary for many years, a middle-aged woman who wore her hair tied back in a bun, answered. Covering the mouthpiece she called out: 'Commander Buchanan of the Yard is phoning you urgently.'

'Bit early, Roy,' Tweed began, after signalling Paula to listen in on her extension.

'It's an emergency,' Buchanan's crisp voice told him. 'I need to ask you an important favour. You've heard of the Main Chance Bank, richest in this country, maybe in the world. Totally independent. No shares on the

Stock Exchange. Controlled by Bella Main. Eighty-four years old with all her marbles. Met you at a party a year ago. Was very impressed. Could you make it down to see her today?'

'Where is she?'

'Hengistbury Manor. Located in an area called The Forest.'

'So where the devil is that?'

Paula, a map open, was signalling. She had already located it. Tweed nodded, spoke again to Buchanan.

'Forget that question. Paula has it. Now why on earth does Bella Main want to see me?'

'I don't know. She wouldn't say . . .'

'Roy,' Tweed growled, 'then why is it important to you, for Heaven's sake?'

'The government thinks there's something funny about that bank.'

'Funny in what way?' Tweed demanded.

'I don't know.' Buchanan was sounding desperate. 'I think maybe several rich ministers have money in the bank. Just a guess. But at the moment I'm choked up with my present job, all my present problems. You know I've been appointed Commander of the Anti-Terrorist Squad? Please make the effort. Could be important . . .'

'In what way?'

'No idea.'

'You're a barrel of information. When does she expect me?'

'This morning, Tweed. As near eleven as you can make it. I've made an appointment on your behalf.'

'Without consulting me? Thanks a lot!'

'I'm sorry, but I'm really in a jam. I told her you might take Paula with you. I do apologize.'

'Get back to chasing terrorists. We'll go. You owe me a big one.' Tweed slammed down the phone before Buchanan could say anything else, looked across at Paula. 'Is it easy to find?'

'No, but I'll get us there.' She turned to Harry, who was peering over her shoulder. 'Why are you so interested?'

'Just curious about where you're going.' He jabbed a thick finger on her map. 'That's it?'

'Yes, it is.' She stood up. 'I'd better put something on. It could be chilly down there. And Tweed is pawing the floor.' Her chief had already slipped on a camel-hair overcoat, was standing by the door. She was inside a fur-lined leather jacket in seconds. She sat on her chair, checked her 6.35mm Beretta automatic was tucked snugly inside the holster attached to her lower right leg. She had earlier checked the 7.65mm was inside her hip holster. She jumped up.

'Ready and willing!'

'Then let's get moving,' Tweed said.

The phone rang. Tweed shook his head as Monica answered. 'I'm not here,' he warned.

'You are for this one,' Monica told him. 'It's Philip

Cardon. From abroad as usual, I expect.'

Tweed perched on the edge of his desk, signalled to Paula, who darted back to her desk. They lifted their receivers at the same moment. Tweed's impatience was replaced by a tone of genuine pleasure.

'Philip, you old dog. Haven't heard from you for ages. How is the world?'

'Is this line secure?' Philip's voice was unusually abrupt.

'If it isn't we're out of business.'

'This call will be brief. I have a deep-cover agent. He tells me Calouste Doubenkian is on his way to Britain. Could be there already. You know who I mean?'

'Vaguely. Never made his acquaintance.'

'You don't want to. He's very dangerous, enormously powerful. My information is that he's on his way in connection with something concerning you.'

'In what respect, Philip? I can't imagine why.'

'Neither can I. But watch your back. I'll call when I've dug up more data.'

Tweed heard a click. Philip had ended the call suddenly. He put down his phone as Paula and Monica replaced theirs. He shrugged as he opened the door, ready to dash down the stairs to his car with Paula at his heels. As Tweed opened the front door she glanced back. Harry had followed them silently down the staircase, was now scuttling out the back way where the transport was kept.

'I wonder what Harry was up to in such a rush?' she mused as she fastened her seat belt.

'Working on some job. You know I give them all latitude to do their own thing.'

'Philip sounded unusually tense,' she remarked as Tweed drove away from Park Crescent, heading towards the motorway which would take them south. 'Maybe we should bother about this Doubenkian,' she suggested.

'Oh, I don't think so,' he said dismissively.

'Well I think we should bother,' she persisted. 'Philip knows what he's talking about. Always.'

'Belt up,' Tweed said cheerfully. 'We're going to have an uneventful day in the country in this lovely spring weather. Relax.'

'Said he was dangerous,' Paula went on.

Tweed looked at her, smiled. He didn't make any further comment, settled down behind the wheel to enjoy a peaceful day.

1

They were driving deep into the countryside, having left the motorway ages ago. The sun still shone out of a clear sea-blue sky. They had met no traffic for a long stretch. Nor were there any more isolated houses with front gardens blooming with spring flowers. Paula's mobile buzzed. She had a short conversation.

'That was Monica,' she said as she pocketed it.

'Really?' said Tweed as though his thoughts were miles away.

'Monica traced where Philip called from. Somewhere in Belgium. Don't know where. They'd only give Monica the country. I didn't think that was one of Philip's happy hunting areas.'

'It isn't normally. But he roams round the Continent.'

'Have you noticed the light aircraft that has been flying roughly on a parallel course to this road?'

'Yes. I have noticed.'

'Maybe it's Marler watching over us.'

'No. Not his aircraft.'

'It's flashing a light now, on and off. What's it doing?'

'No idea.'

'It's stopped. It's flying away north now.'

'So it is.'

She glanced at Tweed. He was answering automatically, as though his mind was elsewhere. He had slowed down as they approached the crest of a high hill, was almost crawling. From the crest they had a panoramic view of the countryside ahead before the lane sloped downwards to a long straight stretch. No more than half a mile ahead, a huge tractor was perched on top of a small hill. The field behind it was ploughed. Large chunks of soil paraded back as far as the eye could see. Tweed stopped, turned off his engine. In the sudden silence the only noise was a faint whine. The digger was stopped but the driver, a vague motionless figure, had kept his motor running. Tweed started his own engine, began moving slowly down the hill. Paula had expected speed. Checking the speedometer she saw they were crawling at a maximum of 25 m.p.h.

Puzzled, she glanced at Tweed. She had never seen him look more relaxed. She was itching to press her foot on the accelerator.

'You could move faster along this stretch,' she suggested. 'We can see miles ahead. Nothing coming the other way.'

'You're right,' he agreed quietly.

They began moving at forty towards the bottom of the hill. Paula sank back in her seat. This was the life. She had her window down and the freshest air in the world filled her nostrils.

They reached the bottom of the hill and Tweed slowed to thirty. Paula glanced at him. He was in a strange mood, but he was probably turning over in his mind aspects of his visit to Bella Main's HQ.

'I'm looking forward to seeing what Hengistbury Manor is like . . .' she began.

'You have got your seat belt fixed properly?' he asked with an edge to his voice.

'Of course I have. Ever since we left Park Crescent.'

'Then sit up straight. And don't chatter. I want to concentrate.'

'All right.' She was peeved. 'I'll be as quiet as a church mouse.'

'Do that.'

They were now moving at forty. Tweed suddenly dropped to thirty again. Then down to twenty-five. He braked suddenly. Paula saw the giant digger just ahead, almost above them, its fearsome caterpillars grinding down through a gap in the hedge. It was making the devil of a noise as it crashed down onto the road.

For a second the massive left-hand caterpillar track, revolving like a terrible mincing machine, filled the windscreen. It passed within inches of their front bumper. Paula was terrified. Tweed sat very still.

The digger's momentum carried it forward across the road as it headed into a gap in the hedge on the other side of the road, out of control. Paula had a glimpse of the driver, wearing a cloth cap and workman's clothes. Panicking, he was desperately trying to find the brake lever, wobbling about inside the cab. Beyond the gap was a smooth slope on the right-hand side, just wide enough for the digger to ascend it to safety.

But to the left of the smooth slope half the gap fell sheer into a rocky gorge. Still panicking, the driver lost control. As the machine mounted the slope the left-hand caterpillar slid over the edge. The whole machine toppled over sideways, plunging into the gorge at speed. Paula had a grisly glimpse of the cab with its driver falling upside down and heard the hideous sound of crushing metal.

The driver had managed to jerk open a window, his head and shoulders projecting. The immense weight of the machine thundered down onto his skull, crushing it to less than half its normal size. Paula let out her breath. Tweed gazed at the carnage for only a brief moment, then drove on down the lane.

'Shouldn't we check on him?' whispered Paula.

'No point. Dead as a dodo. Which was how we were supposed to end up.'

'Maybe we should report it to the police,' she suggested.

'We should *not*! We were supposed to end up inside this car, our bodies flattened like pancakes. Getting involved with the police would cause hours of delay, explanation we don't want to give.'

'Why?' she asked, her voice stronger.

'Obviously someone doesn't want us to reach Hengistbury Manor. It was well planned by a good organizer.'

Paula sensed Tweed didn't wish to pursue this notion. Tactfully she changed the subject.

'Hengistbury is a strange name.'

'Comes from hundreds of years ago. The Jutes – from Jutland – had landed on the Isle of Thanet. Under the command of Hengist and Horsa. They destroyed the Picts who were swarming south to kill the locals. They moved off Thanet and took over large sections of fertile land. It was the beginning of the establishment of the English race. Whoever founded the manor had a sense of history.'

They had reached the top of another hill. Tweed paused. Below the landscape changed dramatically. Instead of rolling open fields they were looking down on an endless sweep of dark green trees as far as the eye could see. Huge tall firs were so close together they looked like an immense cushion, branches often intermingling. Paula almost gasped.

'This must be The Forest, marked on my map. Seems to go on forever.'

'And somewhere inside there is the mansion.'

'Well, I've guided you on the right track.'

As they reached the bottom of the hill she indicated an ancient signpost pointing the way they were headed. *Hengistbury*. The sun, still blazing down, vanished. They were now driving through a dark tunnel, hemmed in overhead and on both sides by stands of firs with massive trunks. Tweed had put on his headlights full beam. Soon a massive ten-foot-high stone wall appeared on their left, continued for a long distance. It was topped by rolls of barbed wire.

'Have we reached Mrs Bella Main's property?' Paula wondered.

'I think so. She must have scores of acres . . .'

He had just spoken when his headlights illuminated closed wrought-iron gates breaking into the sky-high wall. Tweed glanced in his rear-view mirror, slowed, stopped. Paula glanced back, frowned.

'That car has been following us for a while. I saw it earlier.'

'It's Harry. He's pulled up behind us. Here he comes.'

This had happened before when either Tweed or Paula drove off on their own or together. A member of his dedicated staff would quietly follow them. Prior to the digger incident there had been other attempts in previous cases to kill Tweed. Tweed lowered his window as the Cockney arrived on foot.

'Lost you for a short while on the motorway,' Harry remarked. 'Got stuck in a traffic jam. Then caught on you'd taken the side road south-west. I—'

'Harry,' Tweed ordered, 'don't be seen. Creep up to those gates, see if there's a drive leading straight to the manor. Also check that track on the right opposite the gates. I'll want you to park your car out of sight but so you can see the manor if possible.'

Harry was off at a run, keeping close to the wall. He dropped to his knees, crawled a few paces, peered. He jerked his head to the right to glance at the track. Then he was racing back to the cars.

'What are you up to now?' Paula wondered.

'Wait.' Tweed turned to Harry, back at his window. The Cockney was grinning.

'Piece of cake. Drive runs straight to Buckingham Palace. I'll take the car into the undergrowth here, come round onto that track from behind. What's the game?'

'I'm hoping I'll be near a window so I can signal you by flashing my lighter. That is if anyone leaves the manor by car while we're inside. If so, follow them discreetly.'

'I'm always discreet. Have fun . . . Oh, there's a speakerphone in the nearest pillar. Let's hope they think you're respectable enough to let in!'

Tweed was on the move as Harry's car disappeared into a wilderness of undergrowth. Paula shivered. With the canopy of firs overhead it was chilly. Arriving opposite the tall gates, Tweed swung the car round ready for entrance.

'Wow!' exclaimed Paula. 'I see why he said Buckingham Palace.'

A wide straight drive of small pebbles led straight across parkland for a couple of hundred yards to the manor. The HQ of the Main Chance Bank was an ancient and enormous house obviously built in Elizabethan times. Twirly chimneys reared up everywhere from the roof. At each end of the immense span of the manor projected small extensions, the roofs again supporting more palisades of corkscrew-shaped chimneys. Smoke coiled up from many of them into the windless sky.

Tweed had opened his door to get out and approach the speakerphone when a man's cut-glass voice exploded from the instrument.

'Mr Tweed, Miss Grey, welcome to Hengistbury.'

The gates were already swinging open inwards. Slowly Tweed drove forward. In his rear-view mirror he saw them already closing behind him.

'Must be the finest example of Elizabethan architecture in England,' he commented.

'Fabulous,' Paula almost gasped. 'And so is the park.'

On either side of the drive stretched trim green lawn. On their left a tall fountain jetted high into the air, forming the letter 'H'. To their right the lawn was narrower, and beyond it The Forest's giant firs closed in as though ready to swallow up the park. Paula found them sinister.

'Nothing disturbing, I'm sure,' Tweed remarked.

'Don't be too sure,' Paula responded in a quiet voice.

2

Tweed parked near the base of a wide flight of marble steps leading up to a spacious terrace which ran the full length of the mansion. Other cars were parked nearby, including a large black stretch limousine. A uniformed chauffeur with a sneering expression stood by it and ignored the new arrivals.

Arriving on the terrace with Paula, Tweed noted all the small windows had leaded lights. At the top of the staircase was the entrance, a pair of large heavy mahogany doors. The left-hand door opened, and a tall good-looking man in his thirties walked out briskly to greet them. He wore a smart black suit, the trousers sharply creased, the jacket almost reaching his knees and a stiff, peaked collar. The uniform of a servant.

'Mr Tweed and Miss Grey, you are most welcome guests. I will lead the way. You could say I was the butler.'

The voice was the same cut-glass accent which had called to them through the speakerphone.

'Isn't he sure of his status?' Paula whispered humorously as they followed the erect figure inside.

'Shh,' Tweed reprimanded her as they entered a vast square hall with a woodblock floor. In three walls he could just make out closed mahogany doors. The butler led them to a door in the right-hand wall, paused, his hand on the door handle.

'I am Snape, sir. You are most punctual. Mrs Bella Main sends her apologies. She will not be long but one of her important clients arrived without an appointment.' His tone was disapproving. 'She will send him packing very shortly. This is the library.'

They entered another large room, the walls lined with bookcases, the shelves neatly stacked with leather-bound volumes. In an arch-shaped opening a log fire blazed and Paula welcomed the warmth: she was already finding the mansion claustrophobic. The only illumination came from the fire. Hardly any light from outside penetrated the room through the small windows.

A tall man, probably in his late forties, hurried across to meet them. He wore an expensive blue pinstriped suit; his shirt was pristine white, his tie Chanel. White cuffs decorated with gold links protruded from his sleeves. He was smiling and there was something dominant in his jutting jaw.

'I am Marshal Main, managing director of this outfit. You are the most interesting visitors we've had in a long time.'

'Why?' asked Tweed as Main shook hands with both of them.

'What can we offer you in the way of refreshment? I think just about anything is available.'

'Coffee would be pleasant,' Tweed replied.

'Me too, please', added Paula.

'How do you like it, sir?' enquired Snape, standing behind them as erect as a sentry.

'Black as sin. So does Paula.'

'Well –' Main burst out laughing – 'you're in the right place. Plenty of sin round here. Come and sit down.' He took Paula's arm, squeezed it, staring at her. She didn't like it.

As Snape left, closing the door silently, Main escorted them to an antique table circled with four armchairs near the fire. Paula was watching a woman further down the library. She was standing behind a hard-backed chair, listening quietly.

She was in her late thirties, Paula estimated, and extremely attractive. Slim, she had long beautifully coiffeured black hair reaching her shoulders. Her eyebrows were thick and below them her features were perfectly sculpted. Her eyes were large, her nose was straight and just long enough above a firm mouth and determined chin. She smiled at Paula, who immediately smiled back.

Main, who seemed to miss nothing, jumped up swiftly. All his movements were agilely quick.

'Oh, my God! I'm forgetting my manners. Lavinia, do come and join us.' He slid a spare armchair in between Tweed's and Paula's. 'This is Lavinia, my daughter. She's my heart's desire.'

Tweed thought the words odd as Lavinia settled herself next to him. She smiled, gazed at her father.

'Just so long as you don't try and carry that too far.'

'Why?' Tweed again asked Main.

'What?' he replied, puzzled.

'Mr Tweed is referring to your remark that we have the most interesting visitors we've had in a long time. Probably he's wondering if you say that to everyone who comes here,' she chaffed him in her appealing soft voice.

'Stuff and nonsense!' he barked, briefly annoyed. Turning to Tweed he exuded amiability again. 'Because you are Deputy Director of the SIS – and you've brought with you the lady you place most trust in. Also I can tell already you both have exceptional intellects and brainpower.'

'Bella always does her homework before she agrees to meet here,' Lavinia said.

'She always tries to counter me,' Main said irritably.

'I just like accuracy,' Lavinia told him.

'Which is why,' Main told them, 'she is the chief accountant.'

Snape appeared with a silver tray with the coffee. Placing small mats in front of Tweed and Paula, he poured from a large silver coffee pot. The china was Royal Doulton. Snape looked at Lavinia.

'Nothing for me,' she told him.

Snape had just left silently when the room exploded. The door was flung open, banging back against the panelled wall. A young woman flew into the library. Late twenties, Paula estimated. Long red hair, a pretty face with sensuous lips and staring green eyes. Lavinia leaned close to Paula, whispered.

'Sorry about this. She's a bit wild.'

Paula turned round. The redhead wore a low-cut top held up by thin shoulder straps. She had a good figure and wore well-pressed jeans. Paula found herself comparing her attire with Lavinia's: she wore a brown skirt which just reached her knees, and above that was a dark velvet jacket, half-zipped up. Underneath was a white blouse buttoned up to the neck. One hell of a contrast with what had just blown in.

The redhead darted forward, placed both hands on Tweed's shoulders. She was smiling broadly. Her voice was educated and husky as she spoke, hands still resting on Tweed.

'Since no one had the manners to invite me to the party, and no one's introducing me, I'll introduce myself. I am Crystal.' Her voice, aggressive when she arrived, was now quite calm. 'Daughter of the managing director. Not this one.' She glared at Marshal Main. 'My father is Warner Chance. Guess he'll be down in a minute.'

'Get yourself a chair, Crystal,' Lavinia invited. 'Join us.'

'I'm going to show Mr Tweed Pike's Peak. It's unique.' She bent down, her mouth close to Tweed's ear. 'Only view is from upstairs. A quick trip.'

Tweed stood up. He was curious to see more of the mansion and guessed his only opportunity was to accompany Crystal.

'Do excuse me. This sounds a rare sight.'

He followed her to the door which had been closed by Snape. They crossed the hall after Crystal had silently closed the library door behind them. At the rear of the hall she opened double doors with a flourish, stood back.

'It really is rather impressive,' she said in her calm voice.

He had to agree. About twenty feet beyond, a wide magnificent staircase with Elizabethan-style banisters mounted to the first floor. High up was a landing and here the staircase split to the right and to the left. When they reached the landing Crystal led the way up the right-hand section. They turned off a spacious landing and continued down a corridor with a window at the far end. She stopped by a door, took out a key, unlocked the door.

Tweed walked in ahead of her, then stopped. He was standing inside a bedroom with a large canopy bed. Behind him he heard her lock the door. Swinging round, he found her close to him, grinning. His voice was grim as he spoke to her.

'So where's the view of Pike's Peak?'

'That comes later.'

She did two things at once. Her hands slipped the shoulder straps down over her shoulders and arms. Her foot slid between his, her leg shoved against his knees. Caught off balance, he fell back on the bed and she was on top of him, speaking at machine-gun speed.

'I like a mature man. The kids have no *finesse*!'

Her full breasts were half-exposed. She was clawing at his clothes. He didn't fool with her. His hands grasped her bare shoulders, his grip firm. She was strong but he was stronger. He sat up, jerked her hard, pushed her off the bed, stood on the floor himself. A brief expression of disbelief crossed her face. She took a step towards him and he slapped her hard across the side of her face. She blinked.

'I liked that,' she said.

'Get yourself properly dressed. And fast!'

He walked to a cheval mirror, straightened up his clothes. Behind him she was slipping the straps back into their original position. He turned round.

'Your top was higher. Deal with it.'

He walked to the door while she obeyed him. He had turned the key when she ran up alongside him, rested a hand lightly on his arm. She shook her head, then spoke in a calm voice.

'Let me check the corridor. Make sure Snoop isn't prowling.'

'Snoop?'

'Snape. They got his name wrong. He snoops. When I am away I lock my door, take the key with me. Give me a sec.'

Unlocking the door, she strolled out slowly. She looked in both directions. Then she beckoned to him.

'Coast is clear.' She went on talking as she locked the door. 'I don't expect you to believe me but it wasn't my reputation I was bothered about. It was yours.'

'I believe you,' he said, not wanting to start her off again.

'You'd better see the view quickly. Give you something to talk about when we get back to the library.'

He glanced at her as they walked, a foot's space between them, to the window. She was so calm now, a different woman from what he had experienced in the bedroom. They reached the window and he stared.

The solid Forest stretched half a mile away from the extension he'd observed when coming up the drive. Then it stopped. Beyond it reared up a cone-shaped peak of sheer rock. It reminded Tweed of a miniature Matterhorn. He was so hypnotized by the spectacle he stood gazing at it until Crystal plucked at his arm.

'Maybe we ought to get back downstairs now. Any longer and that so-and-so Marshal will start wondering. Considering *his* way of life.'

'You're right.'

As they made their way back to the staircase and down it Crystal began talking in the same calm tone.

'Apparently, umpteen years ago a man called Pike owned the land that strange thing is on. Hence it came to be called Pike's Peak. The best hotel in Gladworth carries its name.'

'Gladworth?'

She sat down on a carpeted tread and Tweed sat beside her. He reached to her back, tucked her top into her jeans.

'Thanks,' she said. 'That wouldn't have looked good. Now, Gladworth. Motor down our drive. Get to the gates and you turn *left*. First place you come to is Gladworth, a very pretty village.'

'I think we'd better get back to the library,' Tweed said, standing up.

They were all there, still gathered round the antique table. In front of Marshal on the table was a bottle of whisky. He had a half-full glass in his hands and he drank the rest as they settled round the table. Paula smiled at Crystal, who smiled back. Tweed began to speak.

'The view was extraordinary. Magnificent and startling – this grim mountain-like rock appearing above the trees.'

'I was telling Mr Tweed its history. How a man called Pike—'

'She's always gabbling on about something.' The insult came from a tall heavily built youth who had just entered. In his early twenties, he had thick fair hair and a longish face with a sneering mouth. He was sloppily dressed in a white pullover half inside and half outside his baggy jeans. His manner had bully written all over it. Tweed glanced at Lavinia, was for the first time aware of the deep blue of her large eyes, as blue as the Mediterranean sea in summer. She raised her thick eyebrows.

'Go get me a chair, Crystal,' the youth ordered.

Crystal stood up, hands on her hips, glaring at him grimly.

'Everybody,' she said, her voice harsh, 'meet my beloved brother, Leo. Only seven years younger than me and hardly out of his nappies. Get your own chair!' she rasped, walking towards him. He raised a large hand to hit her.

A pair of hands descended on his shoulders from behind. A middle-aged man, shorter than Marshal but more heavily built, he had fair hair, a strong face and an air of self-control. At the first moment he saw him Tweed liked what he saw. Turning Leo round to face him, the man spoke quietly but with an air of authority.

'You will now go upstairs. Change into some decent clothes. I'll have a word with you later.'

Leo obediently walked towards the door. When he thought his father wasn't looking he turned, put his tongue out at Crystal.

'Before you go, Leo, apologize to your sister,' the heavily built man said as he walked towards the table.

'Sorry, Crystal. I must be in a bad mood today.'

He left the room as his father was shown to her chair by his daughter. She wheeled another chair close to him. Seated, her father smiled at Tweed.

'An honour to meet you. I am Warner Chance, a managing director.'

Tweed immediately spotted the difference between the two men. Marshal had said *the*, whereas Warner contented himself with *a*. It confirmed to him their clashing characters. Warner wore a neat leather jacket, a cravat at his throat and smart blue trousers. Marshal offered his guest a drink of Scotch, which Tweed refused, then refilled his own glass.

'Here's to Mr Tweed taking up residence with us.'

'That would be wonderful,' Crystal said, leaning on her father's shoulder. 'Then we'd have someone to protect us.'

Tweed said nothing and at that moment Snape appeared, erect as a soldier. He paused.

'If I'm not interrupting . . .'

'Oh, get on with it, man,' Marshal barked.

'Mr Tweed,' Snape said politely, 'and Miss Grey, Mrs Bella sends her apologies and is ready to receive you at your convenience.'

3

Tweed, with Paula on one side and Lavinia on the other, crossed the large, dim hall, following Snape. They appeared to be heading for a panelled wall. Snape turned to speak over his shoulder as he pressed an invisible button in the pannelling.

Two sections of the panelling opened away from each other, revealing a large square lift with a dark beige carpet on the floor, almost a shag covering. Snape spoke.

'Mrs Bella has her study on the first floor, sir.'

'Then why not use the staircase?'

'Mrs Bella prefers visitors to use the lift.'

As they all walked inside Tweed stared at the carpet. There were deep runnels in the shag as though something wheeled had been taken up. He also spotted signs of a vacuum cleaner being used to eliminate the runnels. Snape pressed the second button up in the control panel. Below it was a brown button. They were climbing slowly, smoothly when Tweed spoke again.

'What is the brown button for, then?'

'Emergency,' Snape replied abruptly with a trace of annoyance.

The lift stopped, the doors opened. They stepped into a wide corridor continuing to their left where it ended in a solid panelled wall. A wall-to-wall deep-pile beige carpet covered the corridor floor. Tweed again observed runnels digging deep into the carpet, broken in sections where a vacuum cleaner had attempted to eliminate them. Snape led them a short distance to their right, opened a door, led them into another large room, whose walls were lined on two sides with bookshelves and more leather-bound volumes. On the third wall were two old oil paintings, portraits of two men dressed in the clothes of long ago.

'Ezra Main and Pitt Chance, founders of the dynasty,' Snape explained as he saw Tweed looking at them.

'Mr Tweed,' Lavinia whispered, 'I shouldn't have come so far. If what you are going to say is confidential I'll pop back downstairs.'

'I'd like you to join us,' Tweed replied, touching her arm.

'Mrs Bella sometimes likes me to take notes,' she whispered back, squeezing her notebook under her arm.

'Mrs Bella,' Snape announced after opening a door, 'your guests. Mr Tweed and Miss Paula Grey.'

He bowed, left the room, closed the door. The study was long, the walls panelled and there were leaded-light windows which Tweed, glancing at them, realized looked out straight along the entrance drive. But it was the figure at the far end of the room which gripped him as he walked towards her.

Bella Main, eighty-four years old, sat behind a Regency desk in a tall hard-backed carver chair. Her imposing head and unlined long neck protruded above the back of the chair. He remembered she was over six feet tall.

Her Roman face would be noticed anywhere. Her grey hair was thick, well brushed. Her grey eyes were alert, her nose like a shapely beak, her mouth was firm and she had a good chin. When she stood up to greet them Paula noted she was wearing a fine-cut leather jacket with a white blouse and grey trousers over her long legs. Her grey hair was cut short, her only concession to jewellery a pair of pearl earrings and a brooch with the letters MC in small diamonds attached to her jacket. Coming forward with quick steps to greet Tweed, she hugged him for a few seconds.

'It is so good of you to come and see me. My apologies for keeping you waiting. A client who had a problem he couldn't cope with barged in. I solved the problem and he left a happy man.'

Her presence dominated the room without a trace of arrogance. She shook Paula by the hand and her grip was fearsome. She beckoned to Lavinia to sit with her behind the desk as Tweed replied.

'It gave us time to meet most, maybe all, of your family.'

'Only part of the problem,' she replied as she sat down behind the desk with Lavinia in another chair beside her. 'Now I have to deal with the villain Calouste Doubenkian. I know you come straight to the point and so do I.'

Nothing could have taken Tweed more aback but his face showed no reaction but interest. Paula gripped her knees tightly with both hands to conceal her shock, to keep her expression neutral. Bella frowned.

'I'm getting this out of sequence. First, the Main Chance Bank is private, always has been. We keep well away from the idea of a flotation on the Stock Exchange, although they keep pestering, probably because it's simply the richest bank in Europe, possibly in the world. Founded in 1912 by my fathers-in-law, Ezra Main and Pitt Chance—'

'Excuse me,' Tweed interjected, 'but are their portraits on the wall in the library outside this study?'

'Those are the two brigands. Ezra is the one on the left.'

'Brigands?' Tweed repeated. 'But my reading of history tells me men were tougher in those days. Two world wars softened most of the men. Now in business they trick and cheat.'

'How right you are.' She used a hand to smooth down one side of her hair. 'They had the idea a lot of rich men living in Europe wanted a safe haven for their large sums of money. The Main Chance Bank they founded provided that haven. Has done ever since. Today you need a minimum of a million to join our bank. In dollars, Swiss francs or pounds sterling. We take ten per cent of the first deposit as our fee. They are happy with that because they know their money is *safe*.'

'You take anyone with those funds?'

'We do *not*! My intelligence service vets them first. We're on the lookout for money-launderers, terrorist funds, robbery proceeds. They can all jump in the fountain outside. There is more to the system than that, but first I need to know if you will join us on a permanent basis. As chief administrator with full powers. The salary would be three hundred thousand as a starter. It would go up when you'd settled in.'

'I never guessed you had anything like this in mind.' He paused. 'I take it as a great compliment but I'm dedicated to the work I do now.'

There was a tap on the door and Snape walked in with another silver tray with coffee and separate glasses for water. He placed a large glass carafe near Tweed. They were looking at Snape while Tweed glanced down at the carpet by the side of the desk. The runnels had appeared again, like small wheel marks; two rows, about eighteen inches apart. The sun cast light onto the carpet, reflecting off small and larger specks glittering like gold.

When Snape had left Bella snapped her fingers, checked her watch. She turned to Lavinia, put a hand to her high forehead.

'One day I'm going to get old. Help me find a long stiff brown envelope out of that awkward drawer.'

Both heads dipped as they struggled to open the drawer. Tweed took his white display handkerchief from his top pocket, dipped it, unseen by everyone except Paula, into the open carafe of water. He bent down, spread it widely over the golden specks, pressed hard, screwed it up, returned it to his pocket. What on earth is he up to? wondered Paula. Bella and Lavinia were still struggling with the drawer. Then it came open.

'You really should have that seen to,' Lavinia suggested.

'Then I wouldn't know when someone has been prying.'

Bella held in her hand a long stiff brown sealed envelope, the type used by lawyers. She held it so Tweed couldn't see the side with the address. The side he could see was further sealed with red sealing wax.

'Lavinia,' she said in an unusually slow voice, 'I'm now going to fill in our visitors on the Doubenkian business – which you know all about. Could you please take this to my solicitors, Hamble, Goodworthy and Richter in Threadneedle Street in the City? Get a receipt from them.'

'I'll take it now.' She got up, walked round the desk with her hand held out to Tweed. 'Goodbye, Mr Tweed. I really like your personality.' She turned to Paula, who braced her hand for Lavinia's strong grip. 'I like you equally, Paula. I envy you working for such a remarkable man.'

Tweed noticed that the stiff brown envelope was tucked firmly under her arm so he could see the sealed side but not the address. He waited only a short time before he made his move.

Lavinia, walking briskly, had left the study and Bella was quiet as though deciding how to phrase what she was going to say next. Tweed stood up.

'Do you mind if I smoke a cigarette?'

'By all means go ahead. I think I'll have one.'

Reaching for a silver box on her desk, she lifted the lid and extracted one of her own. She lit it with a silver ball after pressing a button. Tweed was now standing in a dark cubbyhole by the window. The sun had gone in. Looking down he saw Lavinia diving inside a Saab. He was looking straight down the drive to the entrance gates as he pretended to have trouble with his lighter. When a high flame appeared he shook it, dousing it. He repeated the exercise four times before lighting up. Parked in the concealed track opposite the gates he felt sure Harry had seen his signal. He watched as the gates opened automatically and Lavinia drove out, turning left – which was the way to Gladworth, not right to Threadneedle Street in London, the address Bella had spoken aloud so clearly. He went back and sat in his chair.

'Time I came straight to the point,' Bella began. 'Mr Calouste Doubenkian. A billionaire and a crook. Owns large contracts in Eastern oil, an immense steel-works, several banks in the Balkans. All obtained by dubious, not to say murderous methods. To get one bank he had the wife of the owner kidnapped, one of his minor crimes. Now he wants to buy the Main Chance. He's offered a huge sum, about half what we're worth.'

'Normal procedure with those people,' Tweed observed. 'You offer a low price to start with, then they haggle like Arabs in the Mouski bazaar in Cairo.'

'His name sounds Armenian,' Bella remarked.

'Yes, but I doubt it's his original name. He could come from anywhere east of Bulgaria – Georgia, Dagestan, Tajikistan, an oil-rich state.'

'You know something about him, then?'

'No. I've heard the name, know that he's dangerous. That's all. He has never crossed my path.'

'I had him investigated by Medfords Security . . .'

'They've very good,' Paula assured her. 'I was trained by them before I joined the SIS. Who did you deal with?'

'A director called Matteson, who struck me as clever.'

'After my time,' Paula said with a smile.

'So what did he find out?' Tweed interjected.

'Well . . .' Bella sighed. 'He used his best man in Europe, someone codenamed Louis in Paris. Poor Louis ended up in his apartment with his throat cut. He's on my conscience.'

'It goes with the territory. You have a large family working for you. I met them downstairs.'

'It's a dubious tradition going way back. They all want to work for me. They're all bright. Must be a genetic thing lasting for centuries. They know they can't get anything like what I pay them anywhere else. A few wandered off on their own.'

'What is the executive set-up?'

'Marshal Main and Warner Chance are co-directors with equal powers. I was once married to Marshal's father, Charles, deceased. Later I married Rupert Chance, but he was killed in a road accident. So Marshal and Warner are my sons.'

'They choose their clients?'

'They certainly do not! I do that. If they're acceptable I then decide who would handle them best. Marshal is charming and boisterous, very extrovert. Warner is quieter and more deliberate.'

'What made you choose Snape?'

'Good question. Originally he was an officer with the Berkshire Blues, then transferred to the Engineers. Among other duties he can cope with the lift if it goes wrong. He has presence when greeting clients.'

'What about security? When we arrived the gates opened before I identified myself on the speakerphone.'

'We knew you were coming.' She smiled. 'You don't miss much. He spotted you leaving Park Crescent, took a photograph, then tore back here on his motorcycle.'

'He took our photographs?' Tweed was alarmed. 'He wasn't spotted.'

'He's clever.' She chuckled. 'The Invisible Man. When you arrived he was watching from the manor with binoculars . . .'

'He's in charge of security?'

'No. Lavinia, Chief Accountant, is. She's a forensic accountant. So is Crystal, who assists her. Now, Mr Tweed, you have an overall picture, so can't I persuade you to come and live here as Chief Administrator, with total power? Paula would be most welcome as your assistant.'

'Again, I appreciate the compliment.' Tweed had

stood up. 'I am dedicated to the position I hold now. I am sorry.'

'So am I.' Bella rose from behind her desk to escort them to the door. She pointed to the portraits of the two men who had originally founded the bank.

'I couldn't stand having them staring at me in my study. You won't think again about my offer? Mrs Grandy has prepared two large suites which interconnect . . .'

'Mrs Grandy?'

'Our tyrant of a housekeeper. Outspoken too, but so reliable. I do need you, Mr Tweed, to come and protect our treasure.'

She hugged Tweed, then turned to Paula and hugged her. When Snape appeared to escort them to the lift Tweed walked quickly towards him, followed closely by Paula. When the panel doors opened Tweed walked with Paula to the open door into the library. They were greeted by Leo shouting viciously, 'I'll kill you.'

All the family were there. Crystal stood calmly as Leo rushed at her brandishing a knife. She kicked him hard on the leg. He yelled with pain, fell down. Warner appeared, pressed both hands on his shoulders as he slowly clambered upright. Quietly he ordered Leo to his room. Leo limped towards the lift.

They made a point of shaking hands with everyone. As he reached Snape Tweed smiled as he spoke.

'I'm afraid we shan't be coming to protect your treasure, as Mrs Bella expressed it.'

'*She said that to you!*' Snape burst out.

'We're leaving now,' Tweed told him, ignoring the strange outburst.

4

Tweed drove down the drive. The gates had opened, and he turned left into another fir-shrouded tunnel. It was cold again. It would always be cold. Paula stared at him. His expression was grim.

She was looking at a man of uncertain age, of medium height and well built inside his smart navy-blue suit. He had horn-rimmed glasses on his strong nose above a determined mouth and well-shaped jaw. He had changed recently, seemed to her younger and very fit.

'You're going the wrong way,' she ventured. 'We should have turned right beyond the gates for London.'

'You're not as analytical as you usually are.'

'What does that mean?'

'Bella and Lavinia made a great performance about hiding the address on that envelope, the type of envelope which often contains a will.'

'I still don't get it,' she protested.

'Hamble, Goodworthy and Richter, well-known solicitors with offices in Threadneedle Street, London. Bella raised her voice to make sure we heard. I do have an advantage over you,' he admitted. 'Watching her leave in her Saab from that window I saw Lavinia turn *left* beyond the gates.'

'This is the way to Gladworth . . .'

'Precisely,' he went on in the same grim tone. 'I signalled to Harry with my lighter. He'll have followed her. When we find him he'll tell us where Lavinia did go to.'

'Oh, I see.'

'On top of that I don't like people laying plans to kill me, especially when I have you in the car. The attempt on our lives was skilfully planned. Be analytical and you can work it out for yourself.'

'I'm lost,' she confessed.

'*Think!*' he snapped. 'From the moment we left Park Crescent.'

She glanced at him, taken aback. He so rarely snapped at her. She sensed he was concealing a cold rage.

'This must be Gladworth,' Paula said as they emerged from the fir-enclosed tunnel into an old street paved with flat stones. 'Now, to find Harry and see if this is where Lavinia was headed for.'

Tweed had slowed to a crawl. A notice warned

20 m.p.h. maximum speed. Paula had her face pressed to the window. She was searching for his brown Ford with its souped-up engine. Both sides of Gladworth's streets were lined with large expensive-looking terraced houses. Residents obviously occupied the first and second floors, which all had stone troughs perched on the outside ledges, packed with spring flowers – crocuses, daffodils and shrubs. The ground floors were occupied by shops Paula had not expected. Expensive, she spotted Escada where a dress cost a small fortune, then Aquascutum and many more in the same price range.

'There's loads of money somewhere round here,' she observed.

'Probably in big houses hidden in The Forest,' Tweed remarked vaguely. 'What we have to do is to see if Harry is here.'

'There's a sign pointing to a car park down a side street.'

'We'll check that. I don't see cars parked in the street.'

As they turned down a narrow street bordered with grey-stone houses Paula lowered her window. The park was filled with expensive cars neatly slotted in. She saw a Lamborghini and stared at an ancient Lagonda. Tweed found a slot, slipped carefully inside, switched off the engine. He had seen Lavinia's Saab. The number plate was the one he'd memorized while watching her drive off from Hengistbury Manor.

'Now, where's Harry?' she called out.

'The old mucker's here,' Harry's Cockney voice replied, standing outside her window. 'And,' he went on, addressing Tweed, 'if that silver Saab is the one you wanted me to follow you've come to the right place. The girl driving it could drive me nuts. If I put on a decent set of clothes and got educated.'

'She'd probably be fascinated by you,' Paula said, grinning. 'Especially when you started telling her East End jokes.'

'What did she do when she arrived?' growled Tweed. 'Where is she now?'

'First –' Harry ticked off the points on his thick fingers – 'she parks her car here. Second, she darts back into the street and pops into a solicitors – Lowell, French and Browne. Small place in the main street with a big window. A thin streak with a pince-nez is sitting behind a desk. She hands him the long brown envelope she's been carrying. Pince-nez scribbles in a small book, tears out a sheet, hands it to her and she's away.'

'The receipt,' said Tweed.

'Then Pince-nez uses the phone, a short call.'

'Telling Bella it's arrived safely,' Tweed commented. 'What does she do next?'

'Goes into the Pike's Peak, presumably for lunch since she's still there. At least I think so. Not in the dining-room or bar.'

'That posh place with white walls and a doorman?' asked Paula.

'You've got it in one. Best place in town is my guess.'

Tweed was hurrying out of the car as Paula closed the window. When they joined Harry, Tweed's voice was crisp, that of a man who did not waste time. He looked at Harry.

'Guide us discreetly. I'd like to see Lowell, French and Browne without them seeing us.'

'Follow me. Slowly. No one hurries in Gladworth. No one except the glorious dish who drives the Saab. We'll cross to the other side of the main street.'

There was no traffic when they strolled after Harry. Among the few pedestrians were elegantly dressed women gazing into the shop windows. This is better than the Piccadilly end of Bond Street, Paula thought. Harry paused, turned round.

'Other side of the street. That big window.'

Tweed glanced at the window of sheet glass. Inscribed in old lettering was the name. *Lowell, French & Browne. Solicitors*. No one was seated at a large desk at right angles to the High Street. Nor was there any sign of any occupant anywhere in the office. Tweed frowned.

'Don't go to the Pike's Peak for lunch,' Harry warned. 'Your target must be in the restaurant.'

Tweed chose a tea shop which served full lunches. They invited Harry to join them but he had a packed lunch in his car. Paula ordered ham and eggs and Tweed followed suit. He had a faraway look and Paula kept quiet.

'Excuse my not talking,' he said, 'but I have a lot to think about.'

They were driving back towards London through the dark tunnels with Harry a quarter-mile ahead of them when Tweed began talking.

'Worked it out yet?' he asked Paula.

'Yes. My brain must have gone to sleep. That attempt to kill us with the digger was brilliantly organized. First, there must have been someone watching us leave Park Crescent. Then he'd use his mobile to alert a pilot waiting at a private airfield, describing our car and maybe us. Pilot takes off and checks the lane leading to Hengistbury Manor. When he sees us the pilot flashes a signal to the digger driver, already waiting for us.

'Very good. But how did they know we were heading out to see Bella this morning?'

'No idea.'

'*Think!*' he said with a smile. 'There's a traitor inside the Main Chance family. They all knew we were coming. Bella will have told them, maybe days ago. The traitor informed the brilliant organizer of that attack on us.'

'Oh, my God! You have to be right.' She leaned forward. 'There's a police barrier across the road. Very close to where that digger crashlanded.'

'Leave the talking to me,' Tweed suggested as he stopped, but kept the engine running.

A uniformed officer, exuding self-importance, strolled towards them as Tweed lowered his window. He peered into the car and Paula stared back. He then addressed Tweed.

'Driving down from London, sir?'

'I'm driving *to* London from Gladworth. What seems to be the problem?'

'I'm Inspector Tetford from Leaminster. There's been a nasty accident. Fatal. Driver of a large digger missed seeing a small gorge, plunged into it. Weight of the said digger killed him.'

'Really,' said Tweed.

'Coming from Gladworth, would you know a Jed Higgins?'

'No, I wouldn't.'

'Odd business. Digger was stolen from his barn. Earlier the farmer received a phone call saying his wife had been injured in a car smash on the motorway nearer London. So he dashes off and later finds there's been no car smash. Gets back to his farm after the digger was stolen. Finds his wife safe and sound, back from shopping in Gladworth.'

'As you said, odd business.'

'And, sir, none of the locals ever heard of Jed Higgins. I won't detain you any longer.' He stood back, saluted, waved to someone and the barrier was lifted.

Tweed drove on without a glance into the field where a canvas tent had been erected over the digger.

'What do you think of that?' Paula asked.

'I don't like it. The whole thing *was* planned by a brilliant organizer.'

'So are we getting involved with the Main Chance Bank.'

'No.'

'You mentioned a traitor. I'm wondering about Snape. He did take photos of us this morning when we were leaving Park Crescent.'

'The timing is all wrong. They – whoever "they" may be – had to have that data earlier to set up their complex trap.'

'Yes, that makes sense. So you still think we'll never get involved with Hengistbury again?'

'Absolutely not. I'll explain why if you'll come back with me to my Bexford Street house this evening.'

'Of course I'll come. But I still wonder if we've seen the last of Hengistbury.'

5

Norfolk, the Wash.

Thirty-six hours before Tweed and Paula left for Hengistbury, a man called Max was standing in darkness on the seaward side of the great dyke which protected the wilderness known as the Wash, protected the vast area of grassland from the erosion of the North Sea. Max was waiting for the tramp steamer lying just beyond the three-mile limit to reply to his signal.

He held the powerful torch in his large hand. He had flashed one short, two long, one short. He was cold. Despite his fur-lined beaver overcoat, woollen scarf, the cap on his head and the motoring gloves he was frozen in the bitter Arctic breeze. Fortunately the sea was calm. The VIP who would come ashore disliked rough water.

Then the breeze dropped and at that moment the tramp answered his signal. One short, two long, one short. His earlier signal had informed the tramp it was safe, this section of the Wash was deserted.

Dammit, he thought, the whole Wash is deserted. The only buildings were never-used ancient churches scattered across the grassy emptiness, built centuries ago by wool merchants when wool was profitable money. Then the economy changed and the price of wool nosedived. The wool barons disappeared – and so did their workers, abandoning the villages which over a long period had crumbled. Max flashed his torch again as he saw a massive rubber dinghy approaching. This was the only place it could land its powerful passenger.

A crude landing stage with rails projected into the water and Max signalled again to guide the dinghy in. It moved swiftly but its muffled engine made hardly any noise beyond a gentle purr.

Max was over six feet tall, burly, quick with his hands and feet. He had been the most productive lumberjack in Canada. There he had killed one of his fellow workers who owed him money and refused to pay. Removing the knife from the corpse he had used a chainsaw to fell a poor-quality tree, guiding it so it landed across the body. The rest of the crew were working a distance away and Max knew no one would be interested in the fallen tree.

Max immediately went to Vancouver, caught a flight to London. He spent time in the East End where he learned to speak like a Cockney. His next move was to use some of the pile of money he'd earned to buy the best clothes.

He then spent time in some of London's top hotels, listening carefully to how the guests spoke. He was educating himself to mix in any environment. He had an acute brain so he soon boarded a flight to Paris.

He took a job as a bouncer in a high-class nightclub off the Champs-Elysées. His tough but well-shaped features and fair hair appealed to women. He liked women but in his role as a bouncer avoided getting involved. By now he was speaking fluent French.

Late one night when the club closed he walked out, wandered into a classy bar which was empty, he thought, as he ordered a drink from the barman. Normally he was careful, taking euros from a few in his trouser pocket. This time he made a mistake. He took out his wallet stuffed with money. A fat man appeared from nowhere, grabbed for the wallet.

Max held on to the wallet, used his left hand to hurl the thief halfway down the bar where he tripped, fell over. With a savage look on his plump face the thief jumped up after pulling an automatic out of his hip holster. He was aiming the weapon when Max, who had lifted his hands, called out in French.

'*Behind you!*'

The fat man glanced back as Max's right hand slipped a knife out of his pocket. The long blade whipped through the air, penetrated the fat man's throat. He fell forward on the handle and the knife was driven through to the back of his fleshy neck. He lay very still.

Max turned, picked up his glass again, used a handkerchief to wipe off his fingerprints. Which was when four sinister *apache* types appeared all round him. Max was considering how to deal with them when the one in front of him lifted the palms of both hands in a peace gesture.

'The chief was impressed with you. He wishes to talk with you. In that alcove over there . . .'

Which was how Max came to meet and eventually become second-in-command to the man now stepping carefully ashore from the dinghy held fast to the landing stage by its crew.

Calouste Doubenkian walked slowly towards Max. It was impossible to tell what he looked like as he cat-footed onto firm ground. He was short, but he wore a long black astrakhan overcoat which ended below his knees, a Russian-style fur hat which concealed his high forehead, and large dark glasses which concealed his eyes. Long fur gloves masked the shape of his hands. His soft-soled shoes made no sound as he approached Max. His voice was a quiet purr and he spoke in English very softly, which Max always found disturbing.

'Is it safe?' he enquired.

'It was when I last checked . . .'

'Then perhaps you had better check again?'

'Please wait here, Mr Doubenkian,' Max said nervously.

'Have I not told you before never to speak my name?'

'Sorry, sir. Very sorry.'

'I will come with you while you check.'

'If you would please follow my exact footsteps. There is deep marsh just beyond the stepping stones.'

'Useful for hiding dead bodies, my dear Max.'

'I'll lead the way, then, sir.'

The moon that had appeared from behind a cloud and had enabled Max to spot the approach of the large dinghy shed its eerie glow over the vast stretch of grassland behind the dyke. The silence pressed down on them now the faint purr of the dinghy as it headed back for the tramp had died away. The silence disturbed Calouste as he carefully trod from one stepping stone to the next small island of safety. He had a strong nerve but it was tested to the limit as he saw the acid-green grass floating on top of the deadly ooze on either side of the path.

'You have made all the arrangements to eliminate Tweed before he reaches Hengistbury?' he asked softly.

'In thirty-six hours he'll be as dead as mutton,' Max assured him cheerfully. 'I have a network now across Britain. Tweed is a goner.'

He stopped speaking suddenly as they came close to

the solitary road where the cars were parked. A red-haired girl appeared standing just off the road. She wore a windcheater and jeans and was obviously waiting for them. Carol Lynton had lost her way after visiting her boyfriend in his cottage. As Max stopped, wondering whether she had heard what they had just said, Calouste caught up with him.

'Get rid of her,' whispered Calouste. 'Sound carries in this silence.'

'You don't mean . . .' Max began in a similar whisper.

'Obey my order. Eliminate her.'

Max swallowed, gritted his teeth. She was a pretty girl, no more than eighteen. She came down towards him, smiling. He tried to smile back, couldn't. Calouste jabbed him in the back. Max took a deep breath of cold air.

When the girl reached him Max grasped her hard round the waist. She was quite small. As she opened her mouth to yell he uplifted her, swung her upside down, plunged her head-first deep into the ooze. He thought he heard a gurgle. Her legs were waving desperately, then they sank out of sight. A few muddy bubbles appeared on the surface of the green slime. Then nothing.

'Village girls gossip,' Calouste remarked off-handedly.

Max glanced north where, under the moon's ghostly

glow, the Wash had the atmosphere of a bleak and desolate desert. Max couldn't wait to leave the area.

'Sorry we had to land you in a place like this,' he commented, 'but it's one of the loneliest spots in Britain.'

'Nothing wrong with it,' snapped Calouste, who had grown up in the wilderness of Central Asia. 'Where is the car?'

'Only a short walk down the road here. I thought it unwise to park them too close to the path. There they are.'

Stepping onto the road Calouste stared. Parked by the roadside was a gleaming black stretch limousine. Beyond it was Max's second-hand Ford. Seeing their arrival a uniformed chauffeur opened the driver's door, stood to attention.

'The limo is for you, of course,' Max explained. 'Driver is one of my star turns. He's strangled at least one man. Name is Grogan . . .'

'You *idiot*!' Calouste was apoplectic. 'I have told you before, I do not wish attention to be brought to me. Is that limo hired?'

'Oh, yes.' Max was nervous. 'It is.'

'At least you got one thing right. Get rid of this Grogan,' Calouste almost screeched. 'Tell him to return the car to the hire firm instantly. If the police stop him he was to pick up a banker, a Mr Moran in Spalding, and couldn't find the address. I have to cover every bloody angle myself! I will travel beside you in *your* car. I will walk to it. Give me the keys now. And send that limo off this moor *toute suite*. *Move*, damn you!'

Max felt in his pocket for his car keys. In his haste he dropped them, stooped, grabbed them. He ran to the limo, his legs unsteady. He was scared stiff of Calouste in his chief's present mood.

'To the Green Dark Hotel in West Higham. Is that right, sir?' he asked as he drove off with Calouste beside him.

'Correct.'

Max was relieved to find Calouste was in a better mood. He had no idea Calouste had pretended to be in a rage. It was a method he used occasionally on a subordinate to remind them who was boss.

'I drove earlier to the Green Dark Hotel,' Max said casually. 'Just checking so I knew the route. I cruised past. No one seemed to be about. You have booked a suite there, sir?'

'I own the damned place. Bought it through a series of small companies, staffed it with my own people. I will be the only guest. Getting there, avoid King's Lynn. It has a police HQ. I doubt if that peasant girl you had to deal with has yet been reported missing. Why take the risk?'

'Very sensible, if I may say so. You think of everything.'

'If I don't no one else will. Pull up somewhere very quiet before we reach the hotel. I wish to change my appearance.'

No more was said and they met hardly any traffic. No one would be out on such a bitterly cold night. When they pulled up in the middle of nowhere Calouste got out with the suitcase he had hugged on his lap. Max tactfully turned his back. When he turned round he had a shock.

He hardly recognized Calouste, who now wore a tweed overcoat, woollen scarf pulled up to his chin, smart leather gloves and a wide-brimmed trilby pulled well down over his face. The only similarity was a large pair of gold-rimmed dark glasses, different from the pair he'd worn when he had come ashore. His previous outfit was neatly packed in the suitcase. He handed Max a card, keeping his own card in his hand.

'When we enter we go to reception, say nothing, just give the desk man your card. I am in suite three on the first floor. You are in suite four. There is an inter-connecting door. In case of trouble use your fists or your beloved knife. No shooting. A passer-by might hear shots.'

'You are expecting trouble?' Max enquired as they got back into the car.

'Absolutely not, dear boy,' Calouste replied, speaking now in the perfect accent of an Old Etonian. 'But I once read that the maxim of the Boy Scouts' organization was

"Be prepared". Here we are. Afterwards park the car out of sight in the garage at the back.'

The oddly named Green Dark Hotel was a large square building, its plaster walls painted in a light green. There was a spacious park area in front with a pebble drive. Inside, Calouste marched up to the desk, planted down his card next to Max's.

'Parsons, I notice you have omitted an instruction. You really must do exactly as I tell you, please. Outside I want a *No Vacancies* sign erected immediately. I will have a meal in my suite in one hour. There is a menu in my suite? Excellent. I shall phone down my order. Mr Rogers here will make his own arrangements, again for a meal in his suite.'

'Will do, Mr Pennington,' the smartly dressed receptionist assured his guest. 'Will get crackin' at once.'

'The sign outside first, if you please. Immediately.'

'I was goin' to escort you to your suite, sir . . .'

'Not necessary,' Calouste replied in the same lordly manner.

'So you are Mr Pennington,' Max whispered. 'And I'm Mr Rogers . . .'

'Precisely. Kindly do not forget the names. Your suite is the next one. I shall not wish to be disturbed – I have some papers to check.'

Inside his suite Calouste dumped his case in a cupboard. Seated in an armchair he placed a highly sophisticated mobile on a side table. From an inside pocket he extracted several large sheets of paper. Unfolded, they were architect's plans of the intricate layout of Hengistbury Manor. The only section not shown was the labyrinth of cellars underneath the house. Calouste was unaware of their existence. The photostats of the plans had been sent to an address in Brussels by registered mail.

Even Calouste's agile brain had to concentrate hard to memorize the hallways, the large number of apartments, each complete with drawing room, dining room, two bathrooms, two large bedrooms, a spacious kitchen and a small library.

The names of the occupants had been added with a black biro, spelt out in peculiar block letters he suspected were in disguised writing. Hengistbury Manor was more complex and much larger than he'd expected. Removing his reading glasses he glanced at the mobile. It would be at least forty-eight hours before it rang, telling him the first phase of his plan had been completed.

Two days later at eight in the evening the mobile buzzed. Calouste grabbed it.

'Yes, who is speaking?'

'Orion here. The news is not good. Not good at all . . .'

The voice was robotic. The caller was using some kind of instrument which completely distorted the voice. Impossible to tell whether it was the voice of a man or a woman.

'What the hell do you mean?' Calouste demanded.

'The plan failed. Tweed and Paula Grey are alive and well. Back in London, I assume. Alive and well . . .'

'*You said that before!*' he screeched.

He slammed the mobile closed. He was going to have to start all over again. He started to swear in the foulest French.

6

When Tweed and Paula arrived back from Hengistbury all the core staff were assembled. Tweed gazed round at them. Marler, tall and slim, in his late thirties, occupied his favourite position. He was standing up, leaning against the wall next to Paula, now seated at her desk in the far corner by the large windows. He was smoking a cigarette in a long black holder.

As always, he was smartly dressed, his dark hair neatly trimmed. He wore a well-cut beige suit, dark blue shirt, Chanel tie. Marler was reputed to be the top marksman in Europe with his Armalite rifle. Clean shaven, his face was handsome, attracting envious attention from elegant women when he walked down any London street.

'In case you think we've been lounging about,' he began in his upper-crust voice, 'we've all been out and busy. I've been in the East End where agents of a certain Calouste Doubenkian have been recruiting the worst types – brutal thugs, some killers who have never been caught for their crimes. Thought I'd just mention it in view of Philip Cardon's phone call, passed on to me by Monica.'

'*What!*' gulped Paula.

'Don't I speak so good?' Marler enquired cynically.

'You see?' Paula called out to Tweed.

'Harry,' Tweed responded, as though not having heard what had just been said. 'No, I mean you, Pete,' he said to Pete Nield, five feet seven tall and also neatly clad, but without the panache of Marler. 'You have a pal in one of the three gold-bullion merchants. Got something for you.'

Paula jumped up to join him as Pete fingered his neat moustache by the side of Tweed's desk. An educated man, his teammate was Harry Butler, seated cross-legged on the floor. A greater contrast between the two men would have been difficult to imagine. Harry wore a shabby old windcheater, trousers which had seen better days. He was indignant.

'I've got twice the number of underground contacts Pete has,' he grumbled.

Tweed, absorbed, ignored the protest. Laying a sheet of thick white paper on his desk he carefully took his white display handkerchief from his top pocket, emptied the contents onto the sheet. Peter switched on a desk lamp. The specks and one larger piece glittered brilliantly in the light.

'Pete,' Tweed said, 'is that gold?'

'Oh,' said Paula, 'so that's what you were doing. Wetting your handkerchief in the water carafe, then pressing it on the carpet while Bella and Lavinia were struggling to open their awkward drawer.'

'What do you think, Pete?' Tweed asked, ignoring another interruption.

Pete had produced a powerful magnifying glass from a pocket. He peered at each speck for several minutes, spending most time on the largest piece.

'I need to take this to my pal who is an expert,' he said eventually. 'But for my money this is gold.'

'I need to know how long ago it was mined. Also, if it's possible, where.'

'Should be back within two hours,' Pete said, checking his watch. 'My contact works through the afternoons and evenings. Sleeps in the morning.'

As he spoke he converted the paper sheet into a chute, then skilfully emptied the contents back into Tweed's display handkerchief. Screwing it up gently he produced a clean white handkerchief of his own as more protective wrapping.

'Back in two hours,' he promised and was gone.

'Don't tell me anything,' Paula chided.

'Wait until we find out whether I'm right or wrong,' Tweed replied.

'No good pushing Tweed,' Harry warned from the floor. 'He will only talk when he's ready. Should know that by now.'

'And I love you,' she told him with a smile.

The phone rang. Monica answered, waved to Tweed who reached for the phone, heard the voice, beckoned to Paula to listen on her phone.

'Yes,' he said. 'More information about—'

'I'm reliably informed that Calouste Doubenkian is now in England. Arrived several days ago . . .'

'Where?'

'No idea.'

'What route did he use?'

'No idea. Will keep in touch. When I can.'

The phone went dead. Philip Cardon had swiftly ended the call. Tweed raised his eyebrows at Paula. He thought for a moment, then asked Monica to get Commander Buchanan on the line. He opened the conversation by giving his friend Roy a terse report on his visit with Paula to Hengistbury, leaving out any reference to the gold specks.

'I'm sorry,' Buchanan commented. 'I had no idea she was after you as a bodyguard, which is what it comes to as I see it. Of course you had to refuse. Don't like the sound of an offer to buy her out. That could be very dangerous.'

'Thought you didn't know anything about this character.'

'Only rumours, which it's suspected Doubenkian spreads himself.'

'What rumours?'

'Among others he wanted to buy a private bank in Vienna. The owner refused. Next development is his only son – eighteen years old – is kidnapped. Price of his safe release is the sale of the bank. Owner sells, boy is returned unharmed. Then a mysterious buyer, as in Vienna, is offered a price for his private bank in Grenoble. Owner refuses, his wife is kidnapped. Owner, who maybe wasn't too fond of wife, gets her back through the post, a leg at a time, then an arm and in pieces the rest of her.'

'Doubenkian sounds the most cold-blooded villain I have ever heard of . . .'

'Hold on. These are *rumours*. Nothing is ever connected to Calouste Doubenkian.'

'The buyer could be traced by finding out where the sale money ended up,' Tweed insisted.

'The Vienna criminal department tried that. The money was passed through several private holding companies. Ended up in Vaduz, Liechtenstein. You know it's impossible to check accounts in that tiny state.'

'Mrs Bella Main says Doubenkian phoned her himself.'

'That's no proof. We only have her word for that. It is not enough to prove it was him.'

'Doesn't anyone have any idea where his base is?'

'No.'

'What about Interpol?' Tweed hammered away. 'Aren't they at all interested?'

'What I'm about to say is not a joke. You know Interpol out at their quiet HQ at Lyons in France have black notices to list wanted major criminals, with their photographs and whatever data they have? I once asked a contact in Lyons what the position was on Calouste Doubenkian. A black notice is on their walls. Just his name with a query mark. Nothing else, a blank sheet. No photo. Some humorist has scrawled one word on it: *Phantom*. He probably has half a dozen perfect fake passports. All with different names.'

'Why the query mark after his name?'

'Because his real name could be anything. Tweed –' Buchanan became emphatic. – 'Everything I've told you is *rumour*.'

'Well, now you know I'm not going to Hengistbury.'

'How could you? With the present position you hold . . .'

Tweed ended the call, looked across at Paula, who had heard every word. Smiling, he spread his hands in a gesture of forgetting the whole thing.

'What did you think of that?' he asked.

'I found it most intriguing.'

'In what way?'

'We don't yet have a clue as to what Calouste looks like but his *character* is emerging.'

'In what way, for Heaven's sake?'

'In his callous way he is very clever, a brilliant puller of strings without ever exposing himself. I'll bet he never stays in the same place for long. And he'll always appear with a false name.'

'Doesn't get us much further. In any case he's not our problem.' He waved a hand at the pile of files on his desk. 'My job is to deal with these reports from agents overseas. Probably most will have sent meaningless reports to show they are active. I don't want to be disturbed while working on them.'

Robert Newman, a key agent of Tweed's, was sprawled in an armchair near Tweed's desk. Thoroughly vetted long ago, he had once been the most respected international news reporter in America and Europe. His occasional articles had been reprinted in full in the *Washington Post*, *Der Spiegel* in the German Republic and many other influential papers, including London's *Daily Clarion*.

Six feet tall, well built, in his early forties, his strong, good-looking face was often stared at by women when he walked down a street. He frowned at Tweed's response.

'Tweed,' he began forcefully. 'I think what Paula said was very shrewd. Defining the character is halfway towards identifying the man. Give her credit.'

'I asked for no more interruptions,' Tweed said quietly. 'We're not concerned about this Doubenkian. But since you all have him on the brain, everyone can go out and trawl your contacts. Don't go south of the river. Criminals and spies avoid that better-off area. They're worried they would be conspicuous.'

'I'm going to the ladies' room,' said Paula and left the office.

On the morning of the third day after Calouste received the disturbing news that Tweed and Paula Grey were alive and probably back at Park Crescent, he decided to move. He never stayed in the same place for long wherever he might be.

He had spent the whole night out of bed in his hotel room, seated in an armchair, drinking cup after cup of coffee. His agile brain had come up with the only answer to eliminating Tweed. He knew that Tweed was *formidable*. Picking up his case, always kept packed for a swift departure, and sliding back the bolt of the interconnecting door, he opened the door, spoke quietly to Max, standing by a window.

'We are leaving. When will you be ready?'

'Now, sir. Immediately.'

Settled beside Max in the second-hand Ford he spoke as soon as they were in open country. The glaring sun shone low through the windscreen. Calouste pulled down his visor a moment after Max had taken the same precaution.

'We are moving,' Calouste informed his henchman, 'to one of the houses I own outside the village of Leaminster on the borders of Sussex and Hampshire. It's ten miles away from Hengistbury Manor and The Forest.'

He produced a map to hand to Max, who shook his head. 'Just show me. Some of those people who bought second homes out here assume there'll be no traffic, drive in the middle of the road. Young macho types.'

He glanced at the map Doubenkian was holding out for him. His chief's small thumb was pointed to Leaminster, and Max nodded.

'I can drive on a quiet roundabout route. Be there by lunchtime.'

'I have solved the Tweed problem,' Calouste said as he struggled to refold his map. 'Every man had his weak point. Even a man of Tweed's eminence. That is the lever we will use. As we successfully did in Vienna. You will lure Paula Grey out of SIS HQ, grab her, then you phone Tweed. Inform him you have the Grey girl, that she will be tortured for three hours, then murdered unless he comes along within an hour to rescue her. Before you phone him you start the torture, then put her on the phone so he can hear her scream.'

As he explained his plan Calouste was still trying to fold the map. He therefore failed to observe the grim expression which appeared on Max's face.

7

The Park Crescent office was occupied only by Monica, Tweed and Paula when, in the late afternoon, the call came through. Monica waved to Paula.

'It's for you. A Mr Evelyn-Ashton. Posh voice . . .'

'Yes?' said Paula.

'Miss Paula Grey?'

'Speaking. Who is this?'

'Evelyn-Ashton. You won't know me but I have information for you concerning a certain gentleman of Armenian origin.'

The voice was very Old Etonian, bland and superior without being condescending. Paula glanced over at Tweed, who was immersed in his files.

'Well, tell me,' Paula replied.

'Not over the phone. Too dangerous. Can we meet?'

'Where? And when?'

'Now. At the Duke's Head Hotel. In Mayfair, off

Tiverton Street. I'm tall, well-built, wearing a suit with a fake grey rose in the buttonhole. Thick brown hair, clean-shaven. Are you on?'

'Be there in fifteen minutes, roughly.'

'I'll be drinking champagne. Moderately . . .'

Paula had kept her voice low, knowing Tweed wouldn't like an assignation. Paula stood up, put on her leather windcheater, checking her Walther in the hip pocket. While bending to pull up her ankle boots she checked her Beretta tucked inside her leg holster was firmly in position.

'Who was that?' Tweed asked without looking up.

'A firm that's altering a dress for me . . .'

As she drove towards Mayfair, Paula's mind was in a whirl. Was it possible this stranger she was going to meet did have information about Calouste Doubenkian? On previous cases she had known lucky breaks which came when least expected.

Inside the well-appointed bar of the Duke's Head, Max was already waiting for his visitor. He always arrived early for appointments. It gave him time to check the surroundings. The bar was spacious and oblong, the narrower side being the frontage.

He was the only occupant at that hour and had chosen to sit near the door. An ice bucket with a bottle of champagne stood by his side and two glasses were set before him. In his large hand was concealed a small tasteless capsule for her drink. It would swiftly make her feel very sleepy.

Max's mind was in a turmoil. At the Green Dark Hotel he had not had a wink of sleep during the nights he had spent there. Into his mind had frequently crept a memory of the girl he had thrown into the marsh. He had imagined the horror of her opening her mouth to scream. She would have sucked in that foul ooze, then choked on it. He had felt sickened and still did.

It had all happened so quickly. Accustomed to obeying a command from Doubenkian, he had acted on a reflex. Grabbing his victim, upending her, hurling her in. And his paymaster had casually referred to her as a 'peasant'. Max could kill any man and eat a hearty meal soon afterwards. What Doubenkian proposed for Paula Grey filled him with loathing.

Approaching the Duke's Head, Paula, who had parked her car in a free space some distance away, noticed a shabby brown Ford parked almost outside the hotel. She also noticed the driver watching her through his rear-view mirror. He looked away quickly. He sat tensely behind the wheel, North African she thought, dressed in London clothes. She noticed two more things. In the back on the seat was a large travelling rug, and as he sat very still his engine was running. The meter showed he had been there for ten minutes.

She entered the bar and the white-coated man behind the long counter smiled at her and said, 'Good afternoon.'

At a table near the entrance a man stood up and came forward to escort her to his table. Tall, good-looking and heavily built, he was clad in a smart grey suit, white shirt and an old school tie. His smile was cheerful but she thought she detected a hint of strain in it.

'I am Evelyn-Ashton,' he began. 'It is very good of you to take the time to come and meet me.'

'I haven't got a lot of time,' she warned as he pulled out the chair for her.

'Oh, that is quite in order,' he assured her as with unusual agility he was back in his own chair facing her. 'What I have to say is hardly likely to take all week. A tipple of champagne to relax us? We were indeed in the habit of smuggling a bottle into the dormitory when I was no more than a boy at school. Indeed, yes.'

'I'd sooner have coffee, thank you.'

The barman had tactfully moved to the far end of his counter to give them privacy. Max turned round and ordered.

'Coffee for my guest with all the trimmings, if you please.'

Paula already knew something was wrong. Ages ago she had briefly had an Old Etonian as a friend before she escaped his predatory clutches, a man she soon found she disliked intensely. This so-called Evelyn-Ashton couldn't speak Old Etonian correctly. Near, but not near enough. While his back was turned speaking to the barman she dropped her handkerchief. Bending to retrieve it she slid the Beretta out of its holster and kept it in her right hand concealed under the table cloth, the muzzle aimed at her host's legs.

Max was in shock. Facing him was the most beautiful woman, in her thirties he guessed, and with the most entrancing smile. He'd almost decided before she appeared that he couldn't do it. Torture? Hideous. No way.

After coffee arrived a dam broke in his mind. She had to be warned. And certainly after what had happened out on the Wash. She sensed something strange in his manner, leaned forward.

'Is something wrong, something bothering you?'

He opened his mouth, swallowed, then it all flooded out as he forgot to speak like an Old Etonian.

'Miss Grey. Not from me anymore. I've been hired – this will be a shock – to kidnap you, dope your champagne, pretend you're ill, carry you out into that Ford outside, hide you in a travelling rug on the back seat.' He took a deep breath. 'Then torture you in a secret place, get Tweed on the phone to hear you screaming to lure him out. I can't do that to you. Please go now. The barman knows a back way out. Don't use the front entrance.'

'So,' Paula said coolly, 'what is the name of the Armenian?'

'Don't know any Armenians.'

In a strained voice he turned round to call the barman. She chose the opportunity to slip the Beretta back inside her leg holster under her jeans.

Max explained the problem to the barman in low tones but she heard every word.

'This lovely lady's husband is on his way here. Can you quickly show her out of the back way you told me about earlier?'

She laid a hand on his broad shoulder as she stood up to follow the barman.

'Maybe you should get out of the country quickly. Start a new life.'

She was still alert for a more sophisticated trap when the barman led her to a concealed door out of sight at the back.

'Where does this lead to?' she asked. 'And could you check to make sure there's no car or persons out there?'

'Nothing,' he replied, returning from outside. 'No room for a car. Nobody about. You turn left, walk straight down the alley until you come to an even smaller alley. That takes you into Tiverton Street, well away from the Duke's Head.'

'Thank you so much.'

'Good luck.'

It was all in a day's work to him. Paula was not the

first woman he had smuggled out just in time.

Paula had her Walther in her hand, concealed by her shoulder bag as she hurried over the cobbles. Thank heavens for my sensible shoes, she thought. She found the narrower alley and emerged into Tiverton Street, close to where her Porsche was parked.

She glanced down the street to where the brown Ford had been parked. It was gone. She realized then she had walked slowly over the cobbles to avoid twisting an ankle. She heard a familiar sound, a cross between a hum and a whistle. She turned round. It was Marler.

'I've been on the prowl,' he said with a smile. 'You look a bit tense.'

'I'm just going shopping in my Porsche.'

'Give you a hand?'

'Yes, please. The fridge is empty.'

When Max left the Duke's Head he was working on a problem. Taz, the Moroccan who was behind the wheel of the Ford, had been shown a photo of Paula Grey, so it was almost certain he'd recognized her when he saw her enter the bar. If he was questioned by Doubenkian, Max knew his own life wouldn't be worth a penny. Taz was a recent addition to the army of men Calouste had built up in different European countries and now in Britain. In Max's opinion the new recruit was poor quality but he could carry out simple jobs.

When Max opened the passenger door he saw the solution to his problem. Taz, slumped behind the wheel, was holding in both hands a sheet of white paper, carefully folded so it formed a chute. He was holding it up to one nostril while he snorted white powder heavily. He transferred the 'nose' of the chute to the other nostril and snorted again deeply.

He was so absorbed in his indulgence he was not aware of Max until he was seated beside him. Max wet a finger, dipped it into the remnants of the powder still remaining in the chute, tasted it. As he'd thought. Cocaine.

'Needed it . . . to pass . . . the time,' Taz said with a foolish grin. He was slurring his words.

'I will take the wheel,' Max said speaking very clearly. 'So get out, walk round the front of the car and sit in my seat.'

Taz had indulged heavily. He had trouble opening the door. While he did so Max grabbed the chute out of his hands, folded it tightly to keep the remnants of the cocaine inside, then tucked it in the door pocket.

He watched contemptuously while the Moroccan used both hands to hold on to the body of the car while he worked his way round to the passenger seat. As he flopped in the seat, Max lost patience.

'Seat belt, he snapped.

He was forced to fasten the seat belt round Taz himself. Then he started driving, the detailed plan now settled in his head. He took a devious route to Cambridge Circus, turned down Shaftesbury Avenue. It was late rush hour but there seemed surprisingly little traffic. He was approaching Piccadilly Circus when he saw the reason. Road works. The double decker buses were being given priority, two were purring towards him. He slipped into an empty space on the right-hand side, just vacated by a motorist.

'I have another job to do on my own,' he told Taz. 'You get out here. Walk a few metres along the pavement, then you cross the street and there's a Tube station,' he lied. 'Get a train to the lodging house in New Malden. Both rooms are paid for, covering the next two days. Get moving, man . . .'

He had to unfasten Taz's seat belt for him, then open the door on his side. Taz managed to step out onto the pavement and closed the door after him. Max lit a rare cigarette while he watched Taz stumbling along. The two previous buses had passed the Ford but another one was coming.

Taz stepped off the pavement to cross over without looking. The bus, with a clear road ahead, was moving at thirty miles an hour to make the next stop on schedule. It hit Taz – the driver desperately tried to brake but too late. The bus slammed into Taz, brought him down, rolled over his prone body with one wheel. The bus backed, one wheel red with blood.

Max had kept his engine running. He saw a man

dart out, bend down to check the neck artery, then stand up, shaking his head. Max signalled, turned out, drove slowly past a shocked crowd, proceeded on to the Circus.

An hour earlier, facing Paula Grey, he had been shaking inwardly at the prospect at what he was supposed to do. Now he was ice-cold and very hungry.

'I think I'll go to the Café Royal and order a full dinner,' he said to himself. 'At least I'm dressed for a place like that.'

8

'Nice car,' Marler remarked as Paula drove him towards the shops. 'I might think of getting a Porsche myself.'

'Cost a mint, as you probably guessed,' she responded. 'I have a very generous salary, as you'll know, but I saved for months to collect the deposit.'

'If you'd told me I'd have gone halves with you,' Marler joked. 'problem would have been which of us occupied the boot if we'd had a passenger. I think you'd fit better than me.'

She laughed and felt much better. Marler, sensing the tension in her when they'd first met, was talking more than usual. He continued joking, mimicking perfectly the voices of other members of the staff at Park Crescent.

She kept laughing and eventually protested goodhumouredly, 'If you don't stop I'll lose control of this beauty.'

'That's the idea. Then I'll take over the wheel.'

She pulled in a slot outside the large new food shop and Marler jumped out to feed the meter before she could reach it. Then he grabbed a trolley, waved her forward.

'In the Far East they call the servant who helps, boy.'

'Well, boy, I'm a quick shopper so keep moving.'

'And I'm ten years younger than you . . .'

She hauled food off the shelves, out of the refrigerated compartments. Soon the large trolley was piled high. She went to the checkout and Marler stared. A man in a white uniform picked up the purchases as they were checked out, then packed them in a series of strong brown paper bags. He then asked which was their car and wheeled thc large stock to the front of the Porsche where he placed them neatly in the luggage compartment. Marler reached in his pocket for a generous tip. The helper shook his head.

'Thank you, sir, but we're not allowed to accept tips. We get well paid if we're quick. Excuse me, I see another customer at the checkout.'

'Last time I saw that was in California,' Marler commented as he settled in the passenger seat.

'It's a new American food store with American methods.'

She was already driving away from the slot, her speed just below the limit. She slid through a gap in the traffic. A driver of another car shouted at her but she ignored him.

'Going back to California?' she asked.

'I don't think so. Full of blondes with incredibly long legs and not an atom in the brain department.'

Arriving back, eventually, at Park Crescent, Paula parked the Porsche in the yard at the back of the building. It was now dusk and they were followed up the stairs by Pete Nield, holding a small black velvet bag tightly in his hand.

All the staff were inside the office. Harry was seated in his usual position, cross-legged on the floor. He was dismantling a Walther, placing the elements in a plastic tray. Tweed waved a hand at his clear desk.

'Dealt with all the reports. Monica took the replies along to the Communications building further along the street. Ah, here's Mr Pete Nield. Took you a while, not that it matters if you've got the answers to my gold queries.'

'You'll be fascinated. I had to wait while my contact, who was amazed, took this stuff to another analyst.'

At the reference to the word 'gold' everyone gathered in front of Tweed's desk. Harry produced a large piece of black velvet, emptied the contents of the *poche*. With the office lights on, the specks and the larger piece glittered.

'From the Rand in South Africa.' Harry paused. 'Mined well over a hundred years ago. No doubt about it.'

'I had just wondered,' said Tweed, speaking slowly.

*

Before Paula prepared dinner for two at Tweed's house in Bexford Street they had carried the huge stock from the Porsche up to the first floor. Tweed was astonished.

'Why do we need all this?'

'Because both your big American fridges are almost empty. It's essential to keep up supplies.'

'We could run our own supermarket,' he chaffed her.

'I'm cooking. Fancy mushroom soup, lamb chops, potatoes, plus mixed veg, followed by a lemon tart I baked at Fulham Road?'

'My mouth's watering . . .'

When she was well advanced with the meal she came in to set the dining-room table, found everything laid. Two glasses of wine had been poured. She sipped one appreciatively. She peered over Tweed's shoulder at the book he was reading. *The Official History of Gold Bullion.*

They ate in silence, as was their custom. Only when they were perched on the comfortable sofa did Paula tersely tell Tweed about the bizarre Evelyn-Ashton encounter. He looked disturbed so she changed the subject.

'What did you think of Hengistbury Manor and its inhabitants?'

'Seemed like the most luxurious prison in the world. All those people living under one roof. I sensed hatred and maybe an atmosphere of evil. The lid held on by the remarkable Bella.'

'What about Marshal Main?'

'A charmer. Never liked them, probably because it's a quality I lack . . .'

'I've seen women of all ages look at you speculatively. Anything else about Marshal?'

'A ladies' man – and with no qualms when he gets fed up with one. Behind the hail-fellow-well-met flamboyancy I detected a ruthlessness.'

'And Crystal?' she asked, keeping her expression blank.

'Led me into her bedroom, saying the view was best seen from there. Then she tried to seduce me. She's strong but I managed to push her off.'

'And she was furious, even ferocious?'

'Oddly enough, no. She was calm, perfectly controlled. She took me along the corridor to show me Pike's Peak. A very unusual mountain – well, a huge hill. Shaped like a cone at the summit. Sheer sides. Nothing grows on it. I most certainly wouldn't attempt to climb it, not for a thousand pounds.'

'Lavinia?'

'Well . . .' Tweed paused. 'Certainly with the exception of Bella, the cleverest, most controlled person there. I must admit I had trouble reading her. Staring into those enormous glowing blue eyes I couldn't see what was behind them. Strong-willed.'

'And very attractive,' Paula suggested. 'Clever? She is a forensic accountant. The tops.'

'So is Crystal, and she's younger,' he remarked.

'What about the other director, Warner Chance, the father of Leo and Crystal? He's so quiet.'

'Again, excluding Bella, possibly the strongest and the most enterprising character in the whole set-up. I do suspect that he secretly despises Marshal.'

'Two incidents keep coming back into my mind,' Paula mused. 'I was struck by Bella's last comment – "to come and protect our treasure".'

'I noticed that wording.'

'But when you quoted Bella downstairs Snape was appalled. He almost shouted hysterically, "*She said that to you!*" Most odd, I thought.'

'So did I.'

'What does it all mean?' Paula wondered.

'Haven't a clue. Place is like a time bomb ready to explode.'

'Well, we won't be there if it happens. What about Snape?'

'Something odd there. I phoned a friend at the MoD while you were out. He served in Bosnia, was accused of shooting two unarmed Muslims in the back. The only witness was discredited and Snape was exonerated. Soon afterwards he voluntarily transferred to the Engineers. May have felt he was under a cloud. One thing I'm sure of – he knows more about what is going on there than anybody.'

'And that weird business about the gold,' she went on.

'I'll know more about that when I've consulted Bob Newman. After all, he is a reporter, or was before he joined us.'

Tweed suppressed a yawn and Paula realized she'd been asking him questions for a long time. She got up to clear the table and Tweed insisted on helping her. When they had arrived at the house he had taken off his jacket and tie to feel more relaxed.

'Time for bed,' she told him when they had completed the clearance.

'I think so,' he agreed, suppressing another yawn. 'When you can I'd like you to draw an Identikit picture of the head of Mr Evelyn-Ashton, who you met at the Duke's Head. You did spend time at art school in the evenings once.'

'I'll do it first thing tomorrow while he's fresh in my mind.'

Forcing himself to undress, Tweed flopped on the bed. The moment his head hit the pillow he was fast asleep.

Paula was restless. The nerve-racking episode with Evelyn-Ashton kept intruding. She could see his face perfectly, the weird change in his attitude before he confessed why he was really there. She crept into the drawing room. From a drawer she took out an artist's pad of cartridge paper, some sticks of charcoal. She sat down in front of a desk and began. She worked confidently and the sketch was completed in half an hour. She stood up, studied it under the shaded desk light.

'Got you, Mr Evelyn-Ashton,' she murmured to herself. 'First time.'

Which was when she heard a car crawling along the street below. She parted the closed curtains carefully. A brown Ford was stopped. She saw the driver jump out, then arch his right hand back like a cricketer about to lob a ball. Under the light of a street lamp she saw the face clearly. Mr Evelyn-Ashton. She heard the shattering of glass as the object crashed through into Tweed's bedroom.

She ran to the door. Tweed, who woke swiftly, was already out of bed. He had automatically switched on his bedside lamp. By its illumination she saw an object on the carpet shaped like a massive pine cone. A grenade.

'*Get back into the bloody living room!*'

She was frozen still. Frozen with terror for Tweed's life. He rushed forward, bent down, grabbed the object, hurled it out through the window. They both waited for the detonation. The silence was only broken by the sound of the brown Ford racing away up the street.

'I'm calling Harry,' Tweed said. 'He's the explosives expert.'

'What actually happened?' Paula wondered.

'Harry will tell us. After that I'm getting dressed. Won't sleep tonight.'

'Neither will I.'

She fetched a dustpan and brush while Tweed was phoning. She swept up the broken glass, including tiny shards.

When she entered the kitchen, Tweed, fully dressed, was preparing toast, boiled eggs, orange juice and coffee for an early breakfast.

During their meal they heard Harry's square steel-plated truck arrive. Paula got up, rushed to the window. Tweed followed at a steady pace. Looking out, they saw the truck parked and Harry, carrying a metal box in one hand, a powerful torch in the other, walk towards the object lying in the road.

He picked it up after shining his torch on it, raised it to his ear, shook it, placed it inside the metal box. Paula never ceased to be amazed by Harry's insouciance in such situations. Looking up he saw them peering out, walked to the front door which Paula had darted down to open. Tweed followed at his normal deliberate pace.

'Morning folks,' Harry greeted them. 'Grenade? It was a dud. No hole to pull out the pin. A frightener. See you later . . .'

'They knew which window to throw it through,' Tweed commented. 'They know too much,' he concluded as they went back up to the first floor.

'I saw who threw the thing,' Paula told him, producing her charcoal sketch. 'I saw him. Evelyn-Ashton. Here he is.'

'When we get to Park Crescent have a photocopy made for all the members of the team so they'll know who they're looking for.'

The time bomb at Hengistbury predicted by Tweed had detonated within minutes of their arrival at Park Crescent.

9

Paula just had time to obtain photocopies of her sketch of Evelyn-Ashton, then distribute one to every member of the team. Tweed had explained to them tersely the significance of Evelyn-Ashton. 'Very much doubt that's his real name . . .'

'Commander Roy Buchanan needs to see you very urgently,' Monica broke in after answering the phone.

'On the phone, you mean?'

'No, he's just arrived, waiting downstairs.'

'Ask him to come up.'

Paula stood up from her corner desk. Marler, leaning against the wall near her, was by her side when she looked out of the window. An unmarked police car was parked below. Behind it stood a gleaming Rolls-Royce.

'That Rolls belongs to Professor Saafeld, the eminent pathologist,' she whispered. 'I don't like this a bit.'

Commander Buchanan came into the office. Tall and lanky, in his late forties, he was an old friend of

Tweed's. Paula had expected him to be wearing his uniform as Commander of the Anti-Terrorist Squad. Instead he wore a dark grey business suit. Normally his expression was amiable but now it had a grim set to it.

He ignored an armchair, picked up a hard-backed chair, planted it in front of Tweed's desk, folded his arms.

'I am the bearer of grim tidings,' he warned as he placed his briefcase by the chair.

'Then tell me,' Tweed said calmly.

'Mrs Bella Main has been murdered in her study at Hengistbury Manor. The method used is strange and quite horrific.'

A rare and heavy silence descended on the office. They were all staring at Tweed. He had been told about a number of hideous events and his expression had always been impassive. Not this time.

He sat very still, almost like a statue. Brief flashes of different emotions crossed his face. Something akin to grief. Fury. A distant gaze as though he was recalling his interview with Bella, a woman he had admired and liked. Admired for her character, for her brainpower. Eighty-four years old. He'd thought she might live to be a hundred.

'She was so regal,' Paula said very quietly, 'so courteous.'

'*Regal!* That's the word for her,' Tweed agreed,

suddenly alert again. 'Her murderer must be tracked down however long it takes, no matter what risks it may involve.'

'I was just about to ask you,' Buchanan began, 'to take over as chief investigator of the case.'

'I'll do it,' Tweed said quickly.

'I have brought Professor Saafeld with me. He is waiting downstairs in the visitors' room.'

'What the hell has he been parked in that cell for?'

'His idea, not mine,' Buchanan said quickly. 'He thought I should tell you first. He knew Bella. He had a phone call from her about you after you'd left. She was very fond— I mean she had developed an admiration for you. Now,' he went on briskly, opening his briefcase, producing papers, 'in this case you have full powers, even an authorization of the fact signed by the Assistant Commissioner, together with a search warrant covering the whole of Hengistbury Manor and its three-hundred-acre estate called The Forest – or the large chunk of it belonging to the Manor.'

Tweed was examining the thick sheets of paper Buchanan had placed on his desk. The Assistant Commissioner's signature flourished at the bottom of both documents.

'Also,' added Buchanan, 'you have the full backing of the Home Secretary.'

'Who could be one of Bella's depositors,' Tweed said with a smile, his normal iron self-control now recovered.

'I wouldn't know.'

'With all this power I detect a political element.'

'Well . . .' Buchanan hesitated. 'Certain Ministers are concerned that the Main Chance Bank could now be bought out by an immensely rich and ruthless gentleman – who might then use his ownership of this powerful organization to go on to bid successfully for one of our Big Four banks. Which would practically give him control of the country.'

'He is British?'

'No.'

'He originates from the East?'

'He does,' said Buchanan grimly.

'And his name is?'

'I'm not allowed to disclose that.' Buchanan's mood became more light-hearted. 'As assistant you will have Chief Inspector Hammer.'

'Always save the best bit till last, don't you?'

Paula groaned, turned to Newman, who had been comforting her when the news about Bella had been first announced. 'Old Hammerhead,' she rasped well above a whisper.

'I'm very short of senior detective officers,' Buchanan said, turning to shake a friendly finger at Paula. 'And he is very clear he is your assistant,' he went on, turning back to Tweed.

'When does he go down to Hengistbury?' Tweed enquired.

'He's gone down there ahead of you with three photographers, two fingerprint experts and the other technicians.'

'Then we'd better get down there right away. Pete, you stay behind for the moment. My director, Howard, gets back from holiday tomorrow. Explain everything to him in detail and tell him I'll call him by phone soon as I can.'

'Will do, sir,' Nield answered tersely.

'You're in charge here for the moment,' Tweed added.

He walked to where Paula stood with two suitcases, took his own off her and hurried down to the visitors' room with Roy Buchanan and the rest of his team following. Opening the door he found Professor Saafeld comfortably ensconced in a chair, his legs perched on another, reading a book.

'I really think this is dreadful,' Tweed began, 'leaving you in a place like this while Commander Buchanan filled me in on—'

'I've been enjoying Robert Newman's huge bestseller, *Kruger: The Computer That Failed.*' He stood up. 'Isn't that Mr Newman just behind you? Well, Mr Newman, you must be at the least a millionaire from the proceeds. Deserve to be. This is my third reading of your masterpiece. A millionaire at least.'

'I have got a bit stashed away,' Newman said, smiling as they shook hands.

'You two can talk later,' Tweed said firmly. 'Don't imagine you know the complex route to Hengistbury?' he said to the Professor. 'Thought not. So I'll lead the way with Paula in her red Porsche. You follow in your Rolls. Bob, you'll keep behind the Rolls, bringing the team in your Merc. Now we move.'

As they turned out of Park Crescent with the Rolls behind them Tweed issued his warning.

'Paula, Saafeld drives his Rolls at a stately speed, as he should. So time your speed to his.'

'I had already thought of that,' she chastised him. 'If you like you can take over driving this dynamo. Now I'm wondering what horror we'll see at Hengistbury.'

10

'I phoned Snape before we started out,' Paula said.

She had just stopped her Porsche when the tall wrought-iron gates swung inwards. She drove slowly down the drive with the stately Rolls following and Newman's Mercedes bringing up the rear.

'I have the oddest feeling I'm in a dream,' she remarked. 'I suppose it's because we were here so recently.'

Parking near the steps leading up to the terrace, she jumped out to where Saafeld had briskly leapt out with his bag in one hand. Of medium height and in his mid-fifties the pathologist had a shock of white hair, was clean shaven. Below his well-shaped forehead his eyebrows were thick and white, but it was the penetrating grey-blue eyes which attracted attention. His nose was long above a strong wide mouth and the jaw had a pugnacious look, although he was the least aggressive of men except when dealing with fools.

They trooped up the steps and Snape was there to greet them. He smirked and as they entered, Marshal Main, wearing a black suit with a black tie, held out a hand, smiling unctuously. Tweed made a mental note for later that neither man appeared in the least distressed.

Tweed made introductions briefly. From nowhere Chief Inspector Hammer appeared, an even more bulky figure than Paula recalled. His aggressive features appeared even more domineering.

'I'll take you up to where she is, Professor,' he smarmed.

'Has the body been touched by anyone at all?' Saafeld demanded.

'Of course not, sir,' Hammer said with a trace of indignation.

'You are quite sure about that?' Saafeld snapped.

'It's my job . . . sir,' Hammer replied sullenly. 'This way.'

'I would prefer Mr Tweed took me up. Staircase, first floor?'

It was obvious Saafeld had taken an instant dislike to the chief inspector. Which was unusual, Tweed noted, since the Professor rarely showed his reaction to anybody. He led the way across the hall. At the side of the staircase, seated in a hard-backed chair, was Lavinia.

She wore a black dress, underneath which was a white blouse with a ruffled collar. Perfect, Tweed thought, she had not overdone the mourning. He smiled at her and let it go at that.

Saafeld walked quickly, alongside Tweed, while Paula followed them. When they entered the library adjoining the study they found it was occupied by four paramedics in white coats, all standing. Saafeld gestured towards them.

'I arranged for this squad to come here from Leaminster, which is closer to this mansion,' he explained to Tweed. 'They know the way to my place at Holland Park but I'll guide them in my Rolls.'

There were four other men, uniformed policemen. Two had large cameras slung round their necks, the third carried a briefcase. One of the fingerprint experts, Paula assumed. At that moment the study door was opened from the inside and Sergeant Warden, Buchanan's personal assistant, stood in the opening. Paula was surprised. She hadn't seen him for a long time. Buchanan had moved very fast to get this technical team here already. And so had Saafeld, arranging for the paramedics to arrive from Leaminster.

Warden, clad in a business suit, as always had a wooden expression and stood very erect. He addressed Tweed as he spoke.

'Since I arrived no one except myself has entered the study. May I show you in, sir?'

'If I may suggest it,' Saafeld said kindly, looking at Paula, 'it might be best if Tweed and I go in first.'

'I'll come out for you in a minute,' Tweed said quickly to Paula.

Paula did not feel self-conscious, standing in a room with so many strange men. She felt she should say something.

One of the photographers was eyeing her lecherously. 'Not often we get the pleasure of being so close to such a tempting lady,' he said with a leer.

'George,' his fellow photographer snapped, 'clean out your friggin' mouth with a strong disinfectant.'

Paula nodded her appreciation to him, didn't look at the lecherous type. The door from the study opened and Tweed stood there. He beckoned to her.

'Thank you very much,' she said to the man who had told off his fellow photographer.

'Up to you whether or not you come in,' Tweed said to her lowering his voice.

'I'm coming in,' she said firmly.

He closed the door behind her. Sergeant Warden was standing close to a panelled wall. Saafeld was waiting behind Bella's chair. Paula took in a silent breath. Bella was still seated in her chair, her magnificent head drooped forward. Her clothes were drenched with blood and she had a brutal collar round her neck, a collar of barbed wire with vicious spikes. The section of her neck still visible was slashed open with a deep bloodstained wound. It was one of the most horrible sights Paula had ever seen.

When she had entered the study Paula had tucked both her hands inside the pockets of her windcheater and both were now clenched tight. Her expression was calm and Saafeld was watching her closely before he spoke.

'To understand how it was done you need to come behind the chair.'

She walked steadily forward with Tweed close behind her. Joining Saafeld, she saw the ends of both sections of the fiendish barbed wire-collar had small wooden handles. The handles had been drawn close together and the ends of the wire twisted together to tighten the collar.

'I think I see how it was done,' she said, relieved that her voice sounded normal.

'The killer stood behind this chair and dropped the necklace over her head to her neck, then grasped the handles, tied the wire together as you see.'

He spoke as though explaining an anatomical point to a class of students. She nodded as she studied the blood soaking the back of the neck. Saafeld added a comment which was out of character.

'One of the most ghastly methods of murder I have so far encountered.'

'I don't understand how the murderer carried what you call a necklace into the study without Bella seeing it. And whoever did this must have been someone she knew well and trusted.' A thought struck her. 'Of course it could have been carried in concealed in something like a briefcase.'

She looked at Tweed, who was keeping silent, listening to her with an expression of admiration. He nodded agreement.

'But then,' Paula continued, 'the killer had to stand behind her to drop the necklace over her head.' She was glad to see Bella's short grey hair was undisturbed. There was at least some dignity left to her. 'The trim short cut of her hair would help the killer – the necklace would slip smoothly down over it to her neck. Do you think it took long?' she asked.

'Very quick if the killer had strong agile hands. I doubt if she knew what was happening since the carotid arteries are severed.'

Paula realized her hands were no longer clenched. She took them out of her pockets and stared at the carpet as she slowly walked round the desk to join Tweed.

'The rail-like gulleys we saw when we were here have gone,' she observed.

'I noticed that too,' said Tweed. 'Someone has used a vacuum cleaner. I'll find out who did that and when.'

'If you've seen all you need,' Saafeld said crisply, 'I need the police photographer to take pictures. The paramedics can come in. I want a sheet to cover her. I want her moved as little as possible, which means taking her away in the chair. Won't be easy navigating those stairs.'

'There is a lift,' Paula told him. 'It comes up from the main hall, stops just opposite the exit door from the library.'

'That's going to make things a lot easier.'

Tweed and Paula followed Saafeld to the library where he gave precise instructions. Tweed followed Paula onto the landing. She leaned over and saw Lavinia standing up while she talked to Newman. She called down.

'Lavinia, could you arrange for Snape to bring the lift up to this floor? Snape should stand by the open doors until they bring out your grandmother, please.'

'Consider it done,' Lavinia called back in a businesslike voice.

'What now?' Paula asked as they descended the staircase.

'I'm going to start interrogating people immediately. How is Lavinia?' he asked Newman as the granddaughter appeared on the far side of the hall with Snape in tow.

'She's down, naturally. I've been asking her about her trips to London to get her mind on to something else. We seem to get on quite well together.'

'Keep her talking. May stop her thinking . . .'

With Paula he headed for the downstairs living room. As they entered the only occupant was Marshal Main, pacing briskly up and down in his sombre clothes. A glass of champagne, already used, was perched on a round drum table with a bottle resting in an ice bucket. A peculiar drink to be imbibing under the circumstances, Tweed thought. He started his interrogation without formality.

'Mr Main, who discovered the body?'

'Don't waste much time, do we,' Marshal said with a smile as he ushered them to chairs round the drum table and sank into an armchair, the champagne glass in his hands, his long legs sprawled out, crossed at the ankles.

'Some refreshment,' he rattled on. 'Champagne may seem a trifle odd but Bella would have approved. She was never one to make a fuss in an emergency. Coffee instead?'

'Yes, please. For Paula too, I imagine.'

'I'll bring a pot,' a voice said from the door. Tweed swung round and a serious-faced Lavinia was standing by the open door, which she closed.

'Black as sin, if I remember rightly last time you were here. Well, the ultimate sin has been committed now,' he remarked cheerfully, raising his glass to Paula.

'Who discovered the body?' Tweed repeated in a grimmer tone.

'Well, as a matter of fact I did. About eight o'clock in the evening Bella used her desk box to ask me to bring up some accounts at ten o'clock.'

'How did you carry up the accounts?' Tweed enquired.

'How? In that blue folder on that desk over there. The accounts are still inside it.'

'What did you see when you entered her study?'

'Gave me a bit of a turn, I don't mind admitting it. She had her desk lamp on so it shone on her. I knew quickly something awful had happened. I saw that beastly thing round her neck and it was dripping blood . . .'

'You're sure the blood was dripping?' Tweed had leaned forward across the table. 'It's important because it helps to establish the time of the murder. Couldn't have been too long before you arrived when the murder was committed. What time did you arrive in her study?'

'I told you. Ten o'clock. She liked people to be punctual. I actually checked my watch before I knocked on the study door. Ten o'clock. On the dot.'

At that moment Lavinia appeared with a silver tray and the coffee pot with all the accoutrements neatly arranged. Tweed looked straight at her.

'Who discovered the body?'

'Marshal, my father.'

She glanced at him as though surprised he hadn't already told them. Tweed thought the way she referred to her father, using his Christian name, was very odd. He smiled, thanked her for the coffee. She left the room, closing the door behind her.

'Checking up on me, eh?' Marshal said savagely.

'Part of my job. I'll be talking gradually to the rest of

the family and I need to know if they're telling me the truth.' He changed the subject suddenly and Paula smiled to herself, knowing it was a technique he used to throw suspects off balance.

'Bella was, I gathered, Chairman of the Main Chance Bank, so who controls it now?'

Marshal straightened up. 'Well, I am managing director.'

'Co-managing director,' Tweed corrected him. 'There is also Warner Chance. I need to know,' he said emphatically, 'who legally will take over.'

'Well . . .' Marshal stroked his thick hair. 'After I had phoned the Yard and, eventually, been put through to a Commander Buchanan to report what had happened I then at once phoned Bella's solicitors, Hamble, Goodworthy and Richter in Threadneedle Street, to ask them to send her will here. It is being rushed to me by courier tomorrow morning. Then we shall know what arrangements she made in the case of her demise. Good enough for you?'

'I shall need to see that will before anyone else.'

'I say!' Marshal's face had turned red. 'It will have my name on it.'

'And probably Warner Chance's. Perhaps I'd better remind you I am in charge of this murder investigation.'

'So?' Marshal snapped indignantly.

'The will may well have a bearing on leading me to who was the killer of Bella Main.'

'It's not good enough!' shouted Marshal. 'I am entitled to read what is addressed to me. Something I had the wit to ask for.'

'Didn't waste any time, did you?' Tweed said quietly.

'What does that mean, damn it!'

'It means that within a very short period of time after you knew your mother had been foully murdered you were most anxious to see who inherited. That worries me,' he ended grimly.

'You haven't the authority,' Marshal raved.

Tweed produced the document Buchanan had given him. He handed it to Marshal. Paula, watching him read it, saw his hands tremble. Eventually he gave it back to Tweed.

'You are a big bug. Signed by the Assistant Commissioner.'

'So, when the courier arrives you will hand the envelope to me unopened.'

'I'm tired.' Marshal stood up. 'I think I will have my meal in my apartment.'

'Are you married?' Tweed said suddenly.

Paula again suppressed a smile. Tweed had again thrown him off balance. Marshal paused in midstride, turned, returned to his chair.

'Of course I was. You know Lavinia is my daughter.'

'Past tense,' Tweed continued mercilessly. 'So what did happen to her? I need to know everything about you.'

'Don't see that it matters twopence. But as you insist. My wife was killed in a road accident when Lavinia was eighteen. That was sixteen years ago. Lavinia was very upset.'

'As I suppose you were.'

'Oh, these things happen,' Marshal said airily. 'One copes.'

The door opened and Lavinia stood with an apron wrapped round her black dress. She waited to make sure no one was speaking.

'Lunch will be served in the dining room in ten minutes. I am sorry we didn't consult you. I suppose it's because of what has happened. I've told Mr Newman.'

Marshal jumped to his feet, obviously glad of an opportunity to get away from Tweed. He hurried towards Lavinia.

'I'll have mine in my apartment.'

'Mr Main,' Tweed called after him. 'Have you ever heard of Mr Calouste Doubenkian?'

'Sounds like one of those foreigners we keep letting in at Dover. Never heard of anyone with a name like that.'

'What do you think?' Paula asked, keeping her voice down even though the door was now closed and they were alone. 'It's so often the person who discovers the body who turns out to be the murderer.'

'That's a myth. When I was at the Yard I got someone to compute the statistics of murderers who had *not* found the body. They far outnumbered the type you mentioned. Was it my imagination or did Marshal look startled when I asked him about Doubenkian?'

11

Doubenkian's mobile buzzed. He looked at Max, answered it cautiously. 'Dunfield, sales director, speaking . . .'

The voice which spoke to him was again horribly distorted. They were using some kind of instrument: it was impossible to tell whether it was a man or a woman, which irked him.

'Bella Main has died suddenly.'

'Good. How did that happen?'

'Also Tweed has arrived at Hengistbury with Paula Grey. He brought with him Robert Newman, Harry Butler and a man called Marler.'

'You did say Newman?' Doubenkian enquired.

He swore. His informant had gone off the line. He was disturbed, looked round the interior of the cottage for a hammer. Knowing what he wanted, Max handed him the hammer he always kept for these occasions.

They had driven with Max behind the wheel from

the second base in Norfolk that day. They were now ensconced in an isolated cottage, owned by Doubenkian, situated well outside Leaminster, also located within fifteen miles of Hengistbury Manor, just outside the edge of The Forest. Max expected they would soon be moving on.

He watched as Doubenkian, his back to him, removed his dark glasses and replaced them with a protective pair. On a large wooden table he then proceeded to smash the mobile phone to pieces. Substituting his dark glasses for the protective version he turned round to Max.

'Isn't that going a bit far?' Max suggested. 'Once you have used a mobile you destroy the SIM card, then select from your collection a fresh one.'

'The report regarding Hengistbury is good – and bad. You know that Bella Main controlled the Main Chance Bank. She mistakenly refused to sell it to me. She is dead.'

'Murdered?' Max asked.

'My anonymous informant didn't say. Now we have to wait and see who inherits.'

'Who might that be?'

'Either Marshal Main or Warner Chance.'

'And supposing, whichever one it is, also refuses to sell?'

Doubenkian smiled, a horribly sadistic smile. 'Then we use the Vienna method. You remember the bank the owner first refused to sell? Then I had his offspring kidnapped and he agreed to sell immediately – without any reference to the police.'

'I still don't see how you would handle the situation.'

'Simple, my dear Max. If it's Marshal we kidnap his daughter, Lavinia. If it's Warner Chance we kidnap either his son, Leo, or his daughter, Crystal. Whichever it is, we tell the father his child's right hand, cut off at the wrist, will be delivered by courier. Carefully wrapped, of course. We must do the civilized thing.' He grinned.

'I can't do that sort of thing,' Max said firmly.

'You really are soft-hearted. That worries me sometimes. So I'll call in Jacques, the French butcher in Paris. It makes no difference to him whether the meat he is slicing up is dead or alive.'

Max, revolted, changed the subject. 'I still don't know why, once used, you destroy a mobile and use a fresh one.'

'Because of the terrorist threat, the British GCHQ is now monitoring calls at random. One call, recorded, does not arouse their suspicions. More than one might wake them up. So I use a different number each time. My informant has a list of the numbers in sequence. Which is why you need never fear a tough grilling at Scotland Yard.'

Max fetched a dustpan and brush, began scooping up the pieces of the smashed mobile phone. He was stopped in his tracks by Doubenkian's next order.

'Your next job is to kill Robert Newman, who is staying at Hengistbury.'

'Why Newman? He's an international news reporter. Don't see the point,' Max protested.

'Which is why I'm where I am and you are where you are,' Calouste sneered. 'He is now one of Tweed's key team members, but every now and again he writes a big article. It is syndicated all over the world. The moment he finds out I am involved he'll write another sensational article – so then all my plans to control Britain through capturing the main financial centres will be ruined. I want him dead. Preferably due to an apparent accident. But dead however you manage it. He's staying at Hengistbury.'

'I'll get down there in the morning.'

12

'Not thinking of mountaineering, Bob?' Paula teased.

It was the following morning after breakfast. Newman was standing at the end of the corridor beyond the second-floor apartment he had been given. By his side stood Paula while Lavinia, her arms crossed, stood on his other side.

'Bob climbed the Eiger in Switzerland to strengthen his muscles,' Paula explained. 'Can you believe it?'

'Pike's Peak may not be the Eiger,' Lavinia commented, 'but it has already killed three people who attempted to reach the summit. I gather there's only one so-called safe side for an ascent. You can see from here it is like an enormous smooth cone. Nothing grows on it. The rock is brittle so you can't hammer in pitons to hook a safety rope through. It's not so bad, apparently, for the first one hundred feet. Above there it's a death-trap.'

'Sounds like a challenge,' Newman replied with a grin.

'That's the attitude which kills men,' Lavinia warned.

'With a good pair of binoculars,' Newman persisted, 'the summit would be a perfect look-out point to scan The Forest, to see if anything funny is going on.'

'What can you do with men like this?' Lavinia remarked with a sigh.

She turned to study Newman. Early forties, she guessed. She liked his fair hair, his strong head with handsome features, his grey eyes which often had a quizzical expression. His shoulders were broad, his body well built. Everything about him suggested strength and determination. She rather liked him.

'Can you see it from Gladworth?' Paula enquired, hoping the answer would be a negative. 'Bob and I are going in to town on a mission for Tweed.'

'That's where you get the best view,' Lavinia explained. 'You walk down Pegworth Lane, opposite the Pike's Peak Hotel, where you can get the best lunch. The cone rises sheer above you. I've done a bit of climbing in the Italian Alps but you won't get me attempting Pike's Peak.'

'Excuse me a minute,' said Paula. 'I want to go and check something with Tweed . . .'

Left alone with Lavinia, Newman seized the opportunity to chat her up. He found her hypnotically attractive. Her mysterious large blue eyes seemed to swallow him up when he gazed into them.

'Don't you get bored sometimes, locked up in this great mansion?' he suggested with a smile.

'Sometimes,' her appealing voice replied.

'Then why not come up to my place in South Ken? We could paint the town red. Or at least go out to dinner, say at the Savoy?'

'I've been there,' she said, still staring at him.

'Well, what about the Ivy?' he suggested with a wide smile.

'I'd prefer the Savoy,' she countered.

'Anywhere in London that catches your fancy. Here's my card. If I'm out it won't be for long. I have an answerphone,' he pressed.

'So I leave a message. "It's me. At the Savoy,"' she teased him.

'Well, here's my card . . .'

'My hands are sticky from cleaning up the kitchen.' Her smile was wicked. 'Slip it inside the top pocket of my blouse.'

Without hesitation he tucked it inside the pocket. Lavinia's flirtatious personality underwent the swiftest change as she heard the clack-clack of Paula's ankle boots re-entering the room.

'I had got it right,' she told Newman. 'Thought it best to check. Lavinia looks dressed for more housework. We had better get moving, Bob.' She smiled briefly at Lavinia, whose face was now expressionless.

*

'We'll go in my Merc,' Newman said firmly as they walked down the steps from the terrace. 'Better than flying madly along in that macho-style Porsche.'

'I do happen to be a member of the Advanced School of Motoring,' she snapped back. 'I sensed you were taking more than a brotherly interest in the glamorous Lavinia. I thought back in town your girlfriend was Roma.'

'She's getting serious, so I'm beating a hasty retreat. I never saw the ambulance last night taking away poor Bella.'

'Practical Lavinia had told them to park at the back of the manor. Same thing with the police cars bringing that technical team from London. She said it was amazing how the locals heard bad news and gathered like ghouls outside the gates.'

Newman had started the engine when the rear door was opened. Someone jumped into the back, slammed the door shut. It was Crystal. Too late to consider throwing her out: the gates, presumably operated by Snape, were already opening.

'This is great!' Crystal called out as she leaned close to both of them. 'Escape from Belmarsh!' her voice was normal: buoyant and bubbling.

Paula twisted round. Crystal's flaming thick red hair was neatly brushed. She was clad in a riding jacket zipped up to her long neck, jodhpurs tucked into riding boots. Her wide mouth with full scarlet lips was open, exposing her sharp little teeth. She pulled a face at Paula before asking her question.

'Looks like we're headed for Gladworth. We are? Goody. I have loads of shopping to do. Why are you going there?' she demanded, sagging back in her seat.

Girl can't keep still a minute, Paula thought.

'We are also going in to Gladworth to do some shopping,' Paula replied.

'I'm going to sleep till we get there,' Crystal said.

Newman closed the window separating the two compartments. The glass was soundproof.

A moment later a courier on a motorcycle appeared from behind them. He slowed alongside Newman's window and Newman halted the Merc.

'Sorry to bother you,' the courier began. 'I'm looking for a Hengistbury Manor. Can you help?'

'You came past it,' Newman told him. 'Turn round, go back about three miles. Keep an eye open for tall wrought-iron gates on your right. You may have to use the speakerphone.'

'Thanks a lot, guv.'

'He'll have the will,' Paula whispered as they drove on.

'We'll miss the fireworks. Any idea who inherits?'

'Not a clue. Bella was a wily lady.'

'Expect there'll be a queue on the terrace when he arrives,' Newman mused.

'Lavinia will take charge. See it reaches Tweed first. He has already spoken to her.'

'All that money. All that greed,' Newman mused again.

'Way of the world.'

'And they're all being paid huge salaries, I'm sure,' Newman remarked.

'People always want more, more, more.'

'I don't,' he protested. 'That book gave me all I need.'

'They should put you in a museum. The Man Who Doesn't Want More. It's why you're so contented. I've noticed.'

'Did you notice we had hardly any talk from Warner Chance?'

'Another contented man. Just a minute. I could be so wrong.'

'Why?' Newman asked.

He never got a reply. They suddenly emerged from the dark tunnel hemmed in by massive firs on both sides and their dense branches overhead into the village of Gladworth. The sun was blazing and a few shoppers strolled the pavements.

Driving slowly towards them was a brown Ford. The driver had a deerstalker hat pulled down over his face, and was clad in country clothes which helped him to merge into the atmosphere of a country town. Max pulled into the kerb and watched the Merc, waiting.

★

Patiently, he observed. Newman had parked in front of a hardware shop. Attached to its window was a notice. *Climbing Equipment For Your Swiss Holiday.* He saw Newman going into the shop, a man easily recognized from pictures he'd seen in the papers when an article of his in *Le Monde* had been published while he was in Paris. A few days ago, he'd taken his picture secretly when he'd left the Park Crescent building.

He was startled to see Paula Grey by Newman's side. He recalled his encounter with her in the up-market Mayfair pub. Who the third passenger was he had no idea. She was a ravishingly attractive girl with long red hair, but it was Newman who excited Max. His victim had come to him.

Inside the shop Newman had bought a canvas bag with a strap he could sling over his shoulder. He began to collect pitons, two small strong hammers, a pair of climbing shoes.

'What do you want all that clobber for?' Paula demanded. 'You're not really going to climb Pike's Peak, are you?'

'I caught a glimpse of it as we passed Pegworth Lane. I feel like having a go.'

'Don't be so stupid,' she snapped.

Annoyed, she crossed to the pharmacy section, bought a bottle of toilet water. Crystal peered over her shoulder to see what she was purchasing. A faint whiff of Chanel drifted into Paula's nostrils. As she reached inside her windcheater for her purse, Crystal drifted away and she was joined by Newman. Instead of her purse she brought out a folded sheet of cartridge paper, her original sketch of the man who had lured her to the pub in Mayfair. She showed it to Newman.

'We'll know him if we ever see him again.'

'I will. I studied the photocopy you gave me . . .'

Reluctantly she followed Newman as he crossed the High Street. Behind them was a clatter of running feet. Crystal was coming with them. No pedestrians anywhere in Gladworth now. They walked down Pegworth Lane, a narrow cobbled street lined on both sides with old stone terraced houses. No one about. Paula found the heavy silence was getting on her nerves.

Beyond Pegworth Lane was a track, even narrower, hemmed in by trees and undergrowth. Ahead loomed the sheer side of Pike's Peak. Paula moved ahead, then called back.

'This looks like the tricky side you don't attempt.'

Crystal rushed past her. She had lifted the flap of Newman's shoulder bag, had grabbed a hammer and several pitons.

'I've climbed worse than this in Italy,' she shouted.

Agilely, she clawed her way up a good sixty feet. Then she inserted a piton and used the hammer. Newman had rushed forward to stand below her. Crystal hammered away. The rock she was endeavouring to drive the piton into crumbled. The piton dropped to the base.

'No good,' Crystal called down. 'Crumbles like glass . . .'

Then she lost her grip, came tumbling down. Newman had his arms held out, legs braced. He grasped her firmly round the waist, lowered her to the ground.

'No good,' she said breathlessly. 'At least I tried.'

'We're going back into Gladworth now,' Paula said, grasping Crystal by the arm.

Left by himself, Newman wandered round to the easy side. He stopped as he saw a tall heavily built man who had pushed his deerstalker hat over the back of his head – with his left hand. In his right he held a deadly 7.65 mm Luger, aimed at Newman. Magazine capacity eight rounds. The bullet chipped off a tiny sliver of rock as Newman dodged behind the sheer wall. He reached for his Smith & Wesson, realized that in the rush he'd left it in its holster in a locked cupboard in his apartment.

'Take the high ground, soldier,' Max called out in a sneer.

'You'd never reach the summit, you braggart,' Newman shouted back.

He had immediately recognized Max from Paula's sketch and was counting on the bravado he'd observed in his face. He heard the assassin clawing his way up the easy side, heading for the summit. Newman took a deep breath, threw away his shoulder bag, began clawing his own way up, seeking firm handholds, footholds.

He found that he was usually able to detect brittle rock, to avoid it. There was more tough, well-embedded rock than he'd expected. He *had* to reach the summit before the killer, who had the easier climb. But Newman had conquered the Eiger and this gave him caution as well as confidence.

'*Don't look down!*' he kept repeating to himself.

He didn't look up either, zigzagging his way up the smooth cone. It already felt colder, which told him he had gained a lot of height. Systematically he tested each handhold, each foothold, before trusting it. One false move and he knew he was already high enough for a fall to kill him. The worrying thing was he didn't know how his antagonist was progressing.

'Bob, you're nearly there . . .' Paula's voice, echoing a long distance away: but her message was clear.

He was higher up, nearer the summit than his enemy. Paula, brought back by the sound of the single shot, had rushed to the base of Pike's Peak. Circling it, she had seen how high the killer had reached, then run round to find Newman.

The realization sent a fresh flow of energy through him. He increased the pace of his climb, still testing each new hand- and foothold carefully. He was moving up faster. When he glanced up he had a shock – he was almost at the summit.

Suddenly, both hands gripping the lip of rugged rock, he peered over. The summit was a flat platform, about twenty yards in diameter. He hauled himself over and onto it. He would have given anything to lie there, to catch his breath.

Instead he forced himself to crawl a foot back from the rim, listening. He came to a point where he heard agonized movements below. He resisted the temptation to look over the edge. He had no weapon to defend himself. The killer might well still have his Luger. He looked round the plateau for a sizeable rock he could hurl down. No loose rocks.

Then he noticed the summit was littered with rock dust. He used both hands to scoop up a large pile. As he finished, a pair of hands appeared close to where he lay, gripping the rim. The left hand disappeared momentarily, the killer holding on by his right hand and, presumably a firm foothold. The hand reappeared. Holding the Luger. The muzzle was wobbling madly. The killer was trying to do two things at once with his right hand, grip the rim and hold on to the weapon. With a lurching heave more of the killer came into view, his sweating face, the image of Paula's charcoal sketch. Newman, who had moved closer, reacted.

He threw the rock dust, aiming for the eyes. A cloud of dust blotted out the face. Panicking, the killer let go with his right hand to clear his eyes. Then he lost all control. His body began plunging down. Peering over the edge Newman saw the body diving down, turn once in a somersault, then hit the ground. He lay very still.

Paula had seen the body hurtling down, had run back to avoid being hit. Then she ran forward to where the killer lay without a sign of life. She bent over him. Blood was flowing from the back of his head, from his back, from his legs, now misshapen. She felt his carotid pulse. He was still alive.

He opened one eye, stared up at her with an expression of disbelief. He opened his mouth. Nothing came out. He opened it again.

'You . . .' His voice was hoarse and she had to bend closer to hear what he was trying to say. 'Beaut . . . iful sight . . . for a man . . . to see last . . .'

'Don't try to talk,' she said. 'You could be all right.'

'Not this . . . time. Must warn . . . you. Calouste . . .'

'What about Calouste?' she said gently.

'Find bastard at . . . Heather Cottage . . . Fif . . . Fifteen miles . . . this side . . . of . . . Leaminster . . . plans kill . . . you all . . .'

The eye which had opened closed, and he seemed to sag further back. Again she checked his pulse. Nothing. He was gone.

She could hear faint sounds of Newman descending the easy side. She couldn't bear to watch him coming down. She had too clear a memory of the killer falling.

She stayed where she was, hoping to Heaven Crystal would remain in Gladworth shopping. She was so bemused she never heard Newman's footsteps. She jumped when he put his arms round her.

'Take it easy,' he said quietly. 'It's all over.'

'No it isn't,' she burst out as she swung round. Tersely she told him what the dead killer had told her.

'In that case we'd better get back to Tweed, let him know. Mind you don't step back.'

She looked down. A few feet from them was a ravine about a yard wide, seeming bottomless. Paula had not noticed it because the ground was all the same colour. She looked at Newman.

'That could be a big problem.'

'Certainly would be if that Inspector Tetworth was around, or whatever his name was – the policeman who stopped you and Tweed where the digger driver tried to kill you. You go back into the village, find Crystal, wait for me in the car. I've got to collect the piton and hammer Crystal dropped.'

'Well, the sooner Tweed knows Calouste is in the area, where he is . . .'

'So what are you waiting for? Go and find Crystal.'

He waited until she had run out of sight down the track. He put on a pair of gloves, bent down, avoiding the blood, took hold of the corpse, rolled it to the edge of the ravine. He heaved it over, listened for it to hit bottom. No sound at all. The killer's Luger was lying a few feet away. He used his foot to kick it over the edge, listened. It seemed like minutes before he heard the distant clang of metal striking rock. The ravine was frighteningly deep.

Picking up Crystal's piton and hammer, he tucked them inside his shoulder bag. He glanced round carefully. No trace of anyone having been there. He hurried back to the car, where Paula was standing.

'Crystal will be here any moment. She's bought up half a clothes shop . . .'

'Before she arrives, no one climbed Pike's Peak. I didn't like the look of it.'

'Understood. Here's Crystal, loaded with carriers.' She lowered her voice. 'I wonder what's in the will?'

13

When they reached Hengistbury Manor the gates swung open and they drove along the pebble drive. Tweed was on the terrace by himself, pacing slowly in the sunshine, a look of concentration on his youthful face.

Paula dived out of the car as soon as it stopped, ran up the steps. Crystal, climbing out after her, refused Newman's offer to help her with the carriers. Clutching them tightly she was about to pass Tweed when he called out to her.

'You've bought half of Gladworth, I see . . .'

'It's my money,' she snapped, resenting his observation, and disappeared inside the house.

'Can I ask what was in the will?' Paula suggested as Newman joined them.

'You may. I read the will, as I said I would. Quite a few of the family were present – Marshal, Warner, Lavinia (I had to ask her to join us), then Warner's son,

Leo. It was a short and simple will. Control of the bank was divided fifty per cent to Marshal, fifty per cent to Warner, and there was a gift of one hundred thousand pounds to Mrs Grandy, the housekeeper.'

'How did they react?'

'Marshal was furious, stormed out after shouting it would never work. Warner was quiet, remarked it would work and he thought it was typical of Bella's common sense. Leo was outraged, screamed, "Why the hell does that old faggot get all that money?" Warner told him to apologize but Leo was livid, stormed off after Marshal. I told Mrs Grandy myself and she looked astounded, then said it was very generous. You know it all now.'

'Bella was very shrewd. We have urgent information for you.' She explained quickly their experience at Pike's Peak and what the killer had told her before he expired.

'I'm still amazed,' she continued, 'that the man sent to kidnap me in Mayfair, to torture me and presumably kill me, would warn me a second time when he was dying. And tell me where we can find Calouste.'

'Another example of the complexity of human nature,' Tweed observed. 'So many people I've encountered have this mixture of decency and evil.' His manner changed, became commanding. 'Now, action this day, as Winston Churchill used to say. We must immediately try and hunt down Calouste. We'll take a large force. Heavily armed. You'll come, of course, Bob. Harry Butler is helping the police crew to search this vast house, so is Marler, who was investigating The Forest. Heavily armed,' he repeated.

Tweed led the way inside the manor while Newman admitted he'd left his .38 Smith & Wesson revolver and ammo locked in his apartment. Tweed held up a hand before they all rushed into the hall.

'The story is we've had a tip that Bella's killer is hiding in Gladworth.'

Tweed ran up to the floor where Crystal had her apartment, in time to see Chief Inspector Hammer emerging with a disgruntled look.

'Take all week to search this rabbit warren,' he grumbled, then marched off down the corridor, vanished into another apartment.

Tweed caught sight of Sergeant Warden coming up the stairs. He beckoned to him, spoke quietly.

'Could you do me a discreet favour?'

'That's why I was sent here, sir.'

'Find out which apartments the Chief Inspector searched and do the job all over again. He's a good chap but inclined to rush things.'

'I'll tell him Commander Buchanan told me he wanted everywhere searched twice. Good job we had that warrant. Mr Marshal Main is almost going crazy at what he calls this invasion.'

*

Tweed's expedition assembled on the terrace. Marler, wearing camouflage, carried a zipped-up golf bag. Paula stared at it and he noticed her glance. He smiled at her.

'Usual contents in the bag. My favourite Armalite rifle with 'scope and spare ammo, including a few explosive bullets.'

Harry Butler was laden down with a heavy bulging leather bag. She raised an eyebrow and asked him what he was preparing for.

'You saw me having a word with Tweed in the hall. He made it sound like a possible siege of this Heather Cottage. He doesn't think this Calouste character will give up easily – plus the fact he's certain Calouste has a small army of gunmen in this country. So, Paula, what have I got? Grenades, both explosive and smoke. A rocket launcher I can fit together in thirty seconds. Also an automatic weapon firing six hundred rounds a minute. I guess I'm equipped.'

'Equipped for small-scale war,' she commented.

Newman came out looking more comfortable now he could feel a Smith & Wesson in its holster. Earlier Harry had gone to the back of the mansion and driven his brown Ford, parking it behind Newman's Merc. He had then gone back again to fetch a black Audi.

'Too many cars,' Tweed suggested. 'We could use mine . . .'

'May have been spotted,' Harry explained. 'You head the convoy in the Audi, Newman follows in his Merc, I bring up the rear in the Ford. Leaving your car parked out here in front will suggest to any spies you're still here. And the Audi is armour-plated, with bullet-proof windows.'

'Good thinking,' Tweed agreed. 'But if we ever locate Heather Cottage I'll wave this red handkerchief out of the window. When I do Newman and Harry drop back, park where they are. A convoy could alert Calouste. I wave the handkerchief a second time when we are ready to assault Calouste's base. Now all we need is someone to open the gates.'

'Lavinia will do that,' Marler drawled. 'Snape has gone missing.'

At Tweed's suggestion Paula sat beside Marler, who was behind the wheel of the Audi. Tweed chose to sit by himself in the rear. He wanted to concentrate on the complexities of this strange case.

The gates opened before they reached them. Tweed instructed Newman to turn left and head into Gladworth.

'You think that's where Calouste is hiding?' suggested Paula.

'No, I don't. But Heather Cottage will be within ten or maybe twelve miles of Hengistbury. Far enough away to avoid his being seen, near enough to the manor to react to a development.'

'Oh, I said Snape had gone missing,' Marler began. 'I tried to find his cottage in The Forest. Failed. Coming back I thought I saw him on the edge of The Forest overlooking the drive. He appeared to be using a mobile phone. I went over to where I'd seen him and no one was there. Could have been an optical illusion.'

'When we've driven through Gladworth,' Tweed instructed again, 'look for a minor road or lane which turns off to the right.'

'Why not the left?' Paula wondered.

'Because according to the map you gave me, beyond Gladworth the left side is covered with The Forest. No escape route. On the right it's open country . . .'

'Marler,' Paula said tentatively, 'what do you do in your spare time?'

'Fly my plane, look after it. Or I practise shooting on a range. Keeps me in top form.'

'Any girlfriends?' she ventured.

'Well, I do like women. Not infrequently when I'm out and about attractive women smile at me. Some quite a bit younger than me. But there seems to be a sort of barrier between me and women. They like to be amused. I can never think of anything to say. Silly.'

Paula had a shock. She had known Marler a long time and it was only now she realized what he was really like. Marler was *shy*. Where women were concerned.

'Keep your minds on the road – with a right-hand turning,' Tweed growled from the back.

'Oh, don't be so crochety,' Paula snapped. 'Marler *is* checking all the time, for Heaven's sake.'

Tweed had learned that there were times when it was wiser not to respond. A moment later Marler slowed, swung the Audi over to the right up a hedge-lined lane. Beyond the hedges were rolling-green hills. No more fir trees. No houses either.

Marler had pulled down his visor. The brilliant sun blazed through the windscreen. After a while of driving round bends in the lane Marler informed Tweed they had travelled fourteen miles.

'Keep going,' Tweed ordered.

'There's a white brick house on the edge of the road,' Paula called out.

Marler slowed down. Tweed took out the handkerchief to wave and warn the two cars behind to stop. Paula leaned forward as Marler crawled past. She shook her head and told Marler to keep moving.

'No good,' she called out. 'I saw the signboard. Dogwood is the weird name of that place.'

'It's also too close to the road,' Tweed commented. 'I'm sure Calouste would choose a house well back from the road.'

They drove on another mile without seeing another residence. Paula suddenly leaned forward, looking partly to her left. She told Marler to crawl again. Tweed took out his handkerchief, lowered his window.

'Heather Cottage!' Paula called out triumphantly. 'I saw it on the name board . . .'

'Tricky place to assault,' Tweed decided after studying it through his pocket binoculars. 'Open ground up to the place.'

The Audi was parked out of sight a few yards up the lane. Newman had reacted to Tweed's signal. His Merc was parked out of sight of the target, with Harry's Ford parked behind him. Paula borrowed the binoculars. Heather Cottage was a large two-storey thatched cottage with windows open on both floors, its walls painted white.

Marler lifted up the golf bag from the floor under their feet. Unzipping it, he took out the Armalite rifle, carefully attached the 'scope. Getting out, he aimed it at a rock by the side of the lane, adjusted a screw slightly, checked his aim again.

'I'm going up the far side of the hedge running along the edge of the place. There may be a back door they could slip out of.'

'I'll come with you,' said Paula, her Walther in her right hand.

By now Harry, heavy satchel on his back, had crawled to the cover of the front hedge, followed by Newman. Harry extracted two large grenades from his satchel, held one in each hand. He grinned.

'Tear-gas grenades. One through the open window downstairs and one through the upstairs window, same side. I go in through the right-hand window.'

'I come with you,' said Newman.

'I'll watch the front door,' Tweed decided. 'They may come out that way.'

The grenades went in, exploding inside their target areas. Harry rushed forward, dived in through the open right-hand window. A lean evil-faced man wearing jeans and a jacket, neither of which fitted him well, staggered in from the hall, holding a machine-pistol. He tried to aim it.

'Behind you!' Harry shouted.

Instinctively the lean-faced gunman looked back. No one was behind him. He vanished into the narrow hall, ran out through the open back door. He had recovered from the whiff of tear gas he'd absorbed. He saw Paula standing by the hedge, swivelled his machine-pistol to mow her down. Two shots were fired from her Walther. The first bullet hit him in the forehead, the second penetrated his chest. He fell against the cottage wall, slid down it, sagged in a heap.

'You did well,' said Marler. 'My Armalite slipped on my shoulder. Must be losing my grip.'

Paula ran forward, stooped to check the gunman's carotid arteries. She shook her head as she straightened up. Tweed had just appeared round the front corner of the cottage.

'He's dead,' Paula called out. 'From his features he looks French.' She put on a glove, searching his trouser pocket, brought out an almost empty cigarette packet. 'Gauloise,' she called out. 'He *was* French.'

Newman's head poked out of an upstairs window. 'Is everything OK out there? Oh, I see it is. Harry and I have checked the place upstairs as well as downstairs. No one here. What's that motorcycle doing leaning against the wall there?'

'Escape vehicle he won't be needing any more,' Marler replied, pointing to the corpse.

'Kitchen's a real mess,' Newman reported.

Tweed darted inside through the back entrance, followed by Paula. They entered the kitchen. A sudden breeze blew soiled napkins out of the window. The table was laid for three. Plates had remnants of food, two with eggs and bacon, the other with unsavoury-looking sausages. Cups were half-filled with coffee. Paula used a latex glove to pick up and examine a large piece of wrapping paper. It had the name of a butcher's shop in Paris.

'French again,' she said. 'So what happened here?'

'Calouste was warned by his informer we were on our way,' Tweed said grimly. 'Left behind one chap to clean up, the dead one outside.'

'He's going to be difficult to capture,' Paula mused.

'Or kill,' Tweed said. 'After what Buchanan told me about his track record, the bit known, in France and Austria, that would probably be the best solution. He's one of the most ruthless, cold-blooded villains I've ever encountered. In the meantime we search this place from top to bottom. It's obvious he left in an almighty rush, which means he could have left something behind.'

Newman and Tweed disappeared to search the upstairs while Butler and Marler checked the downstairs. Paula stayed in the kitchen. She emptied the food off the plates in the dustbin outside the back door, then closed the window and began a systematic search.

Under the cooker she found a screwed-up piece of paper. Still using the latex gloves, she cleaned a portion of the table and carefully spread out the sheet of paper. It was perforated down one side, which suggested it had been torn from a notebook. A single word had been written on it in black biro.

Sheebka.

Sounds Turkish, she thought. She then went outside to pick up the napkins blown out of the open window. Half under the side hedge she spotted a large coloured sheet. She brought it in, spread it on the table. She was looking at a single page torn from an Ordnance Survey atlas. It was a section of the West Country with a black circle marked round the county of Cornwall. At that moment Tweed returned, followed by Newman, Marler and Butler.

'As I expected, not a thing in the whole house,' Tweed told her.

'You're wrong,' Paula contradicted. 'Look at these two items.'

They all gathered round the table to look at her finds. Tweed picked up the sheet from a notebook with his latex-gloved hands.

'Sheebka? Doesn't mean a thing. Cornwall circled could be significant. Devil of an area to search, but not now.'

'What, then – after this?' Paula wanted to know.

'It's a bust,' said Harry, who had joined them. 'How the hell did Calouste know we were coming?'

'Good question,' Tweed agreed. 'It confirms he has a spy who could be inside Hengistbury. Communicates with him by mobile phone. The only answer.'

'Who could it be, then?'

'No idea.'

'I told you I thought Snape, lurking at the edge of the wood, watched you leave. Can't be sure it *was* Snape,' Marler said.

'So how would he overhear where we were going,' Tweed asked, 'if he was prowling in the wood?'

'He couldn't,' Marler agreed. 'I'm going to give Newman a hand with cleaning up the mess outside. He's moving the corpse of that Frenchman, I'm cleaning blood off the walls he smeared when he slid down them.'

'I was wondering about that,' Tweed commented. 'Then we all go back to Hengistbury.'

Ten minutes later both men appeared. Newman explained he'd hidden the body under the side hedge, Marler reported the cottage wall was as good as new – 'That is,' he added, 'like it was when we arrived.'

Tweed had just settled himself in the passenger seat of the Merc with Marler behind the wheel, when he made his remark, staring at Heather Cottage.

'I wonder what happened here before we arrived on the scene . . .'

About two hours earlier Calouste was seated behind the wheel of his car, parked beyond Heather Cottage, but with a clear view of the road from Gladworth. He was expecting two of his French employees. He was also in a position to drive off if the wrong people arrived. He was not wearing his dark glasses.

A Renault appeared, pulled up in front of the cottage. A man got out. Calouste switched off his engine, which had been running ready for a speedy take-off. He walked back to the cottage. His feet, clad in soft-soled black shoes, moved quickly and he moved with a curious rolling gait. His lack of height was countered by the width of his powerful shoulders, his large nimble hands. He wore a dark trilby hat and an expensive dark suit. If seen by a local they would be sure he was a London businessman.

He had deliberately told his employees he would arrive later so he could check on their punctuality. He approached the two men on the grass as they unlocked the front door.

Despite his silent approach it was, of course, Jacques who swung round, a nasty-looking wide-bladed knife in his right hand.

'Jacques,' Calouste began, speaking in English, 'Pierre has brought a motorcycle? Good. Then he can park it round the back of the cottage. Afterwards he makes breakfast swiftly for us. Bacon and eggs for me and for you, Jacques. For himself I assume he'll want the sausages in that greasy package he's hugging. Inside French wrappings, I see, which was very foolish of him. He must destroy the wrapping before we leave. We may not be here long.'

The lean Pierre, with the evil elongated face, understood English but it was Calouste's technique to keep a man in his place by giving his orders through a third party.

'Very good, sir,' Jacques replied. He used French to repeat the orders to Pierre, adding, 'Get moving, you lazy lout. Motorcycle first out of the boot, parked round the back, then try and prepare a decent breakfast.'

As the two men entered, Calouste stepping inside first, Calouste reflected that Jacques was his prize catch. He owned a butcher's shop in Paris, was a butcher by profession.

Jacques was, in Calouste's opinion, a remarkably reliable personality. His shop was patronized by many of the upper-crust element in Parisian society. Normally servants would fetch what was required, but not infrequently the lady of the house would come herself. Certain ladies like to collect their own meat and flirt with him. He could be so amiable and humorous, and his brutal face could slip into a warm smile.

Jacques, habitually well dressed, had frequented bars and restaurants where he could listen to how the upper class spoke. Soon he was able to speak in the same way.

Once, a guest at a party of several senators and their wives, he had kept them all amused with the stories he related. At one party he had taken a risk, relying on the amount of alcohol that had been consumed.

'There's nothing I enjoy more than slicing up meat,' he had remarked with a grin. 'Whether it's animal or human meat.'

The men had burst into laughter. The women had smiled at the joke. Reluctantly.

Calouste, who had heard of him, was half-hidden away in a dubious bar at a table in an alcove when the key incident happened. Jacques was caught up in a quarrel with a man twice his size and height. His opponent had drenched him with insults, had then walked up to him with an automatic in his hand. He had used the flat of the weapon to slap Jacques a hard blow on the face. Jacques had swiftly produced a wide-bladed knife and rammed it into the ape's chest. As the fatally injured man staggered back, collapsed, everyone in the restaurant had run out. Calouste, wearing his dark glasses, had caught up with Jacques.

'If you work for me I will pay you fifty thousand dollars a year. If you agree to liquidate anyone who stands in my way I will pay you twenty thousand dollars per kill . . .'

That was how it had started, Calouste remembered as he gobbled down his breakfast.

His instinct told him it might be wise to move on soon. He had not had a word over Max's mobile and he was supposed to report regularly. Something must have happened. At that moment his own mobile buzzed.

'Yes?' snapped Calouste.

'Orion here. About half an hour ago Tweed and a large team drove off in the direction of Gladworth.'

'Why not an earlier warning?' Calouste raged.

'This was the first opportunity to call you.' Reception was beginning to fade. 'Marshal Main has a second home at Sheebka.'

'Where?' Calouste scribbled the name on a sheet of his notebook.

'Sheebka. Why don't you listen?' There was a brief moment of clarity. 'Seacove in Cornwall . . .'

The phone had gone dead. Calouste didn't bother writing down Seacove. He tore out the sheet from the notebook, screwed it up, threw it on the table. He was so busy he didn't see the wind had blown the bit of paper onto the floor. Pierre, who had just come in, didn't see it either as his boot kicked it under the cooker.

Calouste picked up the Ordnance Survey atlas he had brought in. Turning to Cornwall, he circled it with his biro, tore out the sheet. It was the only sign of panic he had shown so far. He rushed into the front room to collect his packed bag. The wind which had blown up suddenly lifted the map sheet, floated it out of the window.

'Pierre is almost losing his breakfast since I told him to stay behind and clear up,' Jacques reported.

'We've all eaten only half our breakfast.'

'What shall I tell him,' Jacques persisted, 'if Tweed arrives before he's finished?'

'Tell him to motorcycle across the fields at the back, for God's sake. You and I leave now.'

Calouste was in such a hurry to get away he grabbed the Ordnance Survey atlas. He'd forgotten he'd torn out the map of Cornwall.

He ran across the front garden and up the road to where he'd parked his car. As he moved off Jacques was in his car behind him. They reached a roundabout with five possible routes. 'Which way now?' Calouste muttered to himself. Then he saw a signpost, *West Country*. Cornwall was somewhere down there. He swung the wheel along that route.

14

Tweed had a shock as he climbed out of the car now parked at the foot of the steps leading up to the entrance of Hengistbury Manor. Standing at the top of the steps, arms folded, a smirking expression of triumph on his ugly face, was Chief Inspector Hammer. He couldn't wait until Tweed with Paula, Marler, and Newman close behind him reached the terrace.

'You can all go home now,' he gloated. 'I've solved the case. The murderer was Crystal Chance. Caught her red-handed.'

'Be more specific,' Tweed suggested.

'Come with me, then,' Hammer commanded.

He led them up the wide staircase, almost swaggering. They arrived at Crystal's apartment. The door was closed. Outside stood Sergeant Warden.

'I've left another junior officer inside with her,' Hammer announced.

Junior officer? Tweed glanced at Warden, who raised

his eyebrows. Warden was regarded as a highly experienced officer.

With a flourish Hammer opened the door, entered the apartment. They were in the bedroom. Crystal was seated on the bed, her green eyes glowing with fury as she combed her hair. Seated on a chair facing the bed was a uniformed policeman. Hammer turned to him.

'Well, Parrish, has she moved from the bed since I left? To go to the lavatory, for example – or should I say the loo in these exalted circles?'

'It's called the loo in most places these days,' Crystal snapped at him.

'Not talking to you,' Hammer told her. 'Well, Parrish?'

'Since you left she has remained where she is now . . . sir,' he added after a pause.

'Then shove off. Join the others in searching. Although it's a waste of manpower after what I've discovered.'

'So what have you discovered?' Tweed enquired when Parrish had left the room.

With another flourish Hammer opened the double doors of a wardrobe equipped with old enamel ball-shaped handles.

'Stop!' Tweed ordered. 'Were you wearing gloves when you first opened those doors? You're not sure? Which means you didn't. So it will be useless checking for fingerprints. Yours will have smeared the original ones.'

'He wasn't wearing gloves all the time he was in here,' Crystal said viciously.

'No one was talking to you—' Hammer began, glaring at her.

'Concentrate,' Tweed ordered. 'After you'd opened these doors, what did you do next?'

'Bent down, removed that pile of stuff I've dropped on the left. Hey presto! Look at that.'

Tweed crouched down. He saw two collars of wire with savage-looking spikes protruding. They seemed to him to be replicas of the ghastly collar which had ripped Bella's throat open. Each was complete with a pair of wooden handles to jerk the wire tight. He looked to the left where a pile of blouses had presumably concealed the collars. The top blouse was badly torn and strips of it were attached to the wire of one collar.

'Chief Inspector,' he said, to calm down the officer, 'you were in quite a hurry when you searched this wardrobe.'

'I'll say he was,' Crystal screamed. 'Those are pure silk, those blouses. I bought them in a sale at Harvey Nick's but they still cost a small fortune. I'm suing that policeman.'

'From a police cell?' sneered Hammer as he stood up with Tweed.

'Chief Inspector,' Tweed said grimly, 'I think it's time you joined the others and helped the search. Now! Please.'

Crystal calmed down the moment Hammer had left. She said with conviction, 'Isn't it obvious that someone planted those beastly things on me? Hammer had ordered all apartment doors should be left unlocked. I was working on accounts in the upstairs library when Hammer summoned me back here. Anyone could have slipped in.'

'It's a possibility,' Tweed agreed.

'Something I want to tell you,' she said, lowering her voice.

'Would you sooner I was not here?' suggested Paula.

'No, I want you to hear too. It's about my half-sister, Lavinia. I hate her, but that's not why I'm going to tell you about the secret scandal no one else will tell you.'

'Sisters often don't get on,' Paula mused. 'Sounds as though that's the case with you and Lavinia.'

'Lavinia is the chief accountant. I'm only her assistant. We're both forensic accountants and I could do the top job as well as she does.'

She brushed a curl of red hair away from her face and Paula studied her. She looked perfectly calm, perfectly normal. Perhaps more than Tweed, Paula could understand her fury when Hammer had torn and ruined her new silk blouses.

'Maybe,' Crystal suggested, 'I could meet you both in the library downstairs and tell you what I know down there. I feel the police may come back to search again.'

Tweed knew Sergeant Warden would soon check Hammer's search. He opened the door. At the far end of the corridor Marler and Newman were staring at Pike's Peak. The summit was now covered in cloud. He walked along to them.

'Bob,' he said to Newman, 'a long job for you. I think those fiendish collars – two more have been found in Crystal's room – could have been created from a length of wire taken from the top of the wall guarding this huge estate. Snape probably has a telescopic ladder which could reach the top. Could you check the whole wall?'

'Snape has a cottage in The Forest,' Marler said. 'I'll join you. I know the way to his cottage now . . .'

Tweed and Paula arrived in the library to find Lavinia the only occupant. She greeted them cheerfully, pulling Newman's leg.

'Well, did you climb Pike's Peak? I imagine you could hardly resist the challenge.'

Newman laughed. 'I took one look up and decided I wanted to live a little longer.'

'Then some time you should visit Marshal's hideaway at Seacove down in Cornwall.'

Seacove? *Sheebka*, Tweed muttered under his breath. The weird name Calouste had scribbled on the screwed-up bit of paper found under the cooker at Heather Cottage. Confirmed also by the Ordnance Survey sheet of Cornwall they'd found with the county circled.

'What's down at Seacove?' Newman asked.

'Nothing!' Lavinia laughed again. 'It's minute and wild. He, that is Marshal, has the most amazing small luxury yacht. Designed by Marco Shepherd, the unorthodox designer of ships.'

At that moment Marler appeared at the door. He beckoned to Newman, who sighed.

'Have to go. Work to do. Talk about climbing Pike's Peak.'

'You must excuse me too,' said Lavinia. She gave them her flashing smile. 'A load of accounts to check and they won't wait.'

When they had both gone Tweed and Paula settled at the round table. In a few minutes Crystal slipped into the library, clutching a notebook. She raised her eyes to heaven.

'The library is usually empty mid-morning. Today it was just like Piccadilly circus. I was hiding at the top of the stairs until they'd all gone. This is so secret. It is all about my cousin—'

'What do you mean?' queried Tweed, puzzled.

'Don't interrupt me or I'll lose the thread. Before

Lavinia was born, Marshal and his wife had tried hard to have a child. I heard this from my so-called aunt on her deathbed. Long before, Marshal had been quietly fooling around with any attractive woman who took his fancy. One affair lasted for months and she became pregnant. Marshal told his wife, who was desperate for a child. You can guess the rest but I'd much prefer it if you heard it from her. I think Marshal has been paying her huge sums of money to keep her quiet.'

'Blackmail,' Tweed rapped out.

'Definitely. I found a secret chequebook. He's been paying the real mother twenty thousand pounds a month for ages.'

'Good Lord,' Tweed said. 'That's nearly a quarter of a million a year.'

'It is,' Crystal agreed. 'But, like Warner, my father, he's very rich. The name of the woman is Mrs Mandy Carlyle. She lives at Baron's Walk, Dodd's End, a village this side of Tunbridge Wells. You will go and see her?'

'No time like the present. And you come with me, Paula.' He took the sheet with the address Crystal had torn from her notebook.

'Does Lavinia know this woman is her real mother?' Paula asked.

'I don't think so. It was all done very quietly.'

'Time we set off for Dodd's End,' Tweed decided, standing up. 'If anyone wants to know where we've gone we've made a quick visit to London.'

15

They were getting into the Audi when Tweed changed his mind. He got out again and Paula joined him. Tweed explained as they mounted the steps, 'It occurred to me I've interviewed most of the family prior to a tougher interrogation later. One person I've overlooked is Warner's son, Leo.'

Reaching the top of the staircase they saw Sergeant Warden leaving an apartment. He had just closed the door.

'Any idea which apartment is Leo Chance's?' Tweed asked.

'He's in there.' Warden gestured to the apartment he'd just searched. 'Nothing incriminating. Leo is an odd bod.'

Tweed knocked on the door and they walked in, Paula following Tweed. Leo, neatly dressed in jeans and a T-shirt and with his flaxen hair combed, sat in a wicker chair with a pile of typed sheets perched on a drawing board. He grinned at them.

'Already had one of you in here. Now I get the big guns. Seat yourselves.' He eyed Paula politely. 'Care for a Coke to wet the whistles? Both of you? No? OK by me.'

'Leo,' Tweed began quietly, after they were seated in armchairs, 'could you please tell me where you were on the night Bella was murdered?'

'A night to remember. I was where I am now, checking some balance sheets. Before you ask, no one with me. So no alibi.'

'Between the hours of 7 p.m. and 10 p.m.'

'Same answer.' Leo tucked his hands behind his thick neck. His build was brawny, Paula noticed. 'Again no alibi, folks.'

Leo was restless. He drew up his long sprawling legs and reached for a guitar lying on the bed, began strumming a popular tune from years ago, which Paula recognized.

Then he stood up, still strumming his instrument, and began a little dance, jerking the guitar upright, then down. He appeared absorbed in what he was doing.

'I would appreciate it,' Tweed said, 'if you'd sit down and play your guitar when we're gone.'

'I'm eccentric. Everyone at Hengistbury thinks so. What do I care? I was once grabbed and put in a clinic.'

As he spoke he stopped dancing. Throwing the guitar back on to the bed, he sat down again in the wicker chair. Crossing his legs he waggled one up and down. Can't keep still for a minute, Paula thought. He sat hands clasped together, his fingers interlaced.

'Why were you put in a clinic?' Tweed enquired.

'Thought I was potty. At least Marshal did. Took me to a place in a house the other side of Gladworth. Couple of trick-cyclists, as Churchill called them. Psychiatrists to you. One Mr Kahn, a negro. The other Mr Weatherby, white. I chattered a lot of rubbish to confuse them.'

'Your father took you there?'

'He did *not*! Marshal took me. My father was in America on business. When he got back and found out what had happened he blew his top at Marshal, punched him. Never known Dad hit anyone before. He got in the car, drove to the clinic, brought me home – after telling those two guys they were fakes. Soon afterwards the clinic closed. Weatherby and Kahn disappeared abroad into the wild blue yonder. The rumour was they were caught in a tax fiddle. Have you interviewed the others?' he asked suddenly.

'Some of them,' Tweed replied cautiously.

'So all you've heard is a pack of lies. They're all liars. Bet no one's told you about the back door left open on the night of Bella's murder.'

'You tell me, please.'

'Mrs Grandy, our delightful cook and housekeeper, has the responsibility of checking it last thing. On that night I couldn't sleep. I was thirsty, so I went down to make a pot of tea. Switched on the kitchen light and saw the back door was half open. At two in the morning. I closed and locked it, made my tea, brought it up here.'

'Was anyone else about?' Paula asked.

'No, honey, not a living soul. Although I thought I heard the door to the upstairs library being shut. It creaks. Decided it was my imagination.'

'You have been very cooperative,' Tweed said as he stood up to leave.

A smirk appeared on Leo's face and quickly vanished.

'The kitchen and Mrs Grandy next,' Tweed said grimly as they descended the stairs. 'Someone else I've missed.'

'What did you think of Leo?' Paula wondered. 'I'm sure he's not potty. He seemed to be very articulate.'

'I didn't like the smirk on his face at the end. It suggests "I got away with it".'

At the top of the staircase they met Lavinia. As always, she was smartly dressed. Today she was wearing a pleated blue skirt, a poloneck sweater, gleaming shoes. Her swathe of black hair might have just been attended to by a Mayfair hair-dresser.

'We've just heard disturbing news,' Tweed said. 'How do we get to the kitchen?'

'I'll show you.'

Snape was hanging round in the hall and Lavinia said no more. She waited until they were walking along a narrow corridor, pointing out a narrow flight of steps the servants used. A young maid was passing. Lavinia stopped her, adjusted her cap, smiled and proceeded along the corridor.

Arriving at a heavy door, she pushed it open, led them into the kitchen, a vast oblong room. Here hygiene and hard work took the place of panelling. The walls were of stone, as was the spotless floor. The equipment was very modern, including two mammoth-sized refrigerators.

At the far end was a large wooden table where a well-built woman in her fifties was chopping meat. She ignored the intruders. Lavinia spoke in a clear voice tinged with authority.

'Sorry to interrupt the work, Mrs Grandy, but this is the police. Deputy Assistant, that is Chief of the SIS and his assistant, Paula Grey.'

Mrs Grandy, a hard-faced disagreeable-looking woman with grey hair, tight mouth, aggressive curved nose and dark hostile eyes, turned round. She glared at Lavinia. She raised the meat cleaver, and Paula thought she was going to slice more meat. Instead she swung the cleaver down with a ferocious sweep and thudded it into the table. Other scars in the wood showed where she had performed this act before.

Standing with her arms akimbo, she glared contemptuously at Paula, transferred the gaze to Tweed and finally to Lavinia.

'How in the name of the devil do you expect me to get my work done with these useless interruptions? I have already chased a rude chief inspector out of here with my meat cleaver.'

'You could have been arrested,' snapped Paula.

'Rested, you say? He ran out like a scared rabbit.'

'Mrs Grandy,' Tweed said firmly, 'I'm here to find out who murdered Mrs Bella Main. You will answer all the questions I put to you. For example, where were you on the night of the murder between the hours of 7 p.m. and 10 p.m.?'

'You accusing me of murder?' she growled. 'Get my lawyer on you. That I will.'

'Just answer the question. Unless for some reason you're feeling in need of a lawyer.'

'Mrs Grandy,' Lavinia intervened quietly, 'everyone in this house has had to answer these questions, including Mr Marshal and Mr Warner.'

Not Warner yet, Tweed thought, but kept quiet. 'Between the hours of 7 p.m. and 10 p.m., please?' he repeated.

'All right.' Mrs Grandy drew herself up to her full height. 'I served dinner in the library that night at 6 p.m. They prefer it to the dining room – Lord knows why. The rest of that evening I was in here, eating my own meal, then preparing for the next day.'

'Anyone come in here while you were preparing?'

'They know better.' Mrs Grandy glared. 'Better than to come in while I'm working.'

'Absolutely no one came in here that evening?' he persisted.

'Just told you that, didn't I?'

'Mrs Grandy, I gather one of your duties is to make sure the back door over there is secured for the night. Did you do so on the night Mrs Bella Main was murdered?'

'Course I did.'

'Actually I normally check too,' Lavinia said. 'That night Mrs Grandy was having trouble with a soufflé so I left her to check the door.'

'A soufflé?' Paula frowned. 'Surely that has to be made not long before serving?'

'Oho! We have a cooking expert!' Mrs Grandy sneered. 'I eats the same as my employers. Warner sees to that. So I'm hungry and feels just like a soufflé. First time it flops, so I start all over again. It was half-past eleven before I felt better after eating the second one. A bit tired by then, I was.'

'A member of the household told me when they came down here at 2 a.m. that door was open.'

No one asked Tweed which member of the household had told him, though it was a question he had expected. With Paula he walked over to the now partly open door. There was an ordinary lock and the door itself was made of ordinary wood. He had found the loophole in Hengistbury's security.

He opened it wide, walked out with Paula and Lavinia at his heels. There was a narrow path through grass backed up by the menacing walls of The Forest. Tweed asked where the path led to.

'To Snape's cottage,' Lavinia told him. 'But I'd better come with you. It's easy to lose your way.'

'Thank you, but not now. We have to visit the police in Gladworth to keep them quiet. So you didn't have any opportunity to check this door was locked on the night of the murder?'

'No. I'd been wading through a mass of accounts and I was very tired. When I heard Mrs Grandy was still in the kitchen I didn't want a row. A lapse on my part.'

'You can't be responsible for everything,' Tweed said with a smile. 'Now we really must get into Gladworth before that Inspector turns up here . . .'

At the bottom of the stairs Tweed and Paula met Sergeant Warden. He gestured to them to follow him onto the terrace.

'Thought I should tell you, sir, that soon after the two of you entered Leo's room I saw someone was listening outside the door. Looked as though they might have been there for some time.'

'Man or woman?' asked Tweed.

'Difficult to be sure. I think it was a man. I only saw

a shadow. Then Chief Inspector called to me to help with the search. I'd been leaning over the banister on the upper floor. Not a good viewing point.'

'Who do you think it could have been?' Paula asked when Warden had left them, disappearing into the library.

'I haven't a clue. Place is crawling with people.'

They were nearly knocked down by Snape at the exit as he came rushing in from the terrace. He looked nervous as he apologized.

'So sorry. So much work to do and I'm behind schedule. I don't want Mr Marshal on my back.' He spoke over his shoulder as he hurried to the staircase.

They walked quickly down the steps and jumped into Newman's parked Mercedes. Their Audi was presumably round at the back of the house. Tweed inserted the key into the ignition – he had been handed it before Newman set off to explore the walls with Marler. He tightened his grip to turn the key.

16

Calouste had driven only a few miles down the road to the West Country when he pulled into a lay-by. Jacques stared at him.

'Something wrong?'

'Think like the enemy.'

'I don't understand.'

'You wouldn't,' Calouste sneered and turned to look at Jacques. This was something Jacques always disliked, was nervous about. Two large dark lenses gazed at him, eyeless. 'I have just changed my mind.'

'So what do we do now?' Jacques asked, mystified.

'If Tweed with his team, whom I've been informed left the manor, heading for Gladworth, has located Heather Cottage, he'll find no one there. So, his logical decision is to return to Hengistbury.'

'What if he does?'

'You have used explosives. What did you put in the boot of this car?'

'A carrier of food and a flask of coffee. The bomb is in the leather hold-all I put on the floor behind us.'

'What!' Calouste screamed. 'We have been driving with a bomb barely a foot from us? You are stark raving mad!'

'Calm down,' Jacques replied. 'The bomb is not active. You could drive over a large ramp and nothing would happen. So put away that knife before I get annoyed.'

In his fury Calouste had produced a stiletto with a needlelike blade. It disappeared and Calouste was again in a good humour. He patted Jacques's substantial knee.

'Tell me, please, is this the kind of bomb you attach to a car?'

'It's exactly that.'

'I'm driving back to that roundabout which has many escape routes. You take the bomb with you. Tweed likes travelling in the Mercedes. You walk from the roundabout to Heather Cottage. Check to see if there are signs Tweed has been there. Pierre will have hidden, knowing him. Look at the map. See if the countryside opposite the cottage is level enough for you to borrow Pierre's motorcycle to take you across the fields to Hengistbury. I think you may find the Mercedes parked in front of the manor. Attach the bomb to it. You may have trouble crossing open ground.'

'No trouble. I have some overalls I'll wear. People at this time of day are rarely peering out of windows. So, if they are, they'll see a man like a mechanic in overalls. A mechanic.'

He was getting out of the car when they'd reached the roundabout. Calouste called out to him.

'How are you going to get over that high wall with—'

'You do your job, I'll do my friggin' job. You talk too much.'

Jacques was the only member of Calouste's large team of henchmen who, when provoked, would tell his boss to go to hell.

Jacques had approached Heather Cottage cautiously. He chose the same route Marler had taken earlier, moving behind the side hedge. There were no cars in the road. He found Pierre's body, concealed under the hedge. He was not sorry: in his opinion Pierre had been useless. But he was relieved when he saw Pierre's motorcycle still leaning against the wall.

He wasted no time. The leather hold-all containing the bomb, several wires to be fixed later, a long piece of rope with a hook at one end, were all carefully added to the pannier with the bomb. Finally a neatly folded white coat. He started the machine, headed across the road through a gap in the hedge.

The ground was perfect, rolling green hills covered

with fresh grass. From the crest of an unusually high slope he saw the tops of the manor's Elizabethan chimneys, just in view over the 'barricade' of The Forest. He headed for them.

Leaving the motorcycle concealed in undergrowth, he pushed his way along the track where Harry Butler had waited for a signal from Tweed's lighter. Emerging, hold-all slung over his shoulder, he checked the windows of the manor with a compact pair of binoculars. No sign of anyone.

Carrying the long coil of rope, he walked quickly to where The Forest surrounding the manor masked him. Putting on his white coat, he slung the rope to the top of the wall. Its hook anchored in no time. Climbing the rope he took out a pair of clippers, cut a hole in the barbed wire.

Perched on top of the wall, he hauled up the rope, reversed the hook, dropped the rope down the inner side. He'd get out the same way he'd come in. Descending the rope, he walked confidently across the open space to the foot of the terrace. He was pleased earlier to have seen the empty Mercedes parked below the terrace.

A tarmacadam drive would have helped. On the side of the car facing away from the terrace he dropped to the drive coated with pebbles. His legs sprawled widely behind him as he eased under the car. The wires had already been attached. He heard the magnetic pad click as they clamped to the car. He turned a switch. The bomb was active. As soon as the ignition was turned on, the car and occupants would be blown to smithereens.

He had trouble easing his back from under the car, scattering a wide area of pebbles. He returned the way he had come. Settling himself in undergrowth in the track he waited. Jacques liked to see the results of his careful work.

Tweed and Paula walked down the steps, jumped into Newman's parked Mercedes.

'*Stop! Don't start that car, for God's sake!* Get out of the bloody thing now!'

Harry Butler's warning shout came loud and clear through Paula's open window. She stared at Tweed.

'Do exactly as Harry says,' Tweed ordered her.

'Should we take the key out of the ignition?'

'No! Touch nothing. Just get the hell out of the car.'

They met Harry, who had run down the steps carrying his tool bag. Paula, confused, asked, 'Why? What's wrong?'

'That's wrong.'

Harry pointed to the considerable disturbance of the pebbles on the far side of the car. She could almost imagine the shape of a man in the way they were scattered.

'Someone's been under the Merc,' Harry said. 'I

noticed the pebbles all over the place from a first-floor window, saw you both about to get into the car, grabbed my bag and tore down the stairs . . .' He paused, breathless.

'What now?' Tweed asked.

'You both go inside, to the very back of the hall. You stop anyone coming out onto the terrace while I check under the car. You don't come out until I've come back in. Something is terribly wrong. Go on into the house and stay there.'

'Be careful, Harry,' Paula said as they started up the steps.

'Careful is my second name,' he told her with a grin.

The last they saw of Harry as they looked back before entering the hall was of him sprawled flat, torch in one hand, pair of clippers in the other as he eased his plump body under the car.

They were waiting at the back of the hall when Lavinia appeared, a bundle of papers under her arm. She lifted her eyes to the ceiling.

'Marshal always wants everything done yesterday. I'm off to the dining room for some peace and quiet.'

She disappeared down a narrow corridor towards the kitchen. Tweed, worried, checked his watch, wondering how long Harry would take, whether he was in danger.

Fifteen minutes later Harry appeared at the entrance. He was carrying a metal box which must have been inside his hold-all. He beckoned to them.

'OK now,' he said cheerfully. 'You can drive to Singapore if the mood takes you.'

'Was there something?' Tweed asked.

'Only this,' he said after glancing round the terrace, which was empty.

Tweed and Paula peered inside the metal box. It contained a slim black box with a spray of cut wires. Paula guessed immediately.

'It's a bomb.'

'Give the lady the money! Very sophisticated version. You turn the ignition key – or extract it once inserted – and the Merc explodes, becomes scrap metal. It's totally deactivated now. I'll dismantle it.'

'How on earth could someone get in to plant that?' Paula wondered.

'Sheer cheek and nerve,' Harry replied. 'So much for security at Hengistbury. Enjoy your trip,' he concluded cheerfully.

17

Jacques, crouched in the brambles by the side of the track, was confused. He had been looking forward to seeing the Mercedes blown to smithereens. Perhaps even elevated a few feet before it crashed to earth, a fireball consuming the occupants.

Instead, his vision blurred, he saw activity. Reaching in his pocket for his binoculars, he dropped them. He could not find them in the tangle of brambles. He swore. What was happening?

A patient man, he waited for what seemed a long time. Then, to his astonishment, he saw the gates open. The Mercedes was proceeding down the drive. At the gateway it turned to his right, towards London.

Jacques was shattered. Was the bomb defective? No, that was impossible. He was an explosives expert. Carefully he began his retreat along the track. Getting into the saddle of the motorcycle he drove at high speed, bouncing over hill crests.

He would tell Calouste the truth. It was safer. He knew Max used to lie to conceal a failure. Now, he was sure, the durable, but too human, Max was dead. Arriving at the roundabout he found Calouste waiting in his car. Jacques eased the motorcycle in the boot, climbed into the front passenger seat beside him. Calouste again took the turning to the West Country.

'Tweed is dead,' Calouste hissed.

It was a statement, an expectation.

'No, he isn't,' Jacques said firmly. 'For some reason the bomb I placed under the car did not detonate. It was not a defective bomb—'

'What!' Calouste screamed. 'He must be. I want him dead, so you are wrong.'

'I'm afraid not. I caught a glimpse of him driving away to London. I—'

'It cannot be,' Calouste screamed again as he drove into the lay-by they had parked in earlier. He threw his door open, his stiletto in his hand. Jacques grasped the handle of his wide-bladed knife. Calouste jumped out, began circling the car with his ambling walk.

'Tweed must be dead!' he screeched. 'It was Tweed who told Bella not to sell the bank to me.'

'I thought Bella was murdered before Tweed went to Hengistbury,' Jacques unwisely replied through the half-open window.

'Tweed has a weak spot,' Calouste raved on. He was using his stiletto to stab at the air, at imaginary forms of Tweed. 'That tart he is always with, the one who did not come to meet Max in Mayfair.' He paused. 'At least that is what Max said.' He began dancing round again, stabbing at nothing with the stiletto. 'So,' he raved on, 'we kidnap her . . .'

'Then what do we do?' Jacques muttered, knowing Calouste was not listening to a word he was saying.

'We take her fingerprints on ten different cards,' Calouste screamed from the field of yellow rape he had dashed into, using his razor-sharp stiletto to cut the heads off the flowers.

Jacques sagged in his seat. He had never seen Calouste like this. His green eyes were glowing with hatred. Jacques did not know Calouste, ever cunning, was using green-tinted contact lenses.

'When we have her fingerprints we send one photo marked with a cross on her right index finger . . .'

'What for?' asked Jacques who had an idea of the answer.

'You are a butcher. You chop off the right index finger and we send it to Tweed through the post. To stop any further mutilation Tweed resigns from investigating the case, also resigns as Deputy Chief of the SIS,' Calouste screamed.

'Suppose he refuses?' Jacques yelled.

What was also getting on Jacques's normally ice-cold nerves was Calouste continuing to slash the heads of the rape as he continued his crazy dancing. Jacques had had enough. He shouted his question out of the window.

'What if Tweed still refuses your demands?'

'We continue to slice off parts of the girl's anatomy. That is, after we have sent photographs of her with the relevant sections marked with a cross.'

What was really disturbing was that Calouste's face appeared to have changed. His jaw was twisted to one side, which caused his mouth to twist into the most evil smile Jacques had ever seen.

Jacques determined to react. He made a show of glancing in the rear-view mirror, then shouted at the very top of his voice.

'I think I can hear a car approaching the crest of the road behind us. Sirens blaring.'

Calouste ran to his seat behind the steering wheel. The most extraordinary transformation had taken place. His face, only moments before the devil incarnate, was now quite normal. He glanced in the rear-view mirror, saw no sign of an approaching car. The stiletto had vanished. Reaching into his jacket pocket he brought out a long fat envelope, handed it to Jacques.

'I so appreciate your support that here is a little present. Inside you will find twenty thousand pounds in Swiss banknotes. Now we will drive on. To Seacove.'

18

There was a curious incident as Tweed drove cautiously along the winding road, away from Hengistbury, still under the forbidding canopy of dark fir trees. A Rolls-Royce crept round a bend ahead of them. Marshal was at the wheel. He honked his horn, pulled into the side of the road, waved a hand for them to stop. Tweed drew alongside, lowering his window as Marshal lowered his. Marshal was holding a mobile phone.

'Tweed,' he called out buoyantly, 'I've had a splendid idea. Follow me and I'll take you both down to Seacove, my hideaway in Cornwall. Very remote, and I'd love to show you my beautiful luxury yacht. Very advanced design,' he rambled on. 'Created by Shepherd, the most unorthodox designer in the world. You could turn your car round at a gap in the hedge just beyond the bend behind me . . .'

Before Tweed could reply, Marshal had pressed numbers on his mobile.

'Might be fun,' Paula whispered. 'And I think we ought to see the place. We could go to Dodd's End to see Mrs Carlyle tomorrow.'

As Tweed hesitated Marshal was talking loudly into his mobile. They could even hear the answers from the other end.

'That you, Lavinia? Good. I'm thinking of taking Tweed and Paula down to Seacove now. Where? *Seacove*.'

'Did you say you're taking Tweed and Paula down to Seacove?' she asked.

'Not a good idea,' Warner's voice rumbled. He must have been standing close to her. 'It will be freezing today,' he continued.

Tweed started shaking his head but Marshal was so absorbed he never noticed.

'Mrs Grandy,' Lavinia's voice called out, 'there may be two less for lunch. Marshal is taking Tweed and Paula to Seacove. Yes, I said *Seacove*.'

Tweed at last caught Marshal's attention across the open windows. He had waved a hand up and down.

'We'd love to, Marshal, but another day, please. We've an appointment we can't miss in London!'

Marshal threw the mobile on the seat beside him. His face showed disappointment, then broke into an engaging smile.

'That's a date. Hope your trip is successful.'

'I'm sorry if you're disappointed,' Tweed said before

he drove on, 'but I think we must interview Mrs Carlyle at once – what Crystal told us could have a bearing on the case.'

'I have no idea where Dodd's End is,' Tweed said some time later, 'so it's a good idea you're navigating. It's quite a complex route when you reach Kent.'

'Don't worry,' Paula reassured him. A minute later she pointed to an ancient wooden signpost, the name just readable: *Dodd's End.* Tweed stared at what lay ahead up a small hill.

'It's this place?'

'Only a hamlet. Looks as though the builder who created it about thirty years ago favoured Tudor.'

There were nine houses, each well spaced from the next. All had two triangular roofs over dormer windows with wooden beams attached to the white plaster walls, and all had neatly tended large front gardens. No one seemed to be about. Tweed had the impression they'd been abandoned when a plague came. At the far end, on the crest of the hill, was a larger house facing down the road.

'They've all got numbers, no names. So which one is Baron's Walk?' Tweed complained.

'I saw a woman sneaking a look at us from behind a curtain,' Paula told him. 'The house on the left you're almost past. Let's ask her . . .'

The front door of the house had a brightly polished

handle, which Tweed had to rap on several times before it was opened. A scrawny woman with an unpleasant expression appeared.

'Yes?' she said sharply, arms crossed.

'We're looking for Baron's Walk, a Mrs Carlyle,' Tweed said.

'Are you now?' the woman sneered. 'So why is the girl with you?'

'Sorry, I don't understand.'

'Well, the elegant Mrs Mandy Carlyle normally receives only single male visitors. She never talks to any of us, but then we'd never talk to her.' She stared at Paula. 'Maybe she's taken to having a voyeur watch the show.' She was shutting the door when she looked out again, speaking venomously. 'That big house at the top of the road. You're disgusting.' With this final verbal shot she slammed her door shut.

Tweed shrugged. 'Sorry about that,' he said as they got back into the car.

'Don't be. She's probably the biggest voyeur in Kent herself.'

Reaching the larger house they found the only way in was to drive up a wide area of concrete which led them inside a garage. Paula heard the automatic door closing behind them and grasped the butt of her Walther.

A side door opened, lights came on. A tall woman in her late forties stood in the doorway. Her long hair was bottle blonde, her tight low-cut jumper revealed a good figure. Her face was attractive but showing signs of becoming gaunt.

'Who the hell are you?' she greeted them.

Tweed and Paula had climbed out of the car and showed her their identity folders. The woman's earlier challenging confidence changed.

'Well . . .' She cleared her throat.

'We are investigating the murder of Mrs Bella Main,' Tweed said grimly. 'I believe you've had some friendship with one of that family.'

'I suppose we'd better go into the sitting room.' She led the way up a staircase with an expensive carpet, yellow with purple stripes. Expensive but tasteless. They went into a large living room at the front of the house. Heavy net curtains were half-closed. The main furniture was two long and wide sofas, piled with cushions, also purple.

'Do sit down,' she suggested. 'I'm going to have a brandy, my favourite tipple. How about you two?'

They both refused, sat down in armchairs close to each other while she poured a large amount of brandy into a glass. She was about to recline on one of the sofas when Tweed pointed to an armchair close to them.

'This is an interrogation. Please be good enough to sit there. Thank you. Now, your relationship with Marshal Main. I have been told you became pregnant and conceived a child. Is this true?'

'So Marshal has blown the bleedin' gaff. Much good it will do him . . .'

'So it is true? We are talking about a murder case.'

'Yes, it is true. I'll tell you how it happened. Then I'll phone Lavinia, bring her over here, blow the whole story.'

'You do a cruel thing like that and I'll see you're charged with blackmail. Judges hate that crime, sentence heavily. Marshal has been paying you twenty thousand pounds a month. That's getting on for a quarter of a million a year. Tax free. So it amounts to Heaven knows how much over the years.'

Tweed knew he was walking a tightrope. He hoped to heaven Crystal had told the truth, had seen the monthly withdrawals in Marshal's secret chequebooks.

Mrs Carlyle had, up to now, been sitting upright in her armchair. She suddenly sagged back, her face crumpled, she spilt brandy from the glass she had been sipping, hastily perched it on a table with a trembling hand. Tweed felt relieved. He had summed her up as a hard case on first seeing her.

'I'll tell you,' Mrs Carlyle said in a broken voice, 'if you'll promise to forget about blackmail charges.'

'I promise nothing,' Tweed said remorselessly. 'Just tell your story. The whole truth.'

'At that time, years ago, the doctor told Marshal's late wife she could no longer have the baby she desperately wanted. They didn't want to adopt. Mrs Main worried about what they might get. When he told her about his affair with me, that I was pregnant, she agreed to take it over secretly as her baby. I didn't want the damned thing. We had separate rooms at a crooked clinic. Doesn't exist any more. When the baby was born it was brought to Mrs Main. She loved it. Cost Marshal a fortune, but he's got loads. The birth certificate was faked somehow. Mrs Main arrived back at Hengistbury and everyone was happy. When Lavinia was four her mother was killed in a car crash. I felt relieved.'

'I'd already sensed what a sympathetic person you are,' said Tweed. 'Why were you relieved?'

'Obvious, I'd have thought. I worried that when Lavinia was older she might blow the gaff to her. And how did you find out about me?'

'There's been a murder, in case you'd forgotten. The manor is being searched from top to bottom. I found a hidden drawer with Marshal's secret chequebooks and a diary with your address,' Tweed fibbed.

'Are you telling Marshal?' she said nervously.

'No, it would be pointless. But there is a condition.'

'Which is?' she asked.

'You sit down and write a letter to Marshal. You tell him he is to send you no more gifts – ever. You've met a man who is wealthy. You promise never to reveal what happened years ago. I shall know if you've sent that letter. I examine all mail before handing it to the addressee.'

'I'll do that as soon as you've gone,' she said hastily.

'And don't forget the penalty for blackmail,' Tweed said grimly as he stood up. 'One wrong move and I'll be harder than you are, if that's possible . . .'

'Sneaky is peering from behind her curtain,' Paula remarked as they passed the house where they'd asked the woman the way to Baron's Walk.

She was relieved to leave Dodd's End and soon they were driving well away from the hamlet with open country on both sides. She had her window open and revelled in the fresh air.

'One thing puzzles me about poor Bella's murder,' she mused. 'How was anyone able to get behind her chair to drop that hideous murder weapon over her head and neck? It's close to a corner of a panelled wall.'

'Been puzzling that myself.'

'And,' she went on as they approached the manor, the dark sinister canopy of black fir branches pressing down on them, 'you keep asking suspects where they were on the fatal night between 7 p.m. and 10 p.m. But we know Bella called down to Marshal at 8 p.m. to come and see her at 10 p.m. That is, if she did.'

'She did. I went up on my own to her study and played with that communications box. It's very sophisticated. You can play back what she said and his reply. More than that, it records the exact time. She made the call at 8 p.m. I add on one hour, saying 7 p.m. to find out where people were earlier in the evening.'

'Don't miss a trick, do you?'

'I'm sure that so far I've missed several tricks. Here we are, and the gates are opening.'

Some time earlier, as Tweed and Paula were approaching Dodd's End, Calouste and Jacques were driving west. Ahead they could see the Dorset heights. Jacques was looking forward to a view of the sea. The mobile buzzed. Calouste grabbed it.

'Yes?'

'Orion here. The line is clearer now.'

'Get on with why you called me.'

'Tweed and Paula in the Mercedes were going to Seacove.'

'Are you sure? You mean today? Now?'

'If you will just let me finish. They were going with Marshal Main—'

'Marshal was in the Mercedes with them?'

'I'll have to hang up in a moment, so shut up! Marshal was in his Rolls. Tweed appeared to change his mind. So he is going to London. I'm sure he'll be back at Hengistbury this evening. Maybe earlier.'

The line had gone dead. Calouste hated the way his informer suddenly ended a call. It had been the same distorted voice. Man or woman? Calouste had no bloody idea.

Coming to a roundabout Calouste drove round it

and went back the way they had come. Jacques looked at him, kept his mouth shut. He was still shaken by the extraordinary behaviour of Calouste dancing like a devil in the field of rape.

'Tweed will be back at Hengistbury tonight,' Calouste said viciously. 'You have your rifle in the boot?'

'Yes, I have.'

'He won't expect another attempt on his life so soon. You will shoot him dead. I have a lodge close to that manor. That will be our base. You are the best marksman in all Europe.'

'Not quite,' Jacques admitted, 'the star turn is a member of Tweed's team. Man called Marler.'

19

Tweed had driven through the open gates when a motorcycle followed them in. It flashed at speed past the Mercedes, throwing up pebbles. Paula learned forward.

'Young idiot. Just a sec – that's Leo.'

'Complete with brand-new windcheater and woolly cap.'

'Could he have been following us? I heard a motorbike as we first saw Dodd's End. And I'm sure I heard the same sound twice on our way back.'

'World is full of the things,' Tweed replied.

Leo slowed near the terrace, turned to wave at them, then disappeared on his machine round the back of the manor. The first person they met on entering the hall was Lavinia, dressed in a smart tunic and jodhpurs tucked inside gleaming riding boots.

'You opened the gates for us,' Paula said. 'Thank you.'

'My pleasure. Had lunch? I thought not. I told Mrs Grandy to keep a hot meal. I guessed you might be back soon. That Merc moves – especially on motorways.'

'Luckily,' said Tweed, 'the chap we went to meet lives on the verge of London, so we escaped the traffic.'

'Something I forgot to tell you and should have let you know earlier. I'm talking about Bella's study. There's a secret entrance. After lunch I'll show you.'

'The meal will be delayed half an hour,' the grating voice of Mrs Grandy, who had appeared suddenly, called out. 'If you think heated food can hang about you know as little about kitchens as I think you do.'

'We could go up to the study now,' Lavinia suggested in a quiet voice. She raised her voice as Snape appeared. 'You might take their clothes and hang them up, please.'

She led the way up the staircase and along a narrow corridor with panelled walls, passing the entrance to the library. The rest of the corridor appeared to lead nowhere. It was blocked off by solid panelling. The name of the bank was in raised metal letters: the Main Chance Bank.

'The letters are a code. Care to try your luck?' she asked Paula.

'She had a course in code-breaking,' Tweed said, 'when she worked at Medfords Security before coming to me.'

'It will be simple,' said Paula.

She pressed the 'M' of Main, then the 'a' of the same word. She paused, then pressed the 'n' and the 'e' of Chance. Nothing happened.

'Good try,' Lavinia said, 'now watch me.'

Lavinia pressed the 'M' of Main. She switched to the second word, pressed the 'a' and then the 'n' and the last 'e'. She had spelt out 'MANE' but in a different sequence. The solid panel slid aside and they were looking into the end of the study and the space behind Bella's tall chair.

'You did have the right codeword, MANE,' Lavinia said with a smile at Paula.

'So that's how it was done,' Tweed said under his breath as he walked in and stood behind the chair. Paula and Lavinia followed him then walked further into the study.

'Place gives me the creeps after what happened,' Lavinia remarked.

'Me too,' Paula agreed.

Tweed stood stock-still, trying to reconstruct the murder in the place where it had happened. He heard the panel door closing, turned to look at it. The same lettering was attached as on the far side.

'Same code opens it from this side,' Lavinia called out. 'When Bella summoned someone for a discreet discussion whoever she was calling knew they should use that door.'

Tweed moved from behind the chair, walked to the other end of the study, sat down in a chair close to Lavinia.

'Who else knows the code to open the secret door?'

'There's Marshal.' She counted them off on her slim fingers. 'Then Warner, of course. Plus Crystal – and I'm sure Leo knows it. Once, in a hurry, I didn't check the other end of the corridor before I tapped out the code. I glanced back afterwards and Leo was peeking round the corner. He does have exceptional eyesight. And Snape, of course.'

'Quite a roll call of suspects.'

'Do you mind if we go into the library?' Lavinia suggested, standing up. 'Don't like this room any more . . .'

The three of them settled in armchairs arranged so they faced each other. Lavinia sat opposite Tweed, studying him – her large blue pool-like eyes he found disconcerting.

'You always wanted to work here as an accountant?' he asked her.

'No, I didn't.' She laughed, a pleasant appealing sound. 'Once I'd passed my exams and knew I could stay here if I wanted to I decided I'd explore the real world. Now don't laugh,' she said with a ravishing smile, 'I became an actress, playing in small theatres on the northern circuit. The accommodation was frightful, pokey little rooms, and the food was awful.'

'What parts did you play?'

'Shakespeare. I was in *King Lear* and played all three of his daughters in succession. I really did,' she said with a chuckle.

'Which was your favourite? Goneril or Regan, one of the two evil daughters?'

'Absolutely not, although I coped with the parts. No, my favourite was Cordelia, the sister they so cruelly exploited. Then, I can't imagine why, the company toured Europe. In Denmark the audience hissed me when I played Goneril or Regan, but they applauded Cordelia.'

'Then you came here?' suggested Tweed.

'Not yet. I joined Medfords Security.' She looked at Paula. 'You went there, didn't you. I was taught how to open complex locks, how to shadow suspects without being seen, changing clothes at intervals, the way I walked.'

'I did that too,' Paula chimed in. 'I found that the most difficult part of the course.'

'Me too,' Lavinia agreed. 'I don't think I was very good at it.'

'So play-acting didn't suit you?' Tweed asked Lavinia.

'The travel abroad was interesting. So many different countries. But I didn't like some of my fellow actors. Let's just say they were peculiar.' She leaned close to Tweed. 'And it was after my time at Medfords I came back here. It is so peaceful after the hell of

London traffic and the pedestrians jabbering away on their mobiles and walking into you.' She put a hand on Tweed's knee. 'So now you have the biography of Lavinia.'

'Thank you,' he said with a smile. 'I find it fascinating.'

'Fascinating? Me or the biography?' she asked with an endearing smile as she removed her hand from his knee.

'Both, of course,' he replied gallantly.

Lavinia checked her watch, stood up, her figure erect.

'If we go down now for lunch we should just beat Mrs Grandy using her hooter.'

'Hooter?' queried Paula as they left the library and reached the top of the great flight of the main stairs.

'That's what I call her way of bellowing when a meal is ready.'

As they entered the main library Mrs Grandy appeared with a grim expression. Marshal came bustling in after them, followed by Marler and Newman. Mrs Grandy stood in the doorway, arms crossed.

'Nice when some people are on time. Just. As for the male lot, they're late. And I don't appreciate being told late to prepare for two extras.

She aimed her stubby index finger at both Marler and Newman. Marshal turned on her.

'Instead of bellowing like a baboon, which I'm reminded of, looking at you, do the job you're paid too much for and serve the meal which, I do hope, is edible.'

Marler sat at the laid table between Paula and Lavinia. As Lavinia began talking to Marler, Newman leaned over and whispered to Paula.

'We've discovered something. Later . . .'

20

'I'm going for a walk on the front lawn while the sun shines,' Tweed announced, glancing over his shoulder at the end of the meal. He had announced his intention at the beginning of the meal and was repeating the same words. The lunch had lasted a long time with nearly everyone chattering and joking, a hysterical reaction to Bella's recent death. Tweed had noticed Marler was getting on well with Lavinia, with brief laughter from that direction.

The only exception was Paula, who had been studying Warner. His rocklike head had concentrated on eating and he hadn't said a word. He reminded her of something, then she knew what it was.

During a summer holiday while at Medfords she had flown to America. From New York she had continued on to Rapid City in South Dakota. She'd had a spectacular view of the monument, the famous view of the distant giant cliffs where the heads of four

Presidents had been carved out of the rock on a massive scale. George Washington, Jefferson, Teddy Roosevelt and the other one she couldn't remember. It was these grim rock faces which Warner reminded her of. He had something on his mind – or was waiting for something.

'Excuse me, everyone,' Tweed said standing up, 'I'm going for my walk.'

He had entered the hall when he was aware of someone behind him. Marler, with his golf bag unzipped.

'Coming with you,' Marler drawled. 'No argument.'

They descended the steps with Tweed a few paces ahead of his escort. The sun was blazing again; now it was behind the mansion, shining directly on The Forest beyond the closed gates. Tweed was revelling in being outside, feeling the lawn under his feet. He paused to take in the peace of it all.

Behind the brambles on the other side of the road Jacques aimed the scope of his rifle. He had waited hours hoping his target would appear. Now he had Tweed in his crosshairs. The one thing which bothered him was the sun glaring straight at him. Tweed was standing motionless, hands in the pockets of his country-style jacket. Jacques took a deep breath, prior to squeezing the trigger.

*

'It really is a glorious day,' Tweed enthused. 'Almost makes you forget why we're here . . .'

Marler, on his right, was looking everywhere, as he so often was. His peripheral vision caught the sun's brief reflection off something beyond the gates. His left arm swept round Tweed's waist, pushed him violently to the lawn, flat on his face as Marler himself sprawled beside him.

The bullet passed over Tweed's prone body, making a sharp deadly crack.

'Don't move,' Marler snapped. 'Stay down.'

In seconds he had hauled out his Armalite, the scope attached. He knew where the marksman was. He'd not only seen the sun flash off the killer's scope, he'd seen the muzzle flash.

He aimed swiftly through the upright bars of the gate and beyond at the brambles. He waited a few seconds, then he fired again at the same area. He jumped up, dashed forward with the speed of an antelope, calling back over his shoulder to Tweed, 'Run for the manor . . . zigzag as you run . . . get the gates opened!'

Briefly, Jacques was in a state of shock. The first bullet had passed within an inch of his head. The second bullet had scorched the tip of his hair at the side of his head. And now, from one of the photographs taken of the SIS team emerging from Park Crescent, he recognized the shooter. Oh God! *Marler.*

'Get the hell out of here,' he mumbled.

He was already crashing through the brambles, ignoring the scratches to his face. As he came out into open country he jumped on his motorcycle. It started first time. He headed over the smooth slope rising to a crest. Glancing back, he was appalled to see the gates opening. He swore, increased speed to maximum.

Tearing across the road, Marler charged into the undergrowth as fast as he could. Emerging into open country, he saw the motorcyclist speeding up a rise and shouldered his weapon. He had already reloaded. In the crosshairs he saw the back of the fleeing killer. He had his finger on the trigger when he saw the view through the scope was blank. His target had dropped down the slope beyond the crest.

Marler leaned against the trunk of a huge tree, laughed. 'Next time will be your last time,' he said.

Shortly before, Tweed and Paula had rushed up the steps and inside the hall. Lavinia was standing there.

'Open the gates quickly,' Tweed called out.

Lavinia wasted no time asking why. She used her index finger to press a button concealed in the panelling. Tweed turned round. In the distance through the open door he saw the gates opening, Marler near them.

'Fun and games?' Lavinia enquired with a wry smile.

'An exercise,' Tweed replied. 'We needed the exercise. Now I need to see Newman urgently.'

'He's gone to Snape's cottage in the woods. I'd better lead you there.'

They walked along a corridor and entered the kitchen. Mrs Grandy had just shut the cooker. She glared at them.

'I see the back door is open,' Lavinia told her. 'It needs to be kept closed and locked at—'

'Oh, does it?' Mrs Grandy folded her arms. 'I often have to take rubbish to the bin outside. You expect me—'

'Just so long as you're always in the kitchen.'

They were outside before the cook could answer. To their left at the back of the manor was a hard tennis court. Marshal, looking bad-tempered, had obviously just finished a game with Crystal, who was twirling round, her racquet on top of her red hair.

'*I* won,' she called out.

'No you didn't,' Marshal snapped. 'You cheated!'

'I never cheat and you know it. You just can't stand to lose at anything. Gambling, debating, you've always got to come out tops.'

'I'll come with you,' Marshal said to Paula and Lavinia. 'Anything to get away from that witch.'

Paula was glad Lavinia was leading the way. At intervals other paths curved off through the dark woods. On the ground were piles of pine needles at least ankle-deep. It occurred to Paula you'd never hear anyone coming. Even Marshal, hammering down in his tennis shoes, made no sound.

Turning a corner, Paula saw Snape's cabin, a well-built two-storey structure made of heavy wooden beams. Newman stood in the doorway. Paula sensed someone was behind her. It was Marler.

'Where did you spring from?' she asked.

'I'm the ghost who haunts the woods, especially after dark.'

'Don't,' Paula snapped. 'I find these woods creepy.'

'That's what I do,' Marler continued, 'I creep around the woods after dark, prowling like a wolf.'

'Stop it!' She slapped his face gently. 'You conjure up visions I could do without.'

'I'm really sorry,' he replied quickly, squeezing her arm. 'It was just a joke – and in very bad taste. All right now?'

'Of course.' She kissed him quickly where she had slapped him. 'It's my fault. For some reason I'm edgy, as though something was going to happen.'

'Am I interrupting a lovers' tryst?' asked Marshal, who appeared out of nowhere. He was leering suggestively. 'Might be best if you both took that path, leads deep into the woods.'

'If you think that's amusing it damned well isn't,' Marler told him harshly, standing in front of Paula, close to Marshal. 'Why not go into the village, buy yourself a clean mouth.'

'Hey!' called Newman from the cabin door. 'Come inside here. You, too, Marler.'

Paula walked briskly to the open door. Newman ushered her in with a smile. She'd expected a crude or primitive interior. Instead the room she entered was carpeted wall-to-wall with a grey carpet and the furniture was comfortable, several spotlessly clean armchairs and a highly polished dining table. Along part of one wall was a cupboard with double doors faced with small glass windows. Behind the glass was an array of rifles and shotguns.

Snape, clad in corduroy trousers and a clean blue-striped pullover, stood against one wall, a self-satisfied smile on his face.

'Not bad, Paula, for a butler, don't you think?'

She never had time to reply. Marler scanned the room and strode across to the gun cupboard. He turned the key in the lock, opened both doors, stared for a moment at the weapons, then pointed at one.

'Excuse me,' he said.

All the weapons were secured with clamps. Marler removed the clamp round the gun he'd pointed at, took it out carefully, turned round, the muzzle pointed at the ceiling.

'A stainless-steel Winchester,' he said.

'A shotgun,' Snape replied.

'I know it's a shotgun,' Marler said coldly. 'Is it loaded?'

'It could be,' Snape said irritably. 'Yes, I believe it is.'

'And the safety catch isn't on. That's how accidents happen. I presume you have a certificate for it along with the rest of your arsenal? You have? That wouldn't save you when an inspector calls to check privately held guns. It works like this,' he told his audience after unloading the gun and placing the shells inside a deep ashtray.

Marshal, standing next to Newman, was unusually quiet. He watched closely as Marler, who had first put the safety on.

'First,' Marler began, 'you release the safety, then rack the gun which takes less than a second. Now you're ready to open fire. Press the trigger, rack the gun again, you are ready to fire again and another time and another.'

There was tension inside the cabin. Paula made an attempt to defuse it. She looked at Snape.

'What do you use it for?'

'Ah!' He was grinning sadistically. 'I see a bunch of rabbits clustered together on top of a grassy hill eating. I aim once, fire. I press the trigger and one blast from that shotgun wipes out the lot. Don't even have to clean up the mess. Foxes arrive in the evening and gulp down everything.'

'A massacre,' Marler said in the same cold tone.

'You're in the country here,' Snape protested.

'Then I'll take the city every time,' Paula snapped without looking at Snape.

She turned round and found Tweed standing very still behind her. She couldn't read his expression. Next to him stood Lavinia. Her expression was grim, her lips pursed.

Turning round again Paula saw that Marler had put on gloves, was using a handkerchief to wipe his prints off the weapon. He placed it carefully back inside its clamp, opened a small drawer and dropped the shells inside it with others already there. He locked the cupboard, threw the key to Snape, who missed catching it. As he bent down to pick it up he glared venomously at Marler.

'Tweed, Paula, Marler,' Newman called from the door. 'Let's go for a walk . . .'

'I'm going back to the manor,' Lavinia told them. 'Heaven knows what's going on there.'

'I feel like a bit of gambling,' Marshal decided, then headed back the way they had come.

'Gambling?' queried Paula to Lavinia who was still close to her.

'I'm going to stop it,' Lavinia said. She whispered, 'Another technical team arrived from London very early this morning. Sergeant Warden apologized to me for the delay. They had a photographer who took lots of pictures of those horrible collar things found in Crystal's room. Then they took them away, carefully packed, and also her blouses. I'm so sure someone planted them on her, but who?'

'Are you coming with us or not?' Newman's voice called out from where a path turned a corner. 'You'll be interested.'

With Marler in the lead and followed by Tweed, Newman and Paula walked a devious route through The Forest. Paula had an idea they were heading towards the main road – and the wall. She was right. The Forest ended suddenly. Beyond was open ground and the high wall. A telescopic ladder, fully open, was propped against it. Newman waved towards it and looked at Paula.

'Ups-a-daisy.'

She shinned up the ladder swiftly. Along the top of this part of the wall the barbed wire had a gap. The ends at each end were strung out. Across the road The Forest was a dark barrier. She descended rapidly.

'Someone clipped the wire to make the ghastly collars,' she said.

'Right first time.'

He bent down to pick up a long deep grey metal box, lifted the lid. The box was empty, but the insides were covered with scratches. Newman gestured towards it.

'We found this in a small shed outside Snape's cabin. We borrowed it without asking him. He wasn't there at the time.'

'So,' Paula said thoughtfully, 'the murderer had metal clippers. First to get his raw material, then to convert them into those awful collars. But where did he obtain the wooden handles?'

'We may never know,' said Marler.

Returning to the manor they heard a lot of excited chatter from the main library. Guided part of the way by Newman, Tweed and Paula entered by the back door, ignoring Mrs Grandy's baleful look.

Inside the library was a long square table covered with green baize. On one side was a roulette wheel with Lavinia standing opposite the three players as she acted as croupier.

The three players facing her were Crystal, Marshal and Warner. Crystal had a few chips in front of her to continue playing. Marshal had a fairly large pile. Warner had the largest pile.

Standing next to Paula and Marler, Tweed ignored the state of the game. He had learned long ago it was the faces you watched since this could give you a clue to character.

The game went on for a while without anyone risking much. Then the atmosphere changed, became tense. Crystal laid all she had left on black. Red came up as the ball settled in the slot on the wheel.

'Silly game,' she burst out.

'Of course it's silly,' Lavinia said. 'It's worse when

you have bankers gambling. Shouldn't be allowed.'

'Don't start that again,' Marshal shouted.

'I'll go on saying it until you stop for good. It's wrong.'

'Don't you tell me what's wrong. You're an amateur at everything,' Marshal bellowed.

He pushed his entire pile of chips forward. 'All on the red.'

Just before Lavinia set the wheel in motion Warner pushed his own huge pile of chips forward.

'All on the black,' he said quietly.

The wheel spun, seemed to take forever to slow down, then almost stopped. The ball hovered on the red, then slipped over and settled on the black. Lavinia used her rake to transfer Marshal's chips to add to Warner's pile.

'We need fresh air in here!' Marshal yelled.

Lavinia walked quickly to the window, opened it wide. She was followed by Marshal who snatched up the wheel, hurled it out of the window. They all heard it shatter on the terrace.

'Kids' game,' Marshal shouted as he stormed out of the room.

Warner remained seated. He hadn't moved a muscle or showed any reaction during the game, let alone said anything. Now he turned and his glance caught Paula's. Their eyes met. As Warner's large rock-like head gazed at her he had a strange smile on his face. It was the first time Paula had seen him smile since she'd arrived. It was a peculiar smile, she thought, as his gravelly voice rumbled, 'Winner takes all.'

21

'We're driving down to Seacove in Cornwall today.'

Tweed had waited in the corridor for Paula to emerge from her apartment. From her expression he knew he had taken her by surprise.

'Why are we doing that? I suppose that's why you told me last night to be ready for breakfast at seven-thirty. But why are we going all that way?'

Tweed explained. Later the previous day, after Marshal had hurled out the roulette wheel then stormed out, he had invited Tweed to join him in the smaller library outside Bella's study.

Marshal had recovered, had been in his usual buoyant mood. He had urged Tweed, with Paula, to join him in a trip down to Seacove. Tweed had agreed at once.

'Why?' Paula asked again.

'Because I need to see Marshal – what he is like, away from this manor where the atmosphere is becoming claustrophobic.'

'I need something warm for going down there, don't I?' she asked after eyeing the heavy knee-length overcoat folded over his arm.

'I'd advise it. I'm going down now. See you at breakfast.'

After the meal, Tweed stood with Paula by the Audi at the back of the manor. She took his arm and squeezed it.

'Do you mind if I drive?'

'I was going to suggest you did . . .'

Driving round to the terrace they found the Rolls parked, Marshal at the wheel, Snape holding open a rear passenger door.

Paula parked behind the Rolls, the driver's door flew open and Marshal stormed back to Paula's open window. He glared as he spoke.

'What the devil do you think Snape's holding open the rear door for?'

'I have no idea,' she replied with a smile.

'Because,' he rasped, 'you were supposed to be travelling down with me. Isn't a Rolls good enough for you? What's happened to the beat-up old Merc? Conked out at last?'

'It's Newman's car and he's using it today,' she said with another smile. 'And I prefer independent transport. So does Tweed.'

'If you don't follow me closely you'll never get there . . .'

'You handled that well,' Tweed said quietly as they drove away.

The gates were opening as the Rolls approached them. Tweed glanced back, saw Lavinia in the doorway. She had opened the gates and waved. Tweed waved back.

Driving along the narrow lane to Gladworth, Paula kept her distance behind the Rolls, which was roaring along, headlights on blinding full beam, horn honking nonstop.

'I won't lose him,' she promised Tweed, 'but I need space. Then if he hits something I've time to pull up.'

'Very sensible.'

The Rolls shot through Gladworth's High Street and a pedestrian had to jump clear. Marshal shouted something at her and then Gladworth was behind them.

'Lavinia told me,' Paula remarked, 'that a technical team had photographed Crystal's wardrobe and taken away those two beastly collars. Will they arrest her?'

'Not a chance. Not enough evidence. Her finger-prints were neither on the collars nor on the door knobs.'

'Are we getting anywhere with the case? Any strong suspects?'

'Not really. Yet. Paula, do you mind if I have a nap?'

'I'll be as quiet as the proverbial mouse.'

Tweed relaxed, clasped his hands, closed his eyes.

Paula knew he was not actually sleeping: he was taking the opportunity to sift all the information he'd acquired so far, playing back the conversations he'd had at Hengistbury, searching for something odd, an inconsistency.

They made good progress. The Rolls was going full out; Paula kept within the speed limits but never lost Marshal. She was enjoying herself as they passed from one county to another. The scenery kept changing. Rolling hill country, long flat plains, copses perched on hilltops. The sun continued to blaze down.

They had covered a lot of ground when the weather changed dramatically. The sun vanished. A fierce wind blew up, menacing low thunderclouds filled the sky. Tweed opened his eyes. They were driving along a wide stretch of road when Marshal signalled, pulled up at the side. Paula lowered the window she had earlier raised when the wind started blowing in. She angled the Audi alongside the Rolls, where Marshal had lowered his window on the passenger side.

'Isn't this just wonderful,' he bellowed.

'What is?' Paula asked.

'Stormy weather! Just what we need to demonstrate what the *Star Sprite* can do in a rough sea.'

'I'm so glad someone is pleased,' she retorted.

'You'll both come out with me aboard her. You'll love it.'

'No, we won't,' Tweed said firmly. 'I hate the sea and Paula will stay with me on *terra firma*.'

'Wimps!' yelled Marshal.

He had kept his engine running and suddenly he took off without warning. Paula gave Tweed a look and drove on, seeing Marshal in the distance. Soon they were driving through narrow lanes, only room for one car, with steep banks rising high above them. Devon, she thought. Godawful motoring country. They left it behind fairly soon and entered a quite different landscape. Tweed sat up straight to have a good look.

'Cornwall,' he said.

Inland great stretches of rugged rocky ridges headed westward for miles. Nothing grew. It was a desolate and forbidding desert. Then to the north he saw the sea not far away below them, a raging tumult of giant waves, rolling higher and higher until they hit the shore in a series of thunderous explosions.

They were heading down a rough road towards the sea, had almost reached it when the Rolls swung up onto a small headland. The car stopped, Marshal stepped out, flung his arms wide apart in a theatrical gesture.

'Paradise!' he shouted against the howl of the wind when Paula stopped the Audi and they joined him as Tweed struggled into his overcoat.

'One word for it,' Paula commented. 'What's that?'

She pointed to a long flat area inside a wide bowl

with a shed nearly. A windsock was streaming out, parallel to the ground.

'Bloody private airfield. Not used much, thank God. I tried to have it closed down but the council wallahs refused. Follow me down this path and watch your footing.'

They arrived at a point a few yards above the pebble beach and Paula stared. At three different levels, but built almost on top of each other, were rows of white stone cottages. Below another huge wave trundled in.

'This,' Marshal announced, 'is Seacove.'

'Is this all there is?' Tweed asked bluntly.

'My hideaway is the top level, converted inside at absolutely no attention to expense.'

Between Marshal's cottage and the next one was a wide gap. It continued down between the cottages on the low levels, then increased in steepness as it reached the beach.

'What's that ramp-like thing for?' Tweed enquired.

'You'll see,' Marshal said gleefully.

As he led them to a heavy back door in his cottage Paula thought she heard the faint sound of a plane, then a massive wave broke and she felt spray on her face. Once beyond the back door Marshal had unlocked she almost gasped. The interior was luxuriously furnished, the plastered walls painted a tasteful shade of blue with pictures in gilded frames hung at intervals. The dining table (she presumed) was an antique, as were the carved chairs and an escritoire. Armchairs suggested it was also a living room. Tweed walked over and stared at two portraits of men in strange dress. He looked at Marshal.

'Portraits of your grandfather and his partner, Pitt and Ezra?'

'Right first time.'

Paula jumped as something heavy slapped against the windows on the sea side. Water from the wave was slithering down.

'Couldn't the windows get smashed in?' she asked.

'Not likely, my dear. Armoured glass.'

'You've made an amazing job of the conversion.'

'Not me.' He grinned. 'Lavinia was in charge of that.'

He had taken a large heavy-looking enamel box from the boot of the Rolls and carried it in. He was looking round for somewhere to put it when Tweed grasped the handle to help him. It was *very* heavy. Marshal was stronger than he'd thought. Marshal took the whole weight, dumped the box on a ledge.

'Refrigerated. Lunch for later. Prepared by Lavinia. Don't trust what Mrs Grandy might have shoved in. Now, we'll look at the view, then I'll show you the *Star Sprite*.'

Tweed and Paula gazed out of the window, were appalled at what they saw. They had a clear view down over the tiled sloping roofs of the two levels of cottages below. Then came the pebble beach, half obscured by surf from the recent wave.

Beyond was a small bay. Its distant narrow exit to the ocean was partly enclosed by a cape on either side which made the exit look very constricted. Marshal stood between them, now wearing a blue peaked cap. He pointed to their left. A huge granite buttress with jagged outcrops sat on the mainland as though guarding the bay.

'That's Pindle Rock,' Marshal explained. 'It once had a huge spike, or pindle, projecting upwards. Got blown down by an exceptional storm. OK if you keep clear – and there is another hazard. You've got to watch it sailing our or returning. I'm talking about an underwater current midway across.'

'I know this is Seacove,' Tweed said, 'but where are we on the coast?'

'This –' Marshal embraced the section before the exit into the ocean – 'is Oyster Bay. Because it's shaped like one. Fishermen used to occupy these cottages but the fish went away so I bought their cottages for a song. Surfers used to be a pest, until three were killed out there on the same day.'

'I can well believe it,' said Paula.

She was gazing with fascinated horror at the ocean. A storm was building up. Waves like mobile mountains were building up approaching Oyster Bay. It was sheer havoc.

'Boat's through here,' Marshal said, leading them to a door at the right-hand end of the cottage. They were inside a huge shed with metal walls. Paula stared. Perched on the rail-like structure was what looked like a miniature cruise liner. Marshal handed Tweed and Paula yellow oilskins with hoods. At the same time he must have pressed a button. The huge glass door at the seaward end elevated and the wind had briefly abated, so there was a sinister quiet.

'You'll need these or you'll get soaked,' Marshal insisted, still holding the oilskins. The wind began to rise again.

'We are *not* going out in your yacht!' Tweed shouted. 'And I mean it!'

'Landlubbers,' Marshal said with a sneer.

Paula thought she faintly heard the sound of a plane taking off, then decided it was the purr of the yacht's engine which Marshal had switched on. Proudly, he explained the workings of the yacht.

'Look over the edge of the hull here. See that big lever at right angles to the deck? I press that down and she takes off. The forward hulls, both port and starboard, close in on each other until we leave the shed, then automatically open once we are outside on the ramp.'

'Once *you* are outside,' Tweed corrected him.

'Boat's revolutionary. It's two boats. If the rear half hits another ship the *Sprite* splits immediately. The forward half has its own engine and is completely seaworthy. That is why the bridge is well forward.'

'Sounds tricky,' Tweed observed.

'I need a really big wave coming up off the beach so *Sprite* is carried down the ramp runway on its crest. I think I see what I need coming . . .'

He had thrown the two oilskins on the shed floor in disgust, had donned his own oilskin, not using the hood as he checked the angle of his blue peaked cap. Paula glanced seaward and saw the wave Marshal had referred to approaching. As he climbed aboard and bent down to depress the starting lever he called out.

'Door will close automatically the moment I've left. Best view will be from living-room window. Help yourself to the food.'

They reached the living-room window in time to see *Sprite* emerging from its shed. It moved forward slowly on a level section of the ramp, met the huge wave as it scudded at speed down the tilted section. It crested the wave and plunged into Oyster Bay.

Paula lifted the lid of the enamel box, one eye gazing out of the window. As she'd expected from Lavinia, the box was neatly packed. She called out to Tweed.

'Chicken or ham sandwich?'

'Both.'

She also brought two cardboard cups decorated with a Wedgewood design and a flask of coffee. She had a shock when she stared out of the window. The bridge where Marshal was ensconced had a rear window and she could see him bent forward over the wheel. Her shock was caused by the direction the *Sprite* was taking, heading for Pindle Rock.

'He's going to hit Pindle,' she said tensely.

'No, he isn't,' Tweed replied through a mouthful of sandwich. 'He's steering west to avoid the underwater current.'

He was. The *Sprite* had changed course, then proceeded across the middle of Oyster Bay, heading for the exit into the ocean. The bay was a tumult of large waves following each other. The *Sprite* skilfully crested each wave and disappeared briefly before it mounted the next giant.

'He's got guts,' Tweed commented. 'Guts for anything, I'd say,' he added thoughtfully.

'He's mad!' Paula burst out. 'Mad as the legendary hatter. Look what's waiting for him, assuming he does get through the exit from the bay.'

Tweed had to admit to himself it was a terrifying prospect. Storm clouds had suddenly swept in from the west. The open sea was reacting violently. Mountainous waves were churning up the water, turning it into a maelstrom. Surely Marshal would turn round, come back? Tweed took out his pair of binoculars from his overcoat pocket. Like Paula he had put on his coat because it was cold inside the cottage.

'The fool is going to hit the right-hand cape,' Paula said.

Peering through the lenses, Tweed saw Marshal had adjusted the steering. The *Sprite* passed through the exit with plenty of room on either side. Then it dived into the maelstrom. Paula couldn't watch any longer.

She went back to the enamel box for the third time, collected two more plates and two chunks of Dundee cake well wrapped in greaseproof paper, refilled the cups with more coffee, took them to where Tweed was still standing. He thanked her without taking his eyes off the ocean. Paula felt compelled to watch.

The *Sprite* was being tossed about like a cockleshell, but now it was cresting from one wave to another. Then it turned towards the coast, swept through the exit into Oyster Bay. Passing well clear of Pindle Rock it mounted the crest of an incoming wave. Paula heard the door into the shed rising up.

'How does he do that?' she wondered.

'Probably has a powerful radio control – the sort of thing you use to open a power-operated garage door from the outside. Give him time to get rid of his wet clothes.'

They watched as, on the wave crest, the *Sprite* sailed up the rail-ramp into the shed. The door rattled shut. Paula picked up some plans off the table.

'It's much smaller than it looks but the forepart has two guest suites with bedrooms, living rooms, bathrooms. Same at the part behind the bridge. Do you really think it could split into two in case of an accident?'

'I think so. As it went down the slipway I noticed behind the bridge on the rear deck a wide deep metal band running from port to starboard. That, I think, is where it could split. And there was the top of a second rudder attached just below the bridge . . .'

He stopped talking as Marshal, clad in his country clothes, entered with a rush, slamming the door shut behind him. His face was red, his eyes gleaming with pleasure.

'Bit rough out on the ocean but *Sprite* coped, as she always does. Lavinia will be annoyed she wasn't here.'

'She goes out with you in seas like that as a passenger?' Tweed asked in surprise.

'More than that. She can operate the damned thing better than I can. She's brilliant at steering. So I suppose she must have some talent,' he sneered on a downbeat note.

'I've had an urgent message recalling me immediately,' Tweed said quickly. 'Hope you don't mind coming back by yourself. We have seen the show, for which many thanks.'

'You mean I come back later after I've eaten?'

'We've left you plenty to eat,' Paula intervened, seeing the scowl on his face. 'Thank you for a memorable experience.'

'Then you'd better shove off,' he snapped. 'Other guests always travel down and back with me.'

'What message?' Paula asked when they were well away from Seacove.

'I made it up. Couldn't stand the thought of trailing back behind Marshal's Rolls. And what a weird vessel, the *Sprite*.'

'I wouldn't travel in it for a fortune,' Paula said. 'And you've still got my mobile phone. Why not get one of your own?'

'Because I dislike them, but I need it at the moment.'

'You remember when Marshal was using his mobile and it was so loud we heard not only what he was saying but what people at the other end also were saying? How come?'

'He had the volume turned full up. But why? To show what an important man he is. I think I can remember the way back.'

'I don't think you can. Which is why I'm checking the map. I'll navigate . . .'

A storm broke. Rain lashed so ferociously Tweed had trouble seeing through the windscreen even with the wipers going full blast. It hammered on the roof, stopped as suddenly as it had started. It was beginning to get dark.

When they reached the tunnel through The Forest it

was night and Tweed had his highlights on full beam. Paula didn't like it even with the headlights on. She was relieved when the gates to Hengistbury swung open after a brief delay.

'Peace again now,' she whispered.

It was not long before she regretted making the remark.

22

Climbing the steps to the terrace they saw that all the lights at the front of the manor were on. Standing in the open left-hand door was Leo. His yellow hair was all over the place and he was wearing his usual T-shirt and jeans. He had a silly grin on his face.

'I opened the gates for you,' he said gleefully as they followed him into the dimly lit hall.

'You're not allowed to,' called out Snape, standing at the foot of the staircase. 'I'm allowed to and so is Lavinia. Not you . . .'

'And you're nothing but the friggin' butler,' Leo yelled at him. 'The one who disappears for hours, so push off.'

As Snape, furious, went back up the staircase Tweed was aware that Mrs Grandy was standing near the entrance to the corridor leading to the kitchen.

'You're too late for dinner,' she said with a nasty smile. 'It was served at six. This is my evening off to visit my sister in Gladworth. Best I can do for you two is shepherd's pie and one of Lavinia's fruit things. Ready in a half-hour. Served in dinin' room.'

'Sounds appetizing,' Tweed replied with a smile. 'But what about Marshal?'

'Tried to get 'im on the phone. No reply. So 'e'll 'ave to fend for 'is self . . .'

As she disappeared Leo tugged at Tweed's arm, guiding him towards the library.

'Got something to tell you. Someone you'll want to go and see urgently.'

'What about closing the entrance gates?' Paula suggested. Leo had closed the door into the hall as soon as they were inside.

'Shut them while you were coming up the drive, didn't I?'

Tweed and Paula walked into the library, sat down in armchairs at the round table. Leo, exuding excitement, came bustling in after hanging up the coats he had taken from them. He closed the door carefully.

'Mind if we sit at the far end?' he requested. 'Then if Snape listens at the door he won't hear nothing.'

They stood up, went to a square table near the far end, sat down in tapestry-covered carver chairs with cushions on the seats. Leo sat in the third chair, his long legs in constant motion, his hands clasping, unclasping, then clasping again. Can't he ever keep still for a minute? Paula wondered.

'Where is everyone?' Tweed asked.

'They had dinner quickly, didn't they. Then they trooped off upstairs to their apartments. Lavinia had a pile of papers and said she didn't want to be disturbed. Mr Warner had a big briefcase and told me on no account was he to be disturbed.'

'So what did you want to tell us?' Tweed said impatiently.

'Don't suppose you've ever heard of a Mrs Mandy Carlyle?'

The shock registered with both listeners. Tweed managed to keep his expression blank. Paula clenched her teeth.

'Who is she?' Tweed asked.

'Better go see her and find out for yourself. Here is her address.'

He produced a sheet of folded paper from his back pocket, straightened it, pushed it across the table so both could read it. The words were written in an educated script. *Baron's Walk, Dodd's End.*

'You've visited this place?' Tweed suggested.

'Not me. It's this side of Tunbridge Wells.'

'Who told you all this?'

'Can't tell you that. It's a secret . . .'

'You think so?' Tweed's fist crashed down on the table. It made Leo jump up half out of his chair, then he sank back. 'I'm investigating the brutal murder of your own grandmother. So you *will* tell me now!'

'Well –' Leo's restless hands were performing a variety of movements – 'if you'll promise not to tell a soul . . .'

'That's it. I'm sending you up to Scotland Yard.'

'Oh Lord, not that. It was Crystal.'

'Where did your sister get her information from?'

'I don't know. If you don't believe me you can send me up to your bloody Scotland Yard.'

'All right.' Tweed relaxed. 'Now we'll have Crystal down here for a chat.'

'She's not here. She left after dinner to visit a boyfriend in Gladworth, or maybe outside the village. And, before you ask, *I don't know his name! And I don't know where he lives!*' He quietened down. 'She can be very secretive about her own life.'

'You do realize, Leo, this whole conversation is absolutely confidential? Not a word to Crystal.'

'She'd kill me if I told her. I thought I was being helpful, telling you what I have.'

'You have been. So, not a word to Crystal . . .'

'I've told you. She'd kill me. You've never seen her when she goes *really* wild. I'd like to go upstairs to my rooms to sleep. I'm fagged out.'

'Good idea. Get some sleep.'

When he had gone Tweed looked at Paula, who looked back as he spoke.

'Mrs Carlyle – or Mrs Mandy Carlyle as he said. What do you think of that?'

'Casts a new light on the whole situation.'

Tweed checked his watch. 'Good Lord, it's 8.30 p.m. Where did the time go?'

'Driving carefully back from Seacove, which is a long way off. And it's 9.30 p.m. Your watch has stopped. No sign of our meal. Mrs Grandy has stormed off without bothering to feed us. I'm not hungry anyway.'

'So where is Marshal? He should have been back at least an hour ago. Strange.'

The mobile started buzzing. He answered it. He listened and made very few comments, glancing now and again at Paula.

'We actually interviewed her,' he said at one point. 'Yes, we interviewed her recently. Tell you about it later. I want to leave now.'

He closed the call, sat staring up at the ceiling for a minute. Then he looked at Paula.

'That was Roy Buchanan. Think you could stand a drive across country? Not too long.'

'Something has happened?'

'You could say that. Mrs Mandy Carlyle has been murdered. Same technique as used on Bella. Professor Saafeld is on his way down to Dodd's End.'

'Now that is strange,' Paula said as she stood up. 'After what Leo told us. So soon afterwards.'

'That occurred to me.'

23

When Tweed pulled up the Audi a few yards from the entrance to Dodd's End a dramatic sight met their eyes. The front of Baron's Walk was illuminated in a glare of lights: three police cars, their blue lights revolving, were parked close to the front garden, uniformed policemen with powerful torches were searching the garden and all the windows had their curtains closed but there were lights behind them.

'It's like a circus,' Paula commented.

'It's Chief Inspector Hammer,' Tweed told her. 'He took an earlier call at Hengistbury Manor before we got back. Buchanan spoke to him and Hammer charged over here and started a revolution.'

'He's thick as three posts,' Paula said.

'To be fair he's all right with an open-and-shut case, a murder weapon found with fingerprints, the victim's husband has run off. But he's not so strong when personality and character have to be unravelled.'

'And Hengistbury is all personality and character.'

'I think we'll leave the car here and walk up the left side where the single street lamp is on. The one opposite is not working.'

They were passing the house where the woman who watched behind her curtains had been interviewed on their previous visit. No. 3. She was standing in her open doorway chatting to another neighbour in a dressing-gown. Outside other houses more neighbours in various states of dress were chattering, with frequent glances at Baron's Walk.

'Ghouls,' muttered Paula.

'They probably don't get much entertainment, locked away in this close.'

'You call this entertainment?' Paula snapped.

'They will, in a macabre way . . .'

Tweed and Paula showed their folders to a constable who lifted the police tape for them to duck under. Tweed was heading for the wide drive leading to the open garage, the way they'd entered on their first visit. They reached the garage as Hammer's bulky figure in a crumpled suit rushed towards them from the half-open front door.

'I'm in charge here,' he bawled. 'That's not the way in.'

'You're not in charge,' Tweed told him mildly. 'I am. I know the way in through the garage.'

'I'm in charge of this one,' Hammer bawled for the

benefit of every policeman nearby. 'This isn't necessarily anything to do with—'

'Shut up!' Tweed rapped out, turning on him. 'And under no circumstances are you to mention the name Hengistbury,' he ordered, lowering his voice. 'It's by no means certain the two cases are connected.'

'Well, go up the steps at the back and see her.'

'That her car?' Tweed asked, nodding towards a BMW painted a strong egg-yellow parked in the garage.

'It is.'

Tweed was already halfway up the steps when Hammer tried to push in front of Paula. She reacted by stretching out an arm, pushing him back as she smiled.

'At the top of steps turn right down the corridor,' Hammer called out. 'Last door on the left. She's in the living room . . .'

Tweed paused just inside the entrance. If anything it was worse than what he'd seen in Bella's study. Mandy was sprawled back in an armchair, her legs wide apart, her purple panties thrown on the floor. Round her neck was a wire collar with spikes. That is, what was left of her neck which was little more than a wide gash with a blood-soaked blouse beneath it. Her head was drooped over the back of the chair, her hair awry. Bending over her was Professor Saafeld, who looked up when he heard Tweed.

'He raped her,' Hammer announced. 'Really enjoyed

himself,' with a hint of lasciviousness in his gravelly voice.

Paula swung round in a fury. Hammer was only feet away from her when she lashed out: 'If that's the most decent comment you can make, go and find the bathroom and wash your filthy mouth out with Dettol.'

'You . . .' Hammer stepped back. 'You . . .' Lost for words, he clumped out of the room on his stubby legs and disappeared.

'I doubt if she *was* raped,' Saafeld said. 'Something odd about this whole scenario. The necklace, probably dropped over her from behind, is a replica of the one used to kill Bella. I suspect Mrs Carlyle was at least half-drunk at the time. All subject to examination at my morgue. When the paramedics arrive I want her taken back to Holland Park in the chair. They'll find it difficult but that's what I need.'

'I know you won't want to say yet,' Tweed began, 'but can you give me any idea when the crime was committed?'

Saafeld pursed his thick lips. Paula recalled from earlier cases that Britain's top pathologist never showed any reaction. A team of men appeared at the door, one holding his camera. The technical team had arrived.

'Please take a lot of photographs,' Saafeld said, addressing the young technician with the camera.

'From above, from below, more than usual of the corpse, especially from the front and also several of the chair from various angles. I'm going back now,' he said to Tweed as he removed his latex gloves.

'I didn't see your Rolls when we arrived,' Tweed remarked.

'I had it parked round the back with a constable guarding it. Yobbos are not only in London, more are down in an area like this.'

'Still don't understand how you stand working for Tweed,' he said amiably to Paula as he kissed her on the cheek and left.

He came back almost as soon as he'd left. Saafeld gestured for Tweed and Paula to join him outside. Some distance away tired policemen were still searching the garden with their torches.

'I didn't tell you very roughly when the murder was probably committed. Between 8 p.m. and 10 p.m. subject to—'

He dashed off, holding his bag, round the back of the house where his car was parked. As soon as he'd gone Hammer came out.

'One vital question I didn't ask you,' Tweed said pleasantly, 'who reported the murder?'

'A Mrs Denise Sealle. No. 3, down the right-hand side of the road. The killer left the light on in the living room. He closed the curtains but left a big gap – opposite where the victim was sprawled. When we've done all we can here I'll drive back to Hengistbury.' He addressed his remarks to Tweed and never gave Paula a glance.

They walked down the right-hand pavement, found no one about at No. 3. Tweed pressed the bell, kept his thumb on it. The door flew open and the woman they'd asked the way to Baron's Walk stared at them.

She was wearing a long black velvet dress. Round her plump waist was fastened a gold belt.

'You again,' she rasped. 'I'm going to call the police.'

'They're on your doorstep, Mrs Sealle,' Tweed said, showing her his folder. 'We need a few minutes of your time now.'

'You might have told me before. I suppose you'd better come in. There are no refreshments here.'

They were shown into a living room with undistinguished furniture: hard-backed wooden chairs, two sofas covered with a flowered print. A log fire crackled in the wall facing the road. Mrs Sealle lit a cigarette, waited.

'How did you know Mrs Carlyle had been murdered?' Tweed asked.

'Well, I saw her. Lights on in the living room. A big gap in the curtains.'

'It was dark,' Tweed persisted, 'and your house isn't near hers.'

'I saw her from upstairs, then came down here to get a look from that window.'

Tweed and Paula got up, went over to the window. He frowned, turned round to look at Mrs Sealle, who was puffing madly.

'All I can see is a blur.'

'Use these, then.'

From under a cushion on a sofa she produced a pair of binoculars. Paula smiled to herself. Mrs Sealle probably knew everything that went on in the close. Tweed adjusted the focus. He saw Mrs Carlyle, still in the chair, legs sprawled, her savaged neck, bloodstained blouse.

'Thank you,' he said returning the binoculars, sitting down again on the sofa with Paula. 'Did you see any strangers going towards Baron's Walk, say between the hours of 7 p.m. and 10 p.m.?'

'Yes, I did. The first came on a motorbike. I heard it and he must have left it before he reached the close. Then this man walked quickly up the far side of the road and disappeared when he reached Baron's Walk.'

'Give me a description, please.'

'Wearing a peaked cap, the type they all wear, and jeans.'

'You saw his face?'

'Evil-looking, sharp nose and jaw. I suppose it would be about 7 p.m. Much later the second man arrived.'

'You're very observant. How would you describe the second man?'

'Posh. Tall, slim. Long coat, black, trilby pulled down over his face.'

'What time would this be – when the second man appeared?'

'About 8 p.m., I'd say.'

'Are you really sure of your descriptions?' Tweed pressed.

'Well, I suppose the 8 p.m. man could have been of medium height and rather stocky.'

'Mrs Sealle . . .' Tweed stood up. 'That street lamp on the other side of the street hasn't been working at all this evening. So how could you see what either visitor looked like? It's pitch dark over there.'

'Oh, I see. Calling me a liar, are you?'

Tweed said nothing as he walked towards the front door with Paula. Mrs Sealle already had it open. As they continued down the path to the pavement she shrieked, 'And don't ever bloody come back 'ere.'

On their way back to Hengistbury there was silence in the Audi for some time. Tweed was concentrating on driving along a tricky country road with sharp bends and Paula sat brooding.

'Mrs Sealle would be hopeless as a witness,' she said eventually. 'She's got the right name – Mrs Sea-all. The trouble is she doesn't.'

'The only data we can rely on,' Tweed commented, is that the earlier visitor had a peaked cap, the much later one wore a trilby. I don't think she made up those two items. And Trilby arrived much later.'

'Which gets us nowhere.'

'Maybe . . .'

It seemed to take forever before Tweed drove the Audi at a crawl through the tunnel under The Forest. The gates swung open seconds after they'd arrived. Marshal's Rolls was parked below the terrace steps, Tweed parked behind it, wondering whether Marshal was going off to visit someone at this late hour.

Lavinia met them in the open doorway and Tweed realized she had opened the gates for them. She was clad in a short blue skirt and a white polo-necked sweater which hugged her figure.

'Thank you,' Tweed said, returning her smile. 'Where is everyone?'

'We had early dinner at six so Mrs Grandy could visit her sister in Gladworth. So far as I know they all went up to their apartments, like me, and have been there ever since. I came down to collect some papers in this folder and then I heard you arriving.' She smiled warmly. 'I can recognize the sound of your car. I'd better get on with more work . . .'

After she had taken their coats they went into the library, expecting to find it empty. Marshal stood up from a chair, now wearing a smart business suit. He greeted them affably.

'Been out on the town, you two? I've been back over two hours . . .'

'No! He hasn't!' Crystal had been seated in a deep armchair at the other end of the library, concealed by its high back. She came dancing forward, her expression mutinous. 'Marshal hasn't been back more than ten minutes, if that.'

'If you can't stop telling lies,' Marshal shouted, 'then keep your stupid mouth shut, you idiot child!'

Crystal was close to him now. He raised his hand, swung it back to slap her face violently. If the blow had landed he'd have sent her reeling across the room. Tweed grasped his raised arm in a tight clamp.

'Marshal. First she's not a child, she's a young woman. Second, you do not go round hitting women, whatever age they may be.'

Marshal, his face twisted in vicious fury, jabbed his elbow savagely into Tweed's ribs. That was his intention but Tweed stepped aside, clenched his fist and hit his opponent on the jaw with half his strength. Had he used all his strength the jaw would have been broken. Marshal was thrown back against the panelling where he slid down to the floor. He used a handkerchief to wipe a blood smear from his mouth. Standing up, he smiled engagingly at Tweed and Paula.

'We all have our moments of disagreement but they pass so quickly. I'm going out to park the Rolls round the back, then I'm off to get some shut-eye. Hope you both sleep well . . .'

'Did you see that look on his face before he got to his feet?' Paula whispered. 'Like Dr Jekyll and Mr Hyde.'

'Thank you,' said Crystal as she ran to Tweed and kissed him. 'My defender.' Her expression changed. 'And he got back not ten minutes ago. Nighty-night, and sleep the sleep of the just.'

Then she was gone, closing the door very quietly. Paula sagged into an armchair and Tweed joined her in a facing chair.

'Well,' Paula mused, 'that was quite something.'

'And Crystal told the truth,' Tweed said. 'When we got back I felt the bonnet of the Rolls and it was very warm. Marshal did get back very recently.'

'He had hours to drive back here from Seacove,' Paula said thoughtfully. 'Then drive on somewhere else, say as far as Dodd's End.'

Tweed was about to suggest they might as well get off to bed when the mobile buzzed. As he listened and said very little Bob Newman came into the library, bent down and hugged Paula. Then he sat in an armchair close to them.

Tweed's expression was grim as he finished the call. He sat pondering the conversation and then spoke.

'That was Buchanan. They have now got certain data on the methods Calouste uses. His strategy, if you like.'

'Well tell us,' Paula said impatiently.

'If he's working on a plan, and I think he is over here, he stays in the background. But if it doesn't pan out he gets aggressive.'

'What does that mean?' Newman asked.

'He's likely to move himself much closer to the scene of the action. To supervise it himself, I suppose.'

'What does that tell us?' Paula wanted to know, pushing a lock of black hair clear of her face. 'About here, I mean.'

'We know he's here,' Tweed went on. 'I'm sure we nearly trapped him at Heather Cottage. I'd wrongly assumed he'd then get a long way from Hengistbury . . .'

'We can see that,' Newman intervened. 'What does it tell us?'

'He'll be frustrated. And there was the bullet fired at me outside the Hall.'

'Do get to the point,' Paula urged.

'It's frightening. His normal strategy will lead him to get closer to the target. Me. He's probably close, very close, to Hengistbury now as I speak.'

'Oh, my God!' Paula exclaimed.

'In that case,' Newman said cheerfully, 'we have to think of him biding his time while he's based somewhere near here. Maybe quite near.'

'There isn't anywhere that fits that description,' Tweed protested.

'Oh yes, there is,' Newman said grimly. 'Maybe I'm the only one who's noticed it . . .'

He broke off as Marler entered the room, his flying helmet dangling from one hand. Paula waved a kiss and then spoke to him.

'Where have you been all day?'

'Oh,' Newman replied, 'he's been enjoying himself. Flying over East Anglia and then the Fens.'

'Weather wasn't bad,' Marler told her, 'and I just came in to say good night. I'm off myself for some shut-eye.'

'And where is Harry?' Paula asked when he'd gone.

'Harry,' Newman told her, 'has been prowling The Forest all day. Took a snack lunch with him. He's convinced danger will come through The Forest.'

'And now,' Tweed intervened irritably, 'maybe Bob can go on with what he was saying.'

'I took Harry's car today and motored slowly into Gladworth to get a pack of cigarettes. A distance from here Bella's high wall curves away from the road. Beyond The Forest takes over again. Not far from there is an unmade drive to a small ancient house called Shooter's Lodge. The house is like a lodge.

'I do remember catching a glimpse of it,' Paula confirmed. 'Looks very run-down.'

'And,' Newman went on, 'after hearing Tweed tell us what Calouste's tactics are when a plan isn't going well, he moves in close to the target.'

'Sounds unlikely,' Paula commented as she got up while Tweed also stood up. 'Time for bed,' she announced.

'I'll stay up a bit,' Newman said. 'I'm very alert.'

Tweed followed Paula up the staircase, several paces behind her. She was yards ahead of him along the corridor when he coughed briefly to clear his throat. The door he was passing opened and Lavinia stood just inside. She was still wearing her white polo-necked jumper and short skirt. She stood in her stockinged feet, arms folded.

'I recognized that occasional cough,' she said with a welcoming smile. 'Come in for a minute. I want to talk to you.'

'It's rather late . . .'

She took a step back to encourage Tweed to enter the apartment. He felt disturbed by the sight of her, the deep blue pools of her large eyes. He felt a rising urge to follow her inside.

'I like you,' she said in a soft voice. 'And I think you like me.'

'I do find you intriguing,' he admitted.

'Then we can have a drink of something together. Coffee or something stronger.'

He had both hands inside the pockets of his jacket

and he suddenly realized they were clenched tight. Glancing down the corridor he saw Paula still standing outside her door, her apartment key in her hand. Lavinia caught the glance. She leaned out of the door.

'Hi, Paula. Had a tough day? I'd say Tweed has. Can hardly keep his eyes open.' She smiled. 'Get a good night's kip, both of you.' She gave Tweed a wide smile, then closed her door.

Tweed followed Paula into her apartment, which she had opened by the time he reached it. She was grinning as he sank into an armchair. From a cupboard she fetched a bottle of wine and two glasses, which she filled, placing them on a table. As Tweed reached for his glass she perched herself on the arm of his chair. They clinked glasses, drank.

'What's so funny?' Tweed asked her. 'You were like the Cheshire Cat.'

'She's after you. She likes you. I heard her say it. I can understand it. She's in her thirties and prefers older men. She's also very intelligent and regards younger men as big kids.'

'Well, absolutely nothing happened.'

'You find her intriguing,' she teased him.

He sat up straight, slapped his hands on the table, his face grim.

'She's a suspect in two particularly horrible murder cases, along with a number of other people. If she were guilty I'd give the evidence in the witness box straight.

I would do it, knowing the judge would send her down for life with no option for parole. It's my job. I'm still a policeman at heart.'

'I know you are.' She laid a hand on his shoulder. 'It is one of a dozen reasons *I* like you.'

24

'I'm off to bed, sir,' Snape said to Newman as he entered the library.

'No, you're not. I want you to stay up until I get back. So you can open the gates when I walk out and open them for me when I get back.'

'A walk? At this time of night?'

'That's what I said. So get cracking and open the gates . . .'

Newman left by the exit on the lawn. Walking on pebbles in the drive might be heard by someone. Reaching the road, he turned left towards Gladworth. Walking under the overhead canopy of fir branches was an eerie experience. It was so damned quiet and nothing moved. No breeze. Just the sinister silence.

Arriving at the point where the Hengistbury wall curved away from the road, he slowed down. He moved very cautiously as he reached the unmade drive leading to Shooter's Lodge. The drive was ankle-deep in pine needles. He listened. No sound from the lodge and no lights in any windows. It was too quiet.

By now his night vision was functioning well. The lodge was about ten yards back from the road, on the right of the drive. It was very old, as Paula had said, built years ago of grey stone; it was one storey high with a steep sloping roof and wide stone square chimneys rearing up. The entrance had a long stone-roofed porch protecting it. Too quiet, Newman said to himself again. Yet it had all the appearance of being uninhabited.

With his Smith & Wesson held down by his side he began to walk up the drive, his soft-soled shoes making no sound as they pressed deep into the carpet of pine needles. He thought he saw a movement behind the largest chimney, stopped, waited, stared up. Nothing.

Then he noticed a complex web of radio-like wires attached to the chimney. This was the first sign this place was not all it pretended to be.

Inside Shooter's Lodge an alarm button had flashed red as Newman trod through the pine needles on the sophisticated pressure pad. Two men in the kitchen at the rear looked at each other.

One was dressed in a velvet jacket and trousers. He wore a Jewish-style cap on his head and gold-rimmed pince-nez on the bridge of his long, strong nose above thick lips. He had a professorial look.

His companion, Jacques, was a contrast. Taller and

heavily built, his hands were huge. He produced from a leg sheath an ugly wide-bladed knife. He made a gesture of cutting a throat, pointed outside.

The professor frowned, shook his head, pointed first up the chimney, mimicked taking a photograph. Jacques nodded, then carefully removed a sheet of metal from the base of the chimney. Bending his head, he shinned up a ladder leading up the chimney to the roof.

The Professor bent down, removed a heavy floor rug, dug his fingers into a slot, heaved, hauled up a trapdoor, went down a series of stone steps into the vast cellar. Jacques would follow him by the same route. Warmth from the cellar drifted upwards.

The cellar was luxuriously furnished. Wall-to-wall carpet covered the floor. Heat came from a log fire which the Professor hastily damped down. Then he calmly sat on a sofa and began studying an old book entitled *Weapons in the Middle Ages*.

Jacques took his photo of the intruder walking towards the porch with his non-flash camera. Climbing back inside the chimney onto the ladder, he closed the cleverly designed stone door, descended the ladder, re-entered the kitchen, carefully put back into place the stone-coloured metal sheet.

His only real problem was closing the trapdoor after taking several steps down towards the cellar. The heavy kitchen rug had a strong adhesive attached to its base.

Once this was accomplished he slotted the trapdoor back into its place and descended into the cellar. His large hands were sweaty as he sat down on the sofa beside the Professor, who was calmly reading his book. Without looking at Jacques he took a large blue handkerchief out of his pocket, handed it to him. Jacques used it to dry his hands.

Reaching into his jacket pocket, Jacques produced the small camera, extracted the photo he'd taken from behind the chimney. The Professor always paid for the best – the camera worked without a flash and yet took clear pictures in the dark. He handed the print to the Professor who examined it over the top of his *pince-nez*. Nothing in his expression registered a reaction.

He reached for a notebook on a nearby table. He wrote in it with care. Then he handed it to Jacques, watching him closely as Jacques read the words.

Robert Newman. Key member Tweed's team.

Jacques lurched forward, his wide-bladed knife already in his hand. The Professor reached forward with one hand. With surprising strength he placed it on Jacques's chest, pushed him back into the chair. Then he used two fingers of the same hand, pressed them against his lips. Not one word, his gesture signalled. He resumed reading his book.

On the floor above, Newman was checking each room. When he entered the second bedroom the same atmosphere met him. The bed was made but there was mould on the sheets. And everywhere he went he walked through cobwebs dangling from the ceiling. It seemed even chillier inside the lodge than it was outside.

He entered the last room to check, the kitchen. More cobwebs and again all the surfaces were covered with dust. No aroma of food being prepared, maybe for years. Then he stopped, frowned. Was it his imagination or was there a faint feeling of warmth?

He took off a glove, held his bare hand over the cooker. Nothing. So why had he briefly detected warmth? He swung the beam of his pencil torch round. Unlike the other rooms this floor was covered with plastic sheets instead of stone paving.

Logical, he thought, this being the kitchen. He swivelled the beam of his torch, saw a thick rug in the centre of the floor. He crouched down and felt the corner which was turned up. He frowned. It was sticky, as though covered with an adhesive.

He slowly peeled the rug to one side, exposing the floor beneath. On one side the plastic sheet didn't fit perfectly. There was a deep narrow slot. Carefully, he slid one hand down inside, felt a handle, resisted the impulse to lift. Very carefully he replaced the rug over the whole slab.

His expression was grim as he stood up. There was a cellar below. If opened and closed recently it explained why he had sensed warmth in the kitchen only. As he had examined the apparently uninhabited lodge there had been someone hiding below him. Maybe more than one person. It gave him a creepy feeling.

He walked quietly back to the front door. It was protected by a Keylock, the most complex on the market. On his way in he had used the advanced pick-lock supplied to him by Harry. He had opened it easily.

Now, standing in the long arched porch, he closed the door, which had well-oiled hinges. Harry's instrument locked it silently. He emerged slowly from the porch, Smith & Wesson by his side, listened.

Then he was careful to walk back towards the road down the centre of the drive just as he had come in, his feet again sinking into the carpet of pine needles. He was near the exit when his right foot felt something hard. He crouched down after a quick glance back at the lodge. Using his gloved hand, he swept aside a whole mass of pine needles and there it was.

A wide metal band which appeared to span the drive, a deep trench in the middle of the bar occupied by a thick cable. Whoever was inside the lodge had been warned of his coming by the weight of his foot on the signal cable. Probably a red light came on somewhere inside the lodge.

He took care to sweep back pine needles over his discovery. Then he started the long trudge through the icy night to the manor. He used the speakerphone,

Snape replied immediately, opened the gates.

Newman thanked him for waiting up so late, gave him a generous tip, toiled up the staircase which seemed longer than usual. He paused outside Tweed's apartment door, his hand raised to knock, then decided not to disturb him.

He walked on to his apartment. Once inside he forced himself to take a shower, climbed into pyjamas, flopped under the sheets. The moment his head hit the pillow he fell into a deep sleep. His bedside light remained on all night.

25

After breakfast the following morning Newman described his visit to Shooter's Lodge to Tweed. Marler, Harry and Paula were also present. When he had finished, Tweed's reaction surprised him.

'First, that was good work, outstandingly so, Bob. And the way you handled it was perfect. For the moment we don't go near the place. If we're driving past it no one even glances at it.'

'I don't understand,' Newman protested. 'We may have Calouste in the palms of our hands.'

'I do hope so. So we don't want him slipping away as he did at Heather Cottage. He'll have an escape route. I'm getting to know how Calouste thinks. He's moved in close to me after failing twice to kill me.'

'I think you're right,' said Paula.

They were assembled in the large downstairs library. Before permitting Newman to report, Tweed had checked every distant armchair to make sure neither

Leo nor Crystal were hidden away, listening.

Several were getting up to leave when Tweed's mobile buzzed. He made a gesture indicating they should wait. It was Monica calling from Park Crescent. Tweed listened, said very little, thanked her for the call. Nothing in his expression indicated the call had been important.

'Gather round,' he ordered. 'I'll be speaking very quietly. Disturbing news: Monica has had a call from Philip Cardon on the Continent. Very short. I quote what he said. "Our friend has ordered the elite of his French servants to come over here urgently. They are probably already in England." End of message.'

'I don't get it,' said Harry.

'Philip is warning us Calouste has brought over here the elite of his French killers. I left a bit out. There are six or seven of them, Calouste doesn't do things by halves.'

'They'll come through The Forest to attack here,' Marler warned. 'Obvious line of approach. And unlike us they'll use their favourite weapons – knives. So I suggest the team goes into The Forest, scattered, and now.'

'I'll advise you,' Harry volunteered. 'I probably know the area better than any of you.'

'Wait a moment,' intervened Tweed. 'There's a problem. The bodies. Both the Home Office and the Foreign Office dumbos are playing diplomatic chess with Paris. The French are waiting for some excuse to smear us. Even though you'll be up against murderous thugs, Paris could yell about French citizens being massacred.'

'I have the answer,' Harry piped up. 'I found an ancient and deep stone quarry, its sides crumbling, on the far side of The Forest. Bodies. Need I say more?'

'No,' said Tweed. As his team trooped to the door he called out. 'Be careful – you'll be dealing with professionals.'

'I thought we were professionals,' Harry fired back at him as he left and closed the door.

'Everything is hotting up,' Tweed said to Paula when they were alone. 'The tempo is accelerating. But we have experienced this before.'

'I don't like the idea of our team lost in The Forest,' she said.

'Except they won't be lost, under Harry's guidance.'

A few minutes later the door opened slowly and Leo's head peered round it sneakily. Behind him Crystal's head also appeared.

'Anyone else in here?' he whispered. 'Good. We have an important secret to tell you.'

Not another one, Paula thought. The Mrs Carlyle one was bad enough, but it was important.

With Tweed and Paula the two of them gathered round the table, Crystal looked excited, brushed her hair back off her face, while Leo looked determined.

'You heard our mother died in a car accident,' Leo began. 'I was eleven and Crystal was eight. Mother was driving home by herself using a route she knew well. Coming back from Midhurst she climbed a steep hill with Hook Corner at the top. It's high up, with a drop of a hundred feet on one side and a big warning notice. Hook Corner is a hairpin turn so she drove slowly, I'm sure, as she always did. Are you with me?'

'Yes,' Tweed said, hands perched under his chin, waiting for Crystal to interrupt, which she didn't.

'Coming round Hook Corner,' Leo continued, 'there's a steep hill going down, so you brake. Mother's car went over the edge and ended up a hundred feet down, smashed to pulp. The police under Inspector Trafford—'

'Tetford?' enquired Tweed. 'The man still in charge over at Leaminster.'

'That's him. Tetford. Been here forever. Prior to Mother's so-called accident Tetford reported it as just yet another accident at a dangerous corner. It wasn't. The brake linings had been tampered with. When Mother pressed the brake it didn't work. It was murder.'

'My mother was murdered,' Crystal said. 'Tetford messed it up.'

'How do you know the brake linings were tampered with?' Tweed demanded, leaning forward.

'Leo is a mechanic,' Crystal spoke up. 'Worked for a garage once and was so good they offered him a job. He can take any car to pieces and put it back together perfectly. He could demonstrate on your Audi.'

'No thanks,' Tweed said firmly. 'When did you go down to examine the smashed-up car?'

'The day after his men had made a superficial check.'

'And did you report your findings to Tetford?'

'I did.' Leo's face flushed. 'He told me I was only twelve years old – he even got my age wrong – and warned me not to go spreading silly stories or I'd find myself in serious trouble.'

'And have you told this to anyone else since?'

'Only to Crystal and she's kept quiet.'

'Surely you mentioned it to Warner, your father?'

'I knew he didn't want to discuss it or talk about it to anyone. He's never referred to it since. I'm telling you now so you know everything that might be connected with your investigation.'

'Keep it that way. And I appreciate your telling me.'

They both got up and left the library together. Tweed looked at Paula who had a very serious expression.

'What do you make of that?'

'It could add a whole new dimension to the case. I believed Leo. I've seen him fiddling with his motorcycle in bits, then setting to work to put it together again.'

She stopped talking as the door opened and Marshal breezed into the room, his usual flamboyant self. He wore jodhpurs, tucked into gleaming leather riding boots, and a blazing yellow tunic. In his right hand he held a whip, which he slapped against his boots.

'Mornin', you two detectives. Time you solved the case.'

Tweed was not amused. He stared hard at Marshal before he spoke.

'It's not a flippant matter when your own mother has been brutally murdered. And we are closer to breaking the case than when we arrived. Were you thinking of going riding?'

'As a matter of fact I'm taking a trot through the woods. Lavinia often rides the course laid out beyond the tennis courts which has tricky jumps. She sails over them. I can't watch her. But this morning I'll be on my second horse, Whiskers. A slow plodder so quite safe to take into the woods.'

'In that case, Mr Main, I suggest you postpone your ride, confine yourself to your apartment for the morning.'

'What the hell for? You can't order me about!'

'Some members of my team are in The Forest shooting rabbits to help out Snape. There's a danger the growing population of our furry friends will overrun the place.'

'I haven't seen one damned one of the things on the lawn.'

'And you don't want them invading that lawn, digging up a labyrinth of warrens. Also,' Tweed went on genially, 'I don't want one of my suspects shot.'

'I'm a suspect?' Marshal's face reddened with fury.

'Everyone in this mansion is until we have all the evidence I am collecting almost hourly.'

'Oh, well . . .' Marshal paused uncertainly. 'I do have a whole pile of accounts to check in my apartment. If you'd spoken earlier I wouldn't have had to change my togs.'

With this parting shot he left the library, slamming the door behind him. Shortly afterwards Snape appeared with a telephone he plugged into a wall socket.

'There's a Professor Heathstone on the line. Asked for you personally. Said it was urgent.'

'Hello. Tweed here.'

'Good morning, Mr Tweed, I am a man of few words. I am a rare-book dealer.'

'I don't deal in them.'

The voice was reedy, like that of an old man, throaty and pronouncing every word slowly. As though he had to remember what he wanted to say.

'Ah,' the voice continued, 'an impulsive man. Not what I had expected. I have important information for you. I have a room at the Pike's Peak Hotel in Gladworth. Could you be here in, say, fifteen minutes?'

'No, I couldn't. I'd need to know more about this alleged important information before I come anywhere near you.'

'Very well. I was in a second-hand bookshop in Paris quite recently when, tucked behind some rubbish, I found a first edition of *Ulysses*, by the Irish gentleman. Have you any idea of what that would go for at a London auction?'

'No. And if you don't get to the point quickly I'm going off the line.'

'Patience, Mr Tweed. Just a few moments longer. Inside was a sheet with names typed on it, a new sheet. It gave the names of the members of something called the Red Circle. The chairman, apparently, is someone called Calouste something or other.'

There was silence. Tweed thought he could hear heavy breathing on the line.

'I'll be at your hotel in half an hour,' Tweed said as Harry entered the library.

'There will be a charge, Mr Tweed. I'm a businessman.'

'There always is a charge.'

'What is it, Harry?' Tweed asked as he put down the phone and Marler followed him into the library.

'Thought I'd tell you we're all ready to go at the back door.'

'You have come at just the right moment. A change of plan.'

Newman came in as Tweed began telling them about the mysterious phone call, recalling every word from memory and stating that he was going to meet this professor Heathstone at Pike's Peak Hotel. Paula chimed in that she was going with him.

Marler immediately came up with a detailed plan, reminding Tweed of Philip Cardon's warning that six or seven French killers had arrived. He thought Philip, as usual, had exaggerated the number to put Tweed on full alert. He told Harry and Newman how they should react.

'The car park at that hotel is the danger point, so we must get there first.'

'I hope you're right about this,' Paula said to Marler. 'This could be very dangerous for Tweed.'

'Haven't I always been right?' Marler said with a smile as he put his arm reassuringly round her waist.

'Give me time to think,' she teased him.

'And just before we leave,' Marler continued as Tweed was impatiently waiting by the door.

'What is it now?' Tweed snapped.

'I want everyone to give Harry their handcuffs. He will need plenty.'

26

'This meet at the hotel is a trap,' Paula said as she sat by Tweed driving the Audi through the tunnel road leading to Gladworth. 'I'm not happy about any of it.'

'Of course it's a trap,' Tweed replied.

'A trap for you,' she insisted, 'so why walk into it?'

'Because a trap can be reversed, eliminating the trappers.'

'If you say so.'

Her mood was not helped by the weather change. The sun had vanished. She had the sensation that, even with headlights on, they were driving into a pool of gloom, maybe doom.

A short distance behind them Newman was driving his Merc. As passengers in the rear of the car he had Marler and Harry. Harry had produced from his tool bag a thin long-barrelled weapon, which he handed to Marler. He also gave him a short slightly larger metal barrel with perforated holes at frequent intervals, plus several cartridges.

'An American Colt,' Marler said. 'Not many of them about, even in the States.'

'Pal of mine visiting New York was threatened with that in a bar. He took it off the American. Chap didn't know you don't threaten a Cockney. The shorter bit with a screw lining inside is—'

'A silencer,' Marler said. 'Trouble is they can jam a gun.'

'Agreed. But you could get off two shots, maybe three before you get into trouble.'

'You think I can, if necessary, use it . . .'

'To scare any thug dead.'

'Could come in useful. Thanks.'

Marler's anxiety, carefully concealed, was that they would get to the hotel car park after the French thugs. It would giver the enemy a huge advantage.

Marler had no way of knowing this also was Paula's worry. Calouste had a reputation for brilliant organization. She reminded herself that they still didn't know whether the man who had phoned Tweed was really Professor Heathstone.

She gave the order as they entered Gladworth, which was its normal sleepy self. She scanned the street for parked cars. Not a one.

'Park the car a few yards this side of the entrance to the car park for the hotel.'

'Why?' Tweed asked.

'Do as you're told.'

He parked where she had suggested. To his horror Paula, her Browning hauled out of her leg sheath, jumped out and walked briskly into the car park. She had chosen this weapon because it was easier to conceal, held close to her side.

She walked in slowly, an unlit cigarette between her lips, just a local girl searching for her boyfriend. The car park was deserted. She went back to the entrance, beckoning to Tweed, who drove inside. She pointed to a space under the hotel wall, twirled a hand, indicating he should back in ready for a quick escape.

The Mercedes, driven by Newman, had stopped at the entrance to Gladworth. He had observed Paula's movements and knew there was no danger. Yet.

Tweed walked with Paula out of the car park, entered the large reception hall past a sorry-looking palm tree in a tub to the reception desk. The girl behind the counter greeted him with a welcoming smile.

'If the car park is anything to go by you haven't many guests,' he remarked.

'Only one. It's the time of the year. Come June and we'll be bursting at the seams. A number of those crazy mountaineers eager to scale Pike's Peak.' She clasped a hand to her mouth. 'Oh, have I said the wrong thing?'

'You most certainly have not. The only mountain I want to scale is London's Canary Wharf. In a lift. We are here by appointment to see Professor Heathstone.'

'He's in our best suite, Room 14, first floor.' She sighed. 'Poor man in that wheelchair.'

'We've not met before. Wheelchair?'

'It took the manager and the porter a terrible job to manoeuvre him up those stairs in the wheelchair. Shall I phone him and tell him you're coming?'

'No, thank you. He does know we're visiting him but we'd like to surprise him. He loves that.'

Room 14 was halfway along a wide corridor. There was a peephole in the door, which Tweed kept well away from as he pressed the bell.

Nothing for a couple of minutes, then the door was opened on a chain. An ancient face peered out, nodded, took off the chain, opened the door. Professor Heathstone smiled, manipulated levers as he backed away at speed until he was behind a large desk. He gestured for Tweed and Paula to sit in two comfortable hard-backed chairs facing him. Tweed made the introductions.

'You are most prompt, sir' Heathstone responded. 'I approve of that. And you have made my day by bringing your delightful assistant, Miss Grey.' He managed a small bow towards her. 'They have a well-stocked bar downstairs. What may I offer in the way of refreshment?'

His visitors both thanked him and refused the offer. Paula was nervous and therefore very alert. She bent down to adjust her jeans over her right ankle, checking to make sure her Browning was easily accessible.

Professor Heathstone was not what either of them had expected. First, there was the wheelchair. Then his face was so crinkled, like a crocodile's. His brown eyes peered at them from behind his gold-rimmed *pince-nez*. Tweed noticed his voice was stronger, his accent that of a British public schoolboy of long ago. Maybe he had trouble talking on the phone.

'Now, sir,' Heathstone continued, 'I am a business-man and your swift agreement to come and see me suggests that the document is valuable to you. I trust you will not mind paying me a fee. In cash, of course. Say two hundred pounds.'

'That's a lot of money,' Tweed remarked.

'I assure you, sir, I paid a great deal more for the first edition of *Ulysses* inside which I found this document. Of course I could sell it for three times that amount.' He snickered. 'The bookshop owner in Paris had no idea of its true value.'

'I'll pay your fee when I have examined the document.' He paused. 'What is this organization the Red Circle?'

'I really have no idea. Nor, sir, do I care.'

Tweed nodded. In a recent phone conversation with Buchanan he had been told that the French police had recently found out it was the code name for Calouste's Continent-wide organization.

'I appreciate your time is valuable,' Heathstone said as he placed both hands on the wheelchair's levers. The window behind him overlooked the car park, too far back for either Tweed or Paula to be able to see down into it. They heard the sound of a car entering. Almost at once a second car drove in.

Heathstone expertly swung the chair round, moved it so he could look down through the window. He snickered, swung the chair round and snickered again, then spoke.

'Wedding party. This will be the best day of their lives. Now, to business. The fee is agreeable, sir?'

'After I have seen the document.'

With great skill Heathstone manipulated the chair at speed across the room to a door which obviously interconnected with the next room. As he slid back the bolt he called over his shoulder.

'You *do* have the cash with you?'

'Of course I have.'

The door closed. Paula frowned, lifted her eyebrows as she looked at Tweed.

'Probably has his precious first-edition *Ulysses* hidden in that room.'

Earlier, waiting at the entrance to Gladworth, Harry had made a suggestion to his companion. He wanted Newman to change places, to take over the wheel, while he occupied the passenger seat. Not knowing what he had in mind Newman, always trusting Harry, agreed.

'There's a big Citroën packed with men coming up behind us,' Harry warned. 'Drive into the middle of the car park, well away from the wall. Quickly . . .'

Newman drove the Merc into the deserted car park – only Tweed's Audi occupied a slot. The Citroën drove in at speed, pulled up a few yards to the right of the Merc. The next event happened so quickly it would have been difficult to time.

'Stop!' ordered Harry. As Newman braked Harry was out of the car like a sprinter, his Walther in his hand. He sped across the car park, reaching the Citroën as one of the four evil-looking French thugs, knife in hand, pushed open the front passenger door prior to leaping out. Harry slammed the door shut as the thug had one leg outside. The door hit his leg like an axe blow. The thug screamed with pain, leg still trapped between door and body of the car.

By now Marler had reached the driver's door, a Walther in his hand. The window was down and the driver was about to lunge out, a vicious-looking knife in his right hand. Marler had an unpleasant smile as he aimed the Walther. The driver raised both hands to the roof, dropping his knife.

The two thugs in the back were about to disembark to join in the melee when they heard a loud tapping on the rear window. Looking back they saw Newman, his

Smith & Wesson aimed at them point blank, swivelling the barrel swiftly from one to the other. They sat frozen still.

It was a few seconds earlier when Professor Heathstone had glanced out of the window and made his remark about 'wedding parties'.

Harry now dragged the thug with the injured leg out of the car, pushed him face down on the hard gravel, produced his first pair of handcuffs and clamped them tight round the thug's wrists. He ran round to the driver's seat where Marler had opened the door and pressed the muzzle of the Walther hard against one eye. No point in playing around with lethal scumbags.

Marler was fluent in French and in dirty language the thug would understand ordered him out, to lie stomach-down on the drive. The thug hesitated, still clutching his knife. Harry brought the barrel of his automatic down hard across the thug's fingers, which he broke. The thug screamed, the knife fell, Harry hauled him out, shoved him onto the drive, used a second pair of handcuffs to pinion his wrists behind his back, ignoring the man's moans about his fingers.

Hurrying to the rear, he wasted no time at all while one thug, under the threat of Newman's revolver, meekly stepped out and lay on his stomach on the drive. He had been shaken by the sight of Harry's first captive lying with one leg at an abnormal angle. The remaining thug was made of sterner stuff.

Despite Newman's Smith & Wesson he leapt out of the car, his wide-bladed knife aimed at Harry's stomach. Newman brought the barrel of his gun down on the bridge of his nose, often a lethal blow. He collapsed, half inside and half outside the rear of the car.

'Thanks,' Harry said. 'That was close. He's probably dead. Who cares?'

He checked the thug's carotid arteries. His reaction expressed surprise and something like a hint of regret.

'Bastard's alive. Ticking over nicely.'

He hauled him fully out, turned him over, brought both hands together, clamped another pair of handcuffs on them, stood up.

'Not a bad morning's work, Marler commented. 'Now I suggest we put all the bodies in the back of the Merc and deliver them to Commander Buchanan. They'll all be illegals so he can send them back to France with our compliments.'

In Room 14 on the first floor Paula was getting impatient. She checked her watch, looked at Tweed.

'He's been gone five minutes. I'm suspicious.'

'So am I,' said Tweed. 'We'll go and have a look.'

Paula had her Browning by her side as Tweed threw open the interconnecting door. Professor Heathstone had disappeared. He walked into another bedroom. Nobody. On a table an old copy of *Ulysses*. He opened it to the publisher's data in the preliminary pages. He laughed.

'It's a third edition, not a first. Worthless. And not a document inside. What a surprise!'

Paula ran across to a side door marked *FIRE EXIT*.

Opening it, she saw stone steps leading down. She ran to the bottom with Tweed behind her calling our for her to be careful. Opening the door on the ground floor by lifting a bar she found herself in an alley. Opposite a door led to a garage. She heard a car starting up but by the time she was inside it had disappeared, turning in the direction of Hengistbury.

Tweed led her down the alley into the main street and round into the car park. The Merc, driven by Newman with Marler by his side and Harry between them, was about to leave. In the back, handcuffed bodies were piled on top of each other.

Marler lowered the window. He beckoned to Tweed and Paula.

'This is what it was all about. The gentlemen in the back were supposed to kill both of you. We're taking this lot, all illegals, I'm sure, to dump them in Buchanan's lap.'

'That would be a long drive,' Tweed told him. 'I'll phone Buchanan and tell him to send police cars down to meet you, take your packages off you, then you can drive straight back to Hengistbury.'

'How did you get on with Professor Heathstone?'

Marler asked as Newman started the car.

'It was rather a short conversation, then he slipped away via a connecting door into the next room.'

'So Calouste has escaped once more,' Marler said, lowering his voice.

'He's a persistent rat. He'll be back. I'll be waiting for him.'

27

'There's a sealed envelope waiting for you from Buchanan,' Lavinia greeted them as she opened the door into the hall. 'He phoned and said that it was coming by courier. He spoke to me when I told him you were out with Paula.'

'You told him the rest of my team were also out?' Tweed asked as they entered the hall and she closed the door.

'I did *not*.' She smiled. 'He's a man who uses few words. So am I. I don't pass on information to anyone unless I have to.'

'Well, I'm grateful,' Tweed replied as she handed him the envelope. 'Is there anywhere here where we won't be disturbed?'

'I'd use the smaller upstairs library next to Bella's study. No one likes to go there these days.'

Tweed thanked her again. She was wearing a longer blue skirt, the hem ending just below her knees. Round her waist she had an apron. She touched it.

'Please excuse this. I'm in the kitchen baking more lemon pies. Now, give me your coats then you can hide in the library.

Tweed entered the upstairs library. Sitting down at a table, with Paula by his side, he checked the envelope's seals, which were unbroken. He opened it slowly.

The mobile buzzed. It was Buchanan.

'Tweed? Good. Just to tell you the envelope – it has arrived? Good – contains five portraits of a man Loriot of the French DST believes is Calouste. If so, it's a coup. Sketched by a student in a back-street Paris bar. The subject had a Frenchman with him who might just be his deputy. The sad confirmation is the student was found headless, floating in the Seine. That was after I'd seen him at HQ and he'd told me he heard the deputy address him as Calouste. When I just said "I" and "me" I was quoting Loriot.'

'Why would that trigger off the student?'

'Because Calouste is becoming less invisible. There was an article splashed in *Le Monde* at my suggestion. A blazing headline worded "Calouste Doubenkian: Wanted for Questioning". The reporter who wrote the article is now under police guard in a safe house. Any progress down there about what the reporter Drew Franklin is calling "The Necklace Murders"? Didn't think you'd tell me anything yet. I must rush off now.'

Tweed told Paula the gist of what Buchanan had told him. She nodded impatiently.

'Is it going to take all day to see what's in the envelope?'

'Curiosity killed the cat, to coin a cliché,' he teased.

'Well, women are curious like cats if they've anything up here –' she tapped her forehead – 'except skullbone.'

He withdrew from the envelope five photocopies of the same picture. It was a sketch executed in charcoal and could have been drawn by her. She sucked in her breath. She could tell the poor French student, murdered, might well have developed into a talented artist. But it was the sketches which startled her.

'They're nothing like Professor Heathstone.'

'No, they're not.'

Heathstone had struck her as being in his late seventies or early eighties. The sketch was of someone in his late forties at a guess, an evil-looking man with a spade-shaped jaw, a smooth skin, a crooked nose and wearing dark glasses, which concealed his eyes. Something about the sketch made her suppress a shudder.

'Perhaps Heathstone was a deputy,' she said doubtfully.

'I thought maybe you were going to suggest Heathstone was heavily disguised. The contrast is too great for that.'

'Well, when he fled I heard Heathstone's car heading this way towards London.'

'Or maybe Shooter's Lodge.'

There was a tapping on the door. Tweed slipped the sketches back inside the envelope, then called out, 'Please come in.'

Lavinia appeared, without her apron, carrying a silver tray with Rosenthal crockery, a large pot, a jug of milk, plates, on one of which was a selection of cakes. She arranged them on the table.

'I thought you might like some coffee to keep you going.'

'Yes, we would. How considerate,' said Tweed. 'And now you're here do you mind if I ask you a few questions?'

'Of course not.' She carried a chair over to join them, sat down. 'I can't promise to answer all of them if they concern how the bank operates,' she concluded with a smile.

'I don't want secrets,' he said, turning his chair so her knees almost touched his. 'But Bella gave me no idea at all. You must keep records.'

'We do. In a way you'll think we're old fashioned. We have no computers in the place, no Internet connection. Bella said if hackers were able to penetrate the Pentagon, which quite young boys did, then they could certainly penetrate ours, if we had them.'

Paula was smiling inwardly. Tweed had banned the modern machines from his office for the same reason. After all, overseas agents' lives were constantly at risk.

'If you'll let me go on,' Lavinia said with another smile, 'our records of depositors' amounts are typed on index cards. We employ two bright girls from Gladworth to do the work. They come in several days a week by the back door and work in the east wing. So far I've kept Chief Inspector Hammer out from that part of the building.'

'No point in invading that area,' Tweed agreed. 'I'll have a word with Hammer. Going back to your system, surely you are putting a lot of trust in these two girls from Gladworth, even risk, considering the data they must know?'

'We don't rely on trust.' Lavinia smiled again. 'They work from material I hand them. Each depositor's name is coded, and the amount deposited is coded. I carry the book with those codes everywhere with me.' Her blue eyes seemed even larger as she stared at Tweed with a mischievous expression. 'I even keep that book inside my pillow when I go to bed. So only someone with me might extract it from the pillow when I've fallen asleep.'

The last place Tweed looked at now was where Paula had settled by his side. He tried to think of something to say but nothing would come.

'And now,' Lavinia said, standing up, 'if that is all, then I think I ought to leave both of you in peace. No one else will come up. I wish you positive thoughts.'

After she had closed the door she opened it again quickly.

'If either of you need some bedtime reading matter I'd go to the bigger library downstairs. It is crammed with novels, the latest and classics. This library was Bella's collection of a range of obscure and strange volumes.'

'Thank you,' Tweed said. 'Oh, we have not seen a single newspaper since we arrived.'

'Bella didn't like them. Snape takes a whole variety and keeps them in his cabin in The Forest. 'Bye for now.'

'This coffee is just the right temperature and so welcome,' Paula said after pouring two cups when Lavinia had gone.

Tweed drank half a cup and then wandered over to the glass bookcases lining part of one wall. He could glance quickly along a shelf and absorb all the titles. He stopped, put on latex gloves, unlocked a door, reached for a large leather-bound volume pushed further in between other volumes. Taking the volume to the table he laid it down, gently lifted the front cover and the book opened to a page in the middle.

Paula stood up, joined Tweed at the table. He had closed the book, showed her the title on the well-rubbed spine. *Spanish Inquisition: Methods of Torture*, he translated. Then he let the book open by itself at two pages in the middle. He was wearing latex gloves.

'Oh, my God!' Paula exclaimed.

The right-hand page carried a series of illustrations, each showing from different angles drawings of a spiked collar which was almost a replica of the spiked wire collar which they had seen round the neck of Bella and, later, round the neck of Mrs Carlyle. One drawing showed the back of the collar with wooden handles to draw the collar tight. There was some text in Spanish.

'So now we know where the killer got his idea for the fiendish weapon.'

'Which narrows his identity down to someone inside the manor.'

'Wish I could read Spanish,' Paula mused.

'The pictures are sufficiently self-explanatory.'

Tweed asked her to give him a large transparent evidence envelope. She produced one from a compartment in her briefcase. He slipped the book inside, she sealed it, tucked it into an empty compartment in her case.

'Fingerprints?' she suggested.

'Yes. Give it to Harry. He always carries the kit. Mind you, I don't expect to find any. This killer has already shown how thorough he is.'

'What a weird book for Bella to have in her library,' Paula commented.

'I expect she bought them in job lots to fill the bookcases. Part of her showmanship to impress millionaire clients. When Harry has checked it for fingerprints I want you to bring the book back up here and slip it into place. There's a gap and I found the book pushed back about an inch between the others. As you shrewdly said, it narrows the suspect to someone in the manor. I've had enough of being in here.'

They were walking down the imposing staircase when they met Lavinia coming up. Tweed paused.

'Lavinia, am I right in assuming the only entrance to the manor and its grounds is the main entrance gate?'

'Now it is.' She smiled, her arms full of files. 'But ages ago there was a small pedestrian entrance at the far end of the wall, beyond where it curves away from the road. It was bricked up Heaven knows how long ago. A small arched gateway. Was it quiet for you in the smaller library?'

'Yes, we just rested and talked, which made a change.'

At the bottom of the staircase Marler appeared from nowhere. He looked up to make sure Lavinia had gone, then told them.

'Couldn't help hearing what Lavinia said. I'm sure she thinks what she said is so.' He paused. 'But it isn't.'

'What do you mean?' Tweed asked sharply.

'I've prowled The Forest inside the wall until I almost know every tree. Eventually this morning I found the second way in, what she called the small arched gateway. Bricked up? I think you'd better come and see for yourselves. You are in for a shock.'

28

Marler led Tweed and Paula through the kitchen, ignoring Mrs Grandy's protests. She showed her feelings by raising the meat cleaver she was using and thudding it down deep into an empty section of the heavy work table.

'She'll have trouble hauling that out again,' Marler commented.

'Wait a minute,' Tweed whispered to Marler and Paula ahead of him.

He lingered just outside the back door. He saw the ease with which Mrs Grandy took hold of the handle and lifted out the cleaver. He had realized she was a strong woman but this display of exceptional strength made him frown. He nodded to his companions to keep walking.

It was a long trudge through The Forest before Marler held up a hand. They paused and Marler explained, 'I left Harry to keep an eye on this second entrance. He has his Walther and some grenades. Don't want to startle him.'

Cupping both hands round his mouth he called out: 'Harry, there are three of us coming. I've bought Tweed and Paula.'

His clear voice echoed through The Forest. They crossed a small clearing and there was the wall, curving away from the road a distance back. Tweed stared at an opening with a craftsman-like arch above it. On the manor side, neatly piled against the inner wall, were piles of old intact bricks, the material which had sealed the opening.

'Well,' Paula said grimly, 'that knocks on the head my theory the murderer had to come from inside the manor.'

She had hardly finished speaking when Harry shoved Tweed against her violently. They both managed to keep their balance but ended up clear of the arched entrance. A second or two later a bullet, aimed from outside the arch, passed where Tweed had been standing. Harry's reaction was instantaneous. He had a grenade, taken from the deep pocket of his windcheater, in his right hand, had the pin withdrawn so it was live.

'All right mate,' he said quickly. 'Want to play games?'

He lobbed the grenade into the centre of a clump of bushes on the far side of the entrance. There was a flash, a muffled thump. The next sound was the revving up of an invisible motorcycle, then of it racing full throttle across the open land beyond the deep tangle of bushes. The sound died swiftly.

'Missed him,' Harry said philosophically. 'Sorry for the shove but I heard movement in the bushes over there.'

'It simply means Tweed is still the main target,' Marler said.

'Calouste,' Tweed remarked, 'must think in some degree I'm in his way for his next move.'

'Or,' Paula suggested, 'his informant inside the manor thinks you're now getting too close.'

'Whatever.' Tweed shrugged. 'Harry, did you see the two so-called necklaces found inside Crystal's wardrobe?'

'Yes, I'd walked in, seen them clearly. Then old Hammerhead very rudely told me to get out. I did so but my elbow accidentally jabbed him in the ribs.'

'So how would you carry one of them round the manor without risk of its being seen?'

'Easy. Big briefcase. Both insides lined with thin metal and sheets of leather so no noise as you cart it about.'

'Thank you. Paula, let's get back to the manor. I want to subject Warner Chance to intensive interrogation . . .'

*

Jacques took a deep breath as he descended the steps into the luxuriously furnished cellar running underneath the ground floor of Shooter's Lodge. He was trying to decide whether to tell the truth about his failure.

Once a bricklayer, the previous night he had carefully removed the old bricks from the arched entrance in the wall. After he'd completed this arduous work he'd settled down in the undergrowth opposite the now open arched doorway.

Laying the rifle with the scope sight where he could grab it up quickly, he'd opened his packet of food, gobbled it down, livened it up with a good swig from his flask of cognac, then fallen asleep in the dark.

It had been bitterly cold at night but he'd come prepared for that. Under his windcheater he wore three layers of woollen underclothing. Dawn woke him. He checked his rifle, stared through the crosshairs at the opening he'd created. Calouste's informant had told him one of Tweed's team never stopped searching The Forest.

'When the open entrance is reported to Tweed,' Calouste had predicted, 'Tweed himself will come to see it. That is when you kill him.'

Jacques waited for many hours, frequently shifting his position to fight cramp. The stocky wide-shouldered fat little man appeared first. Jacques did not like the look of him. 'A professional,' he said to himself.

Later, he returned, and with him was a tall slim man who also worried Jacques. Then almost immediately Tweed and 'his tart' were standing there, framed by the arched doorway, a perfect target. Cramp forced Jacques to shift position as he focused the crosshairs on Tweed's chest. He pressed the trigger, stared in disbelief. Tweed and the girl weren't there. He saw Fatty take something from a pocket, guessed it was a grenade, rolled over sideways. A fragment of the grenade sliced a piece away from his windcheater but didn't penetrate the flesh. Jacques fled.

Arriving at Shooter's Lodge by a roundabout route he lowered his motorbike into the deep hole with walls covered with canvas, covered the opening with branches, piled pine needles on top, then let himself into the kitchen.

Calouste was waiting for him in the underground apartment, seated in a tall chair. He wore his coal-black glasses, one clawlike hand under his spade-shaped chin, the other clutching a glass of cognac. The dark lenses Jacques found so disturbing gazed at him.

'Tweed is still alive,' Calouste said.

'How do you know that?' asked Jacques.

'From your expression.'

'I nearly put a bullet through his chest.'

'Nearly,' Calouste sneered.

'One of his team shoved him clear.'

'Because you stupidly made a noise.'

'It's possible.' Jacques was always worried by the way that Calouste could reconstruct what had happened – as though he had been there.

'So I am beginning to think I must kill Tweed myself – with this.'

Calouste was wearing his long black cloak, with its very long sleeves. His right hand slipped up inside his left sleeve, emerged gripping a long slim razor-edged stiletto. He leaned forward, a sadistic smile on his strange face. He placed the point on Jacques's hand resting on the table. Jacques was petrified.

'Do not worry, my dear Jacques,' Calouste said in his soft silky voice. 'Tweed will return to check that new entrance and the trail of blood will lead him to that immense chalk pit.'

'Blood?' Jacques gasped.

Calouste was gently drawing the tip of the stiletto across the back of Jacques's large hand lying flat and tense on the table. The murderous-looking weapon was held so steadily that not one drop of blood surfaced. With a swift movement the stiletto vanished up Calouste's wide sleeve.

'You understand?' Calouste enquired. 'Rabbits.'

'Rabbits?' Jacques repeated in a hollow voice.

'Yes. You go out and shoot three rabbits. Not now, you idiot,' he said gently as Jacques started to get up, thinking Calouste meant him to go out now.

'Tomorrow is the earliest Tweed will reappear.'

'Oh, I see.'

'What does Jacques see at long last?'

'That tomorrow I get up early with my rifle and shoot the three rabbits.'

'But you will need more than your rifle? Yes? No?'

Calouste produced from a pocket a large sheet of transparent material which he unfolded, showing one end was open. He looked at Jacques, who desperately tried to say the right thing.

'After I have shot a rabbit I put it inside that container. Then I squeeze every drop of blood out of the animal. I get rid of the bloodless body where it will not be found.'

'Excellent. Then you take the bag and at intervals along the path leading to the quarry you smear blood for Tweed to track. He will assume the grenade his associate threw did injure you. I shall be waiting for him near the quarry.'

'Where is Mr Warner Chance now?' Tweed asked Snape as they entered the hall.

'In his apartment, sir. He will be working and will not wish to be disturbed.'

'Before I've broken this case all of you will be more than disturbed.' Tweed paused: Snape's complexion had lost colour. 'I have also been told that you are the only person here who has the daily papers.'

'That is so, sir.'

'And that you keep them in that cabin of yours in The Forest. Please bring all those for the past week and leave them for me in the library over there.'

'I will do that as soon as I can.'

'*Now* would be soon enough. Thank you.'

'I find that peculiar,' Paula commented as they climbed the staircase. 'Shuts them off from the outside world.'

'I suspect it was Bella's idea. She probably didn't believe anything in the papers. Also there are no radios or TVs in the place. I think she relied on phoning up her contacts to keep in touch. Here we are.'

Tweed tapped on Warner's apartment door. A strong voice growled from inside, 'Come in, whoever you are, then get out.'

Warner was seated behind a large desk facing the door. It was covered with piles of accounts. The expression on his rocklike face was not welcoming.

'I am very busy, both of you.'

'Murder won't wait,' Tweed said harshly. 'I have questions to put to you.'

'You have five minutes.' Warner folded his arms.

He was wearing a leather windcheater, unbuttoned at his strong, thick neck. He also wore corduroy trousers tucked into knee-length boots. Tweed could see this through the knee-hole in the desk.

'Five minutes?' Tweed repeated. 'We have as long as it takes.'

'You have already interrogated me,' Warner said aggressively. 'So why are you here again?'

'The first time I asked you a few questions they were preliminaries.' Tweed paused. 'More evidence has come to light.'

'What evidence might that be?' Warner asked sarcastically. 'I also object to Miss Grey's presence.'

'Normal procedure. You had a friend, a Mrs Mandy Carlyle.'

'Never heard of a person with that name. You used the past tense.'

'I did.' Warner is very quick-witted, Tweed thought. 'Yes, because she has been murdered. Using the same method that killed your mother. You saw the brutal collars found inside Crystal's wardrobe. A replica of those.'

'Planted on her, of course.'

'Unless it was a case of double bluff,' Paula intervened. 'I did wonder if they were put there so everyone would assume that. If she were involved—'

The communicating door with the rest of the apartment was flung wide open and Crystal stormed in. Her red hair was perfectly coiffeured and she wore a tight red jumper and a skirt of the same colour. This red was nothing compared to the blazing flush of her cheeks. Her expression was livid.

'Are you accusing me of putting those ghastly things there myself?' she screeched close to Paula.

'Been eavesdropping again?' Tweed enquired mildly.

'Damned right I have. Who the hell does Paula think she is? She's been careful not to say that to my face.'

'I can repeat it if you wish,' Paula replied calmly. 'In a murder case all possibilities have to be considered. You, along with others, remain a suspect.'

'What is that room you just emerged from?' Tweed asked to take the pressure off Paula.

'It's the bedroom. Warner's bedroom.' Crystal's expression was hideously suggestive.

Paula froze inside. This conjured up an aspect of life in the manor she had never dreamt of. Tweed sensed her reaction, spoke quickly to change the subject.

'Also,' he said, addressing Warner, 'I understand you drive a green Ford. A witness at Dodd's End,' he continued, making it up, 'saw such a car parked just outside the hamlet. About the time Mrs Carlyle was murdered. And for that evening you – and Crystal – have no alibi. You were supposed to be locked away in this apartment with no one to confirm that.'

'I was at a small party in Gladworth,' Crystal snapped. 'I have told you that.'

'Not a strong alibi, if one at all,' Paula interjected. 'A girl friend or two would support your statement after you'd asked them to cover for you while you joined a boyfriend in his flat.'

For the first time Crystal went silent. She stood staring at a wall. I could have hit the nail on the head, Paula said to herself.

Warner's large hands were gripping the edge of his desk as though about to leap out of his chair. When he spoke, looking at Tweed with eyes which had no feeling in them, 'Who is this Mrs Carlyle?' he thundered.

'She was a lady of flexible morals.' He paused, careful not to mention Marshal. 'There is a direct link with your mother's murder since Mrs Carlyle was murdered using exactly the same kind of weapon. Do you know anyone here who has exceptional mechanical ability when it comes to moulding metal?'

'I don't quite follow you,' Warner said quietly.

'Someone with the ability and nerve to handle barbed wire, to have the equipment – protective gloves, strong cutters – and able to mould it into any shape required like a sculptor.'

'Snape,' Warner said promptly.

'What are you doing?' Paula asked as they made their way down the main staircase.

'I want to accelerate the investigation. The best way to do that is to stir everyone up. Which I'll continue to do.'

'You do take risks. At one moment I thought it was going to end up as a physical struggle between you and Warner, plus a catfight between me and Crystal.'

'That's what I mean by stirring things up.'

'We were on the edge of violence in that apartment,' Paula persisted.

'In other words, I stirred things up there. But when I felt the atmosphere was getting torrid I switched the subject.'

'I did notice that. Here's Lavinia.'

She stood at the foot of the staircase, smiling as always. She pointed to the library.

'I collected the papers from Snape's cabin myself. They're on the round table.'

'I'm most grateful,' Tweed responded. 'Do you read them?'

'Every day. Keeps me in contact with the outside world.' She smiled again. 'It reminds me that there *is* an outside world. I'll leave you in peace now.'

'If you can spare me a few minutes,' Tweed suggested, 'I would appreciate you and I having a quiet talk. In the library, if that would suit you.'

Lavinia laughed. She then curtseyed gracefully. 'My turn to be grilled, my lord. Is it an honour to be left to be the last? From what I've heard everyone else has been subjected to your eagle eye.'

The three of them went into the library. As Lavinia sat at the round table Paula, tactfully, gathered up the pile of newspapers and headed towards the hall.

'I'm sure Tweed would prefer to interview you alone,' she said with a wicked smile. 'I'll take these to my apartment to see what, if anything, has been happening in the world.'

29

Tweed sat down in a chair facing Lavinia. He had never realized how narrow the table was. As he settled himself he felt his knees touch hers. He pulled back his chair.

'Excuse me.'

'You have never done anything which has in the least offended me.'

She was still wearing her white polo-necked jumper. She pulled it down tightly over her figure. Her long slim fingers were clasped lightly together, resting on the table. Her pool-like eyes gazed straight into his. Tweed forced himself to meet the hypnotic stare.

'Actually . . .' He cleared his throat, 'you are not the last to be intensively interviewed. I still have Snape.'

'Our perfect butler,' she replied ironically.

'From your tone I gather you don't trust him.'

'We all have our faults.' Her tone was becoming more husky. Her eyes never left his and he still couldn't read their expression. 'I can rely on him always to be near the hall if someone arrives.'

'What about his lunchtime?'

'He always warns me. He cooks his own meal in his cabin and eats it there.'

'He has no friends?'

'None that I know of.'

'What about everyone else? Surely with the two families someone has a friend?'

'I don't think so.' She lifted a hand and pushed her jet-black hair away from her face. 'Strange, isn't it?' Her smile was enticing.

Damn it! Tweed said to himself. She's playing with me. This was the kind of interview he'd never experienced before. In all other interrogations in his career he had broken through by now. He had a sudden idea that might upset her amazing self-control. She leaned closer to him as though aware he had at long last thought of something.

'Did you know Warner's late wife?'

'Moira was before I came here from Medfords. So I never met her.'

'I have been told that she died in a car crash at Hook's Corner. I have also been told her brakes had been tampered with, which could be why she went over the edge. Warner seems to have adjusted to the tragedy quickly.'

'Now who told you that?' she asked with a smile.

'I'm asking the questions.'

'I have the impression we are having a pleasant conversation.'

Tweed was almost speechless. He forced himself to continue meeting her gaze, to detect a flicker. Nothing. It was as though she was controlling the interrogation. He sat up more erect and his voice was sharper.

'What about Marshal? You must know he plays around with any attractive available lady, then drops her for the next one. A kind of movable harem.'

'I love that last phrase.' She laughed. 'Yes, of course I know about Marshal's roving eye. It's common knowledge. Men are like that. At least some men. By no means all men.'

'Well, at least you're not cynical.'

'I didn't want you to think I was being personal.'

Tweed's mind whirled. She had stopped him in his tracks. He made himself say something.

'There's been a second murder. A Mrs Carlyle at a cramped hamlet called Dodd's End. I'm wondering about Marshal. We have a definite connection – the same method was used that was employed on your grandmother.'

'I know.'

At last he had her. He became aware his clasped hands had been tightly clenched. He relaxed, leaned closer to her.

'So how do you know that?' he snapped.

'It's in the newspaper. Today's. Paula can show you.'

Tweed sighed inwardly. She had trumped his ace. Rapidly he listed the other occupants of the manor. While she waited Lavinia leant back and put her arms behind her neck, then stretched her body. A normal reaction, Tweed told himself quickly. She had remained previously in exactly her original position. It was a natural act of exercise. She then leant across the table, her hands lightly interlaced.

'I get the impression there is intense rivalry, verging on physical violence at times. What is their relationship? Crystal and Leo,' he said.

'Brother and sister.' She smiled to show she wasn't making fun of him. 'The trouble is Crystal is the younger, twenty-eight. She always thinks Leo gets more attention from her father. She doesn't like it.'

'Why not?'

'Because . . .' She smiled again. 'She expects plenty of attention from men.'

'At times Crystal seems almost savage.'

'That's simply her vitality.'

'Mrs Grandy,' he said suddenly. 'I admit I've overlooked her. Presumably Bella had her vetted before she employed her. Where does she come from?'

'No one knows. She appeared in Gladworth five years ago. She's a marvellous cook, always punctual, acts also as the housekeeper. At 5 a.m. a small group of girls come in from Gladworth. They clean the whole house, leave by 6.30 a.m., which is probably why you've never seen them. We are well organized here.'

'One last question, Lavinia.' Tweed paused to see her reaction.

He waited. She waited. Her blue eyes seemed to swallow him up. He was developing a tingling sensation. Thank God we're in a public room, he thought.

'One last question,' he repeated. 'You know these families and everyone else in this vast mansion better than I ever will.' He paused. 'So who do you think is the most likely suspect responsible for the murders?'

As soon as he'd asked the question he regretted doing so. It was inappropriate, to say the least. She was a suspect as were all the others in the place. Why had he done it? Some invisible bond seemed to have brought them together.

'I've thought and thought about that,' she said slowly. 'But thinking as hard as I can I don't find myself pinpointing one person. Sorry.' She stood up, smoothed down her skirt. 'And now I think I'd better ask Paula to come down to see you with the newspapers.'

He stood up to thank her. She was round the table and next to him in a flash. They were about the same height.

'Thank you for your patience and consideration,' she said. She kissed him briefly, full on the mouth. 'I do like you,' she said and strode on her long legs to the door.

30

Tweed felt exhausted. He walked over to the drinks cabinet, took out a glass and the cognac bottle. He poured himself a modest drink. He had not slept well. The faces of the different inhabitants of the manor had kept appearing. Which one?

The door opened quietly and Paula came in, the sheaf of newspapers tucked under her arm. She paused as Tweed turned, sipped at his drink. She chuckled.

'She roadblocked you, didn't she?'

'The most unsatisfactory interrogation I've ever conducted. Yes, she roadblocked me every time,' he admitted as he sat at the table.

'I thought she would,' Paula observed, sitting opposite him. 'She's the cleverest person living here. Shall I wait before I show you the papers?'

'No. My head has cleared. Show me them now.'

'Typically, Lavinia arranged the papers in date order, so the most recent comes last . . .'

Tweed took the pile of newspapers from Paula and began to skim through the front pages of each paper. The headlines were huge.

RICHEST BANKER IN WORLD HORRIFICALLY MURDERED

MAIN CHANCE'S BELLA MAIN: THROAT BRUTALLY SLASHED

LADY OF NIGHT MURDERED BY SAME METHOD AS BELLA MAIN

'Oh Lord,' Tweed muttered, 'and now we have Drew Franklin after us. How the devil did he find out so quickly about Mrs Carlyle? In three days he's blown the lid off the case. We can expect trouble from London.'

The phone rang. Tweed glanced at Paula, picked it up. It was Lavinia, calm as ever despite the news she had to impart.

'Commander Buchanan is on the line. He does sound a bit worked up. I'll put you through then get off the line.'

'Yes?' said Tweed.

'What the devil's going on down there?' Buchanan shouted. 'Have you see the papers, the headlines? All hell is breaking loose up here. I've had a cabinet minister on the phone – he is probably a discreet depositor in the Main Chance. He urged me to take you off the case, to hand it over to Chief Inspector Hammer. I refused his request, explained you now knew more about the case than anyone. But have you a suspect? Can you break the case in the next twenty-four hours? The City are getting nervous. Somehow they have picked up a rumour that a fabulously rich foreigner is going to bid a fortune for the bank. That would put whoever it is in a position to use Main Chance to buy up some of the big British banks. This case is now becoming international. Tweed, are you still there?'

'Yes,' Tweed replied calmly. 'Have you got the spleen out of your system? I've sent my Director, Howard, reports early in the mornings. You know he never gets to bed early. And he's good at soothing down politicians, so suggest he has a chat with this anonymous cabinet minister. I have no more to say. Thank you for the call.'

'There's a lot of detail in the text,' Paula told Tweed. 'Bob Newman, a top reporter, is a friend of Franklin's. Maybe he could get Drew to go easy.'

'Not possible,' said Newman who had entered, had heard her suggestion. 'Drew is a friend of mine but basically he's a reporter. He won't soft-pedal a big story like this for anyone. He's a real professional.'

'We're in a real mess then,' Paula commented.

'No, we're not,' Tweed said decisively. 'The problem is still the same. Clearly Drew has an informant here, so who is it? Someone Drew offered a tempting sum of money to tell him when given a hint of the scope of the story.'

'So what do we do?'

'Nothing about the leak. For the moment. But I'm going to continue stirring everybody here up. Something is going to break . . .'

He stopped talking as Harry hurried into the library and began speaking quietly close to Tweed.

'Something's happening. You know that arched entrance we found had been unblocked? Well, outside now there's a trail of dried blood leading along the path to that big chalk pit.'

'Alert the whole team.'

'I have done. They're all on their way there.'

'So are we.'

Marler, holding his Armalite, and Newman were on the manor side of the arched gate when Tweed arrived with Paula. Harry pushed past them, peered out, Walther in his hand. He nodded. All clear.

'The path leads direct to the big chalk pit. Abandoned long ago would be my guess.'

'We'll follow it,' Tweed ordered.

'Could be another trap,' Harry warned.

'Good. Time we met the enemy face to face.'

Harry led the way, crouched over the trail, followed closely by Tweed and the rest of the team. The weather had changed drastically. The sun was gone. In its place a still white mist enshrouded The Forest. Trees were vague silhouettes. Tweed paused, bent down, ran his finger lightly over one of the occasional large dried splashes of blood. He sniffed it, cleaned his finger quickly with his handkerchief.

'Funny sort of blood,' he told Paula and Marler who had now caught up with him. 'Not like human blood.'

Then he began running to catch up with Harry. Behind him Paula marvelled at the speed and agility Tweed was moving at. Not long ago they had attended a refresher course at the secret training mansion hidden away in Surrey – climbing ropes, crawling through large drainpipes and all the rest. They always called the chief trainer Sarge but the normal trainer had been on holiday. In his place was another tough Sarge who liked martial arts. Tweed disliked martial arts, regarding them as a waste of time. As the new Sarge was dancing about prior to attack Tweed had leapt straight at him fist clenched, hitting him a heavy blow on the jaw. The trainer collapsed, was taken to hospital with a broken jaw. End of course.

Paula recalled this as she saw Tweed catching up with Harry who was now moving fast. She didn't like the atmosphere as they continued along the snaking path. The mist made it difficult to see what was a tree or a man.

They had covered a long distance when Harry stopped, held up a hand.

'We're very close to the huge chalk pit. The Forest stops suddenly and there's a clear ground, an open slope to the edge of the pit.'

'It isn't just huge,' Marler drawled. 'I've seen it. More like an amphitheatre. There's a small hilltop over to the right. The perfect lookout point. I suggest we get up there first.'

Harry led the way up to the hilltop followed by the others. Tweed ignored the advice. He paused to glance round. Over to his left a remote stand of giant firs extended towards the edge, creating large black shadows. One especially dark shadow he assumed was a large boulder. Walther in his right hand, he began to descend the slope alone.

An amphitheatre? Marler had been right. The pit was vast and deep. On the far side were the remnants of a rusty crane. It had, years ago, obviously been used to haul up chalk and drop it into waiting trucks.

There was a sinister silence over the whole abandoned area. Tweed continued walking down the slope. He waited to check the interior of the pit. There could be men with rifles waiting down there. His boots crunched on chalk as he reached the edge, peered over. Lord, it was over a hundred feet down. At the base to his right and left were immense piles of powdered chalk. He heard something to his right.

On the hilltop Marler had restrained Paula from calling out. He had simply placed a hand over her mouth.

'Do not distract him,' he warned.

'But Harry has just said the cliff is unstable,' she

whispered furiously from behind the hand.

At the edge, Tweed stared at the black shape he'd assumed was a boulder. Something large – a black cloak – was thrown to one side and a man with a face of crinkled skin was on him, a large wide-bladed knife in one hand, raised to strike. It happened very quickly. Calouste himself.

Tweed dropped his Walther. Calouste was too close to use it. His right hand whipped up, grasped his opponent's knife hand, slid instantly higher to the forearm, pressing a certain nerve. They were struggling on the edge of eternity, swaying back and forth. The brutal knife was still in the hand of the killer. Tweed was surprised at the killer's strength.

His left hand darted upward, two stiffened fingers extended, aimed at his opponent's eyes. His right hand tightened its grip on the nerve. His opponent grunted with pain and his fingers clasping the knife loosened their grip. He jerked his head back away from Tweed's pointed fingers.

Tweed jabbed them savagely forward, still aimed at the eyes. Both men were arched backwards over the precipitous drop. Tweed forced himself back. His opponent came with him. Tweed's right hand dug deeper into the nerve. The knife fell from the hand, slithered down into the chalk pit. Loss of his weapon seemed to take the strength out of the killer.

On the hilltop Paula suddenly started running down

the slope in a desperate effort to save Tweed. No one had been able to shoot. The bodies of the two men struggling were too close together.

Marler took off, his long legs taking giant strides. Reaching Paula, he fell on her, pinning her to the ground. She yelled at Marler, '*Bastard!*'

'You'll distract Tweed if he has to worry about saving you,' Marler told her.

Tweed raised one leg, scraped his boot down the killer's shin. A grunt of pain. Tweed's boot continued down the shin. He put all his force into crushing the killer's foot. A scream of agonizing pain. The killer's arms gripping Tweed's body released him. At that moment Tweed's left hand clawed at the killer's face, felt softness. The leather mask he had been wearing came away in Tweed's hand, exposing the face of a younger man.

The killer's back was now facing the edge. Tweed used both hands to shove hard against his chest. The killer's body sailed over the brink, legs twirling as he sank down and down. Tweed watched as the body reached the bottom, falling on a rock. The body, legs splayed, lay very still. He heard Harry shouting, both hands cupped round his mouth.

'Get well back *now*! The cliff's unstable!'

Tweed turned round, took a mighty leap, his legs trembling as he landed on hard rock. Behind him he heard a rumbling sound. He glanced back. At least a foot of where he had been standing had disappeared. There was a deep thud from the base as tons of cliffs reached the bottom, engulfing the body of the killer forever.

Marler had released Paula. He was trying to help her up, but she brushed aside his helping hands. Instead she used her own to wipe remnants of chalk off her clothes.

'Who the devil was that?' Tweed asked, still holding the pliable mask in his hands. 'I thought it was Professor Heathstone we met at Pike's Peak Hotel.'

'Look at it,' said Harry.

A white cloud of powdered chalk was rising above the brink, the result of the enormous fall of the chalk cliff. Tweed nodded, his manner fresh and brisk.

'Our next job is to kill the real Calouste. I'm sure he's still hidden away at Shooter's Lodge, awaiting the good news that I'm dead.'

31

Tweed was walking up the main drive to the manor with Paula and Marler. It had been his decision to return by this route. He'd wanted to conceal from the inhabitants the fact that he had left by the arched gate and visited the chalk pit.

'I've changed my mind,' he told them as they mounted the steps. 'We'll let Calouste stew a few hours. Harry is going to Shooter's Lodge to keep an eye on developments.'

He had just spoken when they heard Harry, who had run ahead of them start up his motorcycle behind the manor. He appeared on his machine, sped down the drive. Glancing back, Tweed saw the gates swinging open again. It did not surprise him when Lavinia opened the door. Her reactions were impressive. She had opened the gates for him before he'd used the speakerphone. The gates had closed automatically once they were inside. Now she'd immediately reopened them to let Harry out.

'Harry's off to Gladworth to fetch some things,' he told her.

'Welcome back,' she greeted him with a smile. 'And the sun has come out again. That's for your benefit.'

'You got here to open the gates twice,' he remarked. 'Where is Snape?'

'The idiot saw you coming, said he'd got something cooking on his stove and rushed off to the cabin.'

'Lavinia, excuse me, I've got to attend to something.'

Tweed tore off out of the hall, down a corridor, followed by a puzzled Paula and Marler. He was rushing through the kitchen when Mrs Grandy glowered at them.

'If you want a late lunch you'll have to ask me nicely.'

'Yes, please,' Tweed replied over his shoulder. 'Ravenous.'

He dived through the open back door and hurtled along the path leading to the cabin. Both Paula and Marler had trouble keeping up with him. He slowed his pace, held up a hand to warn his companions. He crept up to the cabin door.

Paula peered over his shoulder. Snape was standing by the table with his back to them. He had a mobile phone pressed to his ear. They could hear every word.

'Capricorn reporting. Tweed is alive.

'Yes, you heard me correctly. I've just seen him . . .

'I promise you I have, sir.

'No, no, sir. It was only a few minutes ago. I thought you said he'd be dead this morning . . .

'No, sir, I can't help that. No, he wasn't wounded. He was walking briskly. Even hurrying. Hello? Hello? Are you still there? Damn him, he always does that.'

Snape slipped his mobile into a side pocket, turned round. His expression of surprise and horror when he saw Tweed was quite a picture.

'Don't worry. We heard every word. How is Calouste?'

'Who? . . . Who did you say?' Snape blustered.

'Handcuff him, Marler,' Tweed snapped. He advanced on Snape as Marler forced the butler's hands behind his back and cuffed his wrists tightly. 'You are under arrest,' Tweed said, his voice grim, 'for obstructing the course of justice in a major murder investigation. Anything you say may be taken—'

'I took down every word he said,' Paula reported, waving her notebook.

'Well,' sneered the butler, 'your lady friend who also—'

Tweed slapped his face hard before he could utter the obscenity. He stared at Snape with detestation.

'We have three witnesses to your treachery. I doubt whether any barrister will be keen to defend you. I predict the judge will send you down for ten years without the option of parole.' He turned away. 'Paula, could you search his cabin for any more evidence while we're all still here.'

Marler had been searching Snape. Inside one pocket he found a bunch of keys, handed them to Paula. She examined them carefully. She inserted one of the cheap keys into the lock of the gun cupboard. It opened the door.

'Not much security for all those weapons,' she observed.

'And that shotgun,' Marler added, 'is a very ugly brute.'

Paula moved swiftly round the room, ignoring the flimsy locks. During her training at Medfords she had learned a lot about locks. She stood, staring round the room, then put on latex gloves and felt underneath the table. 'Ah,' she said to herself, bending down. There was a secret drawer out of sight, about six inches beyond the table edge. She inserted the Banham key, opened the drawer, brought out a long, wide fat envelope.

Laying it on the table top, she extracted a large bundle of high-denomination Swiss banknotes. She looked at Snape, who couldn't meet her gaze.

'The wages of treachery,' Tweed remarked. 'He's going behind bars for a very long time. Paula, when we get back to the manor please call Buchanan, tell him what we have found, ask him to send a two-man police car down quickly to pick up Snape. Marler, I suggest you take him back to the kitchen, tell Mrs Grandy he's a spy and is not to be given anything to eat. As much water as he needs.'

*

'Next,' Tweed told Paula as they walked back to the manor, 'I want to interrogate Warner Chance intensively. He was short on answers the last time I interviewed him . . .'

While Paula went into the downstairs library to make her call to Buchanan, Tweed ran up the stairs, heading for the smaller library. At the top of the second flight he met Lavinia.

'Would you mind giving me a hand?' he suggested.

'At any time, day – or night,' she replied with a Mona Lisa smile.

'This box of tricks Bella used to summon people,' Tweed began as they stood by the murdered woman's desk. 'It's far more sophisticated than I'd realized. I came up on my own and fiddled with it. There's a system which records all calls she made and the response of the person she was calling inside the manor. In addition it records the exact time of the conversation.' He pressed a small lever.

Bella's request to Marshal to come and see her at 10 p.m. came over.

He glanced at Lavinia, who had placed a hand against her throat.

'I don't often show emotion,' she apologized.

'Sorry, my fault, I should have warned you . . .'

He stopped talking as they heard Marshal's agreement to be there by 10 p.m. Tweed pointed to a clock sunk into the desk which showed the timing of both people. 8 p.m. for Marshal answering.

'Which shows what happened took place between 8 p.m. and 10 p.m. Tweed remarked. 'Now I'll want to speak to Warner Chance. So which of the numbered buttons is he?'

'Number two.'

'Thank you.'

'And now I'll give you privacy to talk to him,' Lavinia said and left, carefully closing the door.

Tweed hauled two armchairs close together so they faced each other. He was curious to see which door Warner would use to enter the study as he settled in one of them. The secret door slid back and Warner entered, walking behind Bella's chair. He wore a velvet jacket and velvet trousers, looking very smart but not best pleased. He sat in the chair facing Tweed, very erect.

'What is it now?' he growled. 'And I hear Snape has been arrested. You've caught your murderer?'

'Not yet, but I'm getting close. Snape is just a greedy sneak.'

'I always thought that about the fellow.'

'Mrs Bella Main was murdered between 8 p.m. and 10 p.m. We know that definitely now. You say you were in your apartment then. Surely someone must have come to say good night, or you had a phone call.'

'Do you mind if I light a cigar? Thank you.'

He produced a morocco-bound case, took out a

cigar, a pair of clippers. He took his time slicing off the end of the cigar, then more time lighting it with a match. Time for him to decide what to say, Tweed thought, but the blank grey eyes in the large head never left Tweed's.

'No one came to see me. I received no phone calls. So no alibi. But I gather all the main members of both families also have no alibis.'

A defensive note was creeping into Warner's voice, Tweed noted from his fresh remarks.

'When Bella died she left a will appointing you and your brother as co-directors of a fabulously rich bank. Should something fatal happen to Marshal the whole business would fall into your lap.'

'Now listen to me, Tweed.' Another whiff of brandy floated into Tweed's nostrils. He had been drinking and this was increasing the ferocity in his voice. 'You may make a major assumption there – that another will would hand over everything to me. There is Lavinia, an enormously capable lady whom Bella admired – and who is in charge of the assets in her position as Chief Accountant.'

Now a new manoeuvre, Tweed thought – the casting of suspicion on someone else.

'You do have a most desirable motive,' Tweed insisted.

Warner was puffing furiously on his cigar. He stood up. 'I challenge you to charge me with murder on the basis of no evidence whatsoever. I've had enough of you. Any more of this and I shall complain to Commander Buchanan that you are harassing me. Good night to you, sir.'

Warner stormed out, this time using the main door into the library. Typical of Warner, Tweed thought, to use the device of threatening him to escape the interrogation. Had he been feeling the heat?

Walking into the library he met Harry rushing in. His face was damp. He was also breathless and it took him a minute to burst out with the news.

'He's gone!'

'Take it easy, Harry. Who has gone?'

'That swine, Calouste. I've really messed up this one.'

'I doubt that, Harry. Would you like a beer? Plenty in the drinks cupboard.'

'No thanks. I arrived at Shooter's Lodge, took me a while to hide my motorbike in some brambles. Then I walked a bit further, found a good hiding place from where I could see the lodge. No sign of life at all. No lights on in the place. Then, after a little while, it happened.'

'What did, Harry?'

'A bloody great black car with tinted windows comes from the back somewhere. Roars straight out into the road and drives off towards London. Uniformed chauffeur driving, with one passenger in the back. Couldn't see who it was.'

Calouste has eluded me again, Tweed said to himself. This is the result of Snape's phone call to him. He rested a hand on Harry's shoulder as he sat hunched in a chair.

'Come and join us for dinner. Tomorrow is another day.'

When he said that Tweed had no inkling that the following morning everything was going to explode.

32

Tweed was settling down to his meal in the breakfast room – as opposed to the dining room – when the mobile buzzed. He listened to Monica calling him from Park Crescent.

'I have Philip Cardon on the line. Very urgent.'

'Tell him to give me thirty seconds while I go somewhere quiet.'

He hurried to the empty dining room. Closing the door he sat in a chair.

'Philip, Tweed here . . .'

'A priority-one crisis – if you wish to eliminate Calouste Doubenkian. I've booked all of you on the last Eurostar this evening to Brussels. He's at his HQ a long way outside the city.'

'We'll come,' Tweed decided immediately.

'I need to give you special instructions . . .'

Tweed noted down what Philip said, then he was off the line. Philip had abruptly broken the call. He made a brief call to Park Crescent, then walked back quietly to finish his breakfast with Paula and Newman. On a sheet from his notepad he had scribbled brief instructions. He handed them to Marler, who read the notes, then left the table immediately.

'Trouble?' Paula whispered as Mrs Grandy brought in more plates of eggs and bacon.

'Mrs Grandy,' Tweed said with a smile, 'could you help me by serving those breakfasts in the dining room?'

'If you say so,' she grumbled. 'Means laying a table with a cloth and the cutlery.'

'Of a sort,' he whispered to Paula, answering her earlier question. 'I'll explain when the whole team is assembled. In the meantime I suggest we enjoy a leisurely breakfast.'

After breakfast he strolled with Paula into the dining room. Marler had moved fast. Seated at the dining table, eating the last of their meal were, besides Marler, Newman and Harry.

Tweed's first move was to close the heavy oak soundproof door and perch a large tilted chair against it. Then he sat at the head of the table with Paula on his right.

'First,' he began, 'I'll tell you what Philip said when he opened the conversation, then his specific instructions . . .'

When he had finished, Harry asked, 'What about Pete Nield now holding the fort at Park Crescent?'

'I've already informed him and he'll be joining us.'

'I like that,' Harry replied. 'He watches my back and I watch his.'

'I'm putting Chief Inspector Hammer in charge while I'm not here. I've also warned Buchanan to forbid him from arresting Crystal – on the basis there's not enough evidence. Yet.'

'Is Snape confessing now?' Paula wondered.

'Buchanan interrogated him and couldn't get a word out of him. So he's parked in a cell.'

'Well, we've got rid of the spy who was informing Calouste,' Paula mused.

'One of the spies,' Tweed corrected her. 'I'm convinced there is another one hidden away in this manor. The main spy.'

'Any idea who that is?'

'I haven't a clue,' Tweed told her. 'Incidentally, I'll be telling Marshal, Warner and Lavinia that we have a lead in London and have to search different localities. Also that we shan't be back tonight. One more thing, Philip warned it's very cold in Belgium now. So wrap up well.'

They were on the verge of leaving, gathered in the hall, when Leo appeared. He plucked at Tweed's sleeve. 'Could we talk together, just the two of us? I've stumbled on something very important.'

'Tell me when we get back. I'm behind schedule.'

'I wonder what he was on about?' Paula asked as they walked down the steps.

'Another of his fantasies, I imagine.'

'Well, nothing serious can happen here while we're away.'

It was a remark she was later bitterly to regret making.

33

'The last Eurostar tonight leaves at 7.15 p.m.,' Tweed reminded his fully assembled team at his office at Park Crescent. 'So you all arrive in separate taxis at different times. Monica has distributed the return tickets she had brought over by courier. And maybe you should get some sleep. When we get over there I suspect it will turn into a dogfight.'

'Can't I take my tool-kit bag?' pleaded Harry.

'*No!*' Tweed was at his most emphatic. 'I've already explained Philip's warning. Calouste has under his control a certain highly corrupt section of the Belgian police run by an Inspector Balouster Benlier. We shoot a policeman, they catch us, and we could be in a Belgian jail for six months. Yes, sleep would be a good idea. You need to be on maximum alert for the whole trip.'

'You will be taking those deadly hands, old chap,' Pete Nield teased his partner.

'No nap for me,' Paula remarked. 'I can last out for thirty-six hours.'

Everyone except Paula left the office to go home. Pete Nield came back immediately.

'I've checked the reports from overseas agents, sent replies after showing them to Howard, who approved. The tricky one was our main in Marseilles, who said he'd been spotted.'

'I see you ordered him to board a cruise liner as a waiter, then leave the ship at Gibraltar,' said Tweed.

'Which he has done. We can't afford to lose Roger. And we must guard his safety. He is one of our best agents.'

'I congratulate you on your decisiveness.'

'Maybe we could go up and see Howard with the reports?' Nield suggested.

'We'll do that now.' He checked his watch. 'Time is flying. We will get something to eat on Eurostar. This expedition is going to be interesting.'

'Interesting?' Paula queried sceptically.

'Calouste has been a nuisance. He's diverted time I needed to investigate two murders.'

'A nuisance?' She sounded indignant. 'He's tried to kill you four times.'

'That's what I meant when I said nuisance.' Tweed stood up. 'I suggest, Paula, you go home and collect some warm clothing. When Philip says "cold" he probably means Siberian. On the way back I suggest you call in at my Bexford Street place and collect some things for me.'

'What I need is already at Bexford Street, so it will mean one round trip. In case you hadn't noticed, my desk is piled up with reports I must deal with before we leave.'

'Leave it to you. Pete, I see you have an armful of reports. Time we went up to Howard and reassured him. And Monica is going to the deli to bring back hot food for the three of us later. Napoleon said an army marches on its stomach, a most undignified way of going to war, I'd have thought.'

It was dark and 7 p.m. exactly when the taxi transporting Tweed and Paula pulled up at the foot of the steps at Waterloo.

'You go first on your own,' he whispered to Paula as they alighted.

She ran up the steps which led across the concourse to the Eurostar. Tweed deliberately took several minutes sorting out change to pay the driver and give him a generous tip.

He knew the rest of his team would have arrived earlier, each by himself and at intervals. More of Philip's exact instructions. They knew the coach to board since the number was on the tickets.

Tweed was wearing his fur-lined overcoat with an astrakhan collar, which Paula had brought him from

Bexford Street. Mounting the steps, he descended the escalator and the gleaming train extended down the platform. Passing through security, Tweed boarded the correct coach. Second class, it was occupied only by his scattered team.

Paula was seated in the rear aisle seat. Opposite her sat Newman, studying a book on radio technology. Marler was two seats ahead. Nield was halfway down the coach while Harry sat at the front, watching the door.

'No trouble with security?' Paula asked as Tweed settled in the window seat. 'What's in that bulging briefcase?'

'I simply said "business" and opened the briefcase. It's stuffed with files of useless papers Monica typed for me, plus pyjamas, shaving kit, a fresh suit. The things a businessman would carry for a trip abroad. How did you get on?'

'I told the miserable old officer I was going to meet my French boyfriend. Wedding ring on his finger. Probably nagged to death by his wife. Hence his scowling at me.'

The train was gliding out of the station when Newman got up, gave them a little salute as though being polite to strange passengers.

'Tweed, I'm sorry I forgot to tell you something. When I was scouting Shooter's Lodge early on I told you about the sophisticated wireless system perched by a chimney. I got up there and clipped two key wires, which would ruin his system.'

'Not to worry,' Tweed said with a smile as Newman began heading for the loo to cover his action.

'Now he tells me,' Tweed whispered to Paula. 'That's why we're here. I'd wondered about his communications. He'd need them to issue instructions to all the banks he owns on the Continent. He's hustled back to his HQ to sort out his communications system.'

'A lot was happening then,' Paula said and put up a hand as she yawned. She closed her eyes and rested her head on his shoulder. In no time she was fast asleep. The train stopped briefly at Ashford and then raced on across Kent. There was a moon up and Tweed gazed at the orchards, their stark silhouettes beginning to show signs of life. He'd travelled a lot but he loved England best.

Another treat was moving through the tunnel. He hated the sea. On any boat the damn thing was always wobbling and he suffered from sea-sickness, until Paula forced him to take a Dramamine. Then he'd be on deck, watching the rolling waves. He lost interest as the train emerged and they entered France.

The train was approaching Brussels Midi station when Paula woke. She went to the loo to splash water over her face, returned fully alert as she stretched arms and legs.

'Don't forget,' Tweed reminded her, 'Philip will be

wearing a red peaked cap with an artificial carnation in his buttonhole. In other words, this is where the trouble starts. We are now in no-man's-land.'

As they alighted Philip appeared, his manner brisk and quick-moving.

'That's the exit. Outside get in the first of three Land Rovers. Get moving . . .'

Then he was gone. Tweed was relieved. The approach to Brussels was no better than to any other terminus. They had been hemmed in by endless tall cheap apartment blocks. It was bitterly cold and within minutes they were inside their Land Rover, which had a blue tail-light. Inside the second Land Rover, Newman sat behind the wheel with Marler. Harry was behind the wheel of the third vehicle with Pete beside him. They were ready to go.

Paula stared out at the galaxy of lights which were almost blinding. Restaurants were lit up and inside people were eating dinner, laughing, raising their glasses. Nightclubs with glaring lights. Outside them were huge pictures of semi-clad young girls. Several had queues as garishly dressed couples waited for tables. The whole city seemed like a blaze of neon.

'We're on the famous Boulevard de Waterloo,' Philip explained as he kept the Land Rover moving. 'I have booked a room, or I should say rooms, for all of you at this monster we are coming to.'

'We are not staying there,' Tweed said firmly.

'I have also booked a large dinner table for all of you at the best restaurant in town, in Grand Place.'

'We will not be dining there,' Tweed told him. 'In any case you are now driving east and that restaurant you mentioned is behind us.'

'Precisely. On both points,' Philip agreed. 'Inspector Benlier, who runs the most corrupt police unit in Belgium, has contacts everywhere. We are heading straight for the main HQ of Calouste which is also his communications centre. What I said earlier about the hotel and the dinner is throwing dust in Benlier's eyes!'

'Smart of you,' Paula commented.

She glanced at Philip, the best agent Tweed had in Europe. In his late thirties, he had a strong, clean-shaven face with trim brown hair and looked younger than his age. She had always liked him. He took one hand briefly off the wheel to squeeze her arm.

'There is nothing to worry about.'

'I'm not in the least bit worried,' she fibbed.

He took two small leather bags out of his pocket, gave one to her. She delved inside and brought out a small spike held firmly upright by a heavy curved rubber base. There were plenty more inside the bag.

'What is this?' she asked.

'Engineer pal of mine in Rotterdam made them for me.' He smiled. He was always smiling, she remembered. 'Clever little jigger. If a police car appears behind us you throw a few out of your window. However they land, because of the curved rubber base they always immediately stand upright with the steel spike vertical. Don't do tyres any good. I've given Marler his own bagful.'

The road was sloping now and they raced through an underpass. Emerging from the other side they met a glare of lighting from oncoming traffic from the opposite direction. Paula lowered the visor. Philip had put on tinted glasses.

'This is a wide road,' she remarked. 'Like an autobahn or a motorway.'

'Main drag in and out of the city.'

'I don't like Brussels,' she mused. 'It's boring.'

'It is,' Philip agreed. 'I much prefer Ghent and the Flemish area to the north-west. The Flems are much more friendly and welcoming. That area should be part of Holland. Down here it's French-speaking. Need I say more?'

There was silence for a while. They had left the city behind. On both sides the moon shone down on more open country. Less traffic was coming towards them heading for Brussels. Paula sighed with relief.

'Well, it's quieter now. I'm glad—'

She never finished her sentence. The increasing wail of a police siren shrieked through the night behind them. Then another. And another. Their roof lights were flashing.

'Smart Inspector Benlier has caught on to my diversions, so get ready with the spikes,' Philip warned.

'Three police cars and they're all passing Harry and Bob Newman,' Paula warned after glancing at the rear-view mirror. 'We're their target.'

'Open your window,' he said, 'they're coming up off-side.'

She did so and then stared at a uniformed policeman, also with his window down in the police car alongside. He was grinning, had something in his hand, was about to hurl it. She closed the window quickly. A second later the missile hit her window and a cloud of white vapour floated outside.

'Tear gas,' said Philip.

'Nice people,' Paula snapped.

He handed her a small instrument like a miniature fire extinguisher. It had a long slim nozzle. Philip was grinning as he rammed his foot down, accelerating well beyond the first police car.

'See that button on that thing? It's filled with oil, you place the body on the window edge, press the button and a jet sprays the road. You do that when I say "now" for the second time. When I first say "now" you hurl a load of spikes out. See that large black limo coming from the other way? It's wobbling all over the place. Driver's drunk. This is where we create chaos,' he said gleefully.

'Paula, give me that spray gun now,' Tweed called out

from the back. 'You have too much to time properly.'

'Good idea,' agreed Philip. 'Just look at that limo.'

It was swerving from left to right, then back again after crossing lanes. For some reason the driver had his interior light on. She caught a vague glimpse of a fat man togged up in evening dress.

'*Now!*' yelled Philip.

The lead police car had almost caught up with them, again approaching on the offside, its siren a hellish scream. Paula had her window down, threw out two handfuls of spiked caps.

'*Now!*' Philip yelled for the second time.

Tweed already had his window down. The spray gun was perched on the window's edge. An amazing amount of oil jetted out on to the road, creating a black lake in the moonlight.

There were a couple of loud bangs as the spikes destroyed two tyres on the lead police car. It swung round and smashed into the rear section of the limo, swivelling it round. The second police car skidded on the oil, rammed into the side of the first police car. The third police car tried to swerve too late, ploughed into the side of the second police car. The fat driver of the limo staggered out, unhurt, and shook his fist, his mouth moving.

'There you are. Chaos,' said Philip.

Leaning over to look through the rear-view mirror, Paula saw a mass of twisted metal which reminded her of a car-crusher yard. Skilfully, Newman swung in a wide arc, followed by Harry, avoiding the wreckage completely.

'Not bad timing,' Philip, 'it all depended on assessing the position of that limo.'

'Well, that's behind us,' said Paula. She had closed the window quickly. Arctic air had entered their Land Rover. Philip had the heating turned full up and soon she was comfortable again.

'We've beaten Inspector Benlier,' she remarked with relief.

'Oh, that was just the opening shots,' Philip replied.

'What do you mean?' asked Tweed.

'I call that the prelude. Ahead we go up into the Ardennes to Calouste's HQ at the Château les Rochers to destroy him. Don't expect a Christmas party.'

34

The Ardennes.

'I'm turning off the main road in a minute, heading across the Ardennes,' Philip said. 'It's some of the bleakest land I've seen in Europe. Remote. Tourists never come here.'

Paula lowered her compact powerful binoculars. She had aimed them ahead while they were still on the main road.

'I think you ought to know I saw a lot of headlights coming this way from the direction of Liège.'

'That's good news,' Philip said ironically as he turned to the right off the main road. 'Benlier has a section of his corrupt unit temporarily stationed in Liège.'

'Where does this lead us to?' Tweed asked.

'It's the direct route to Namur and Marche, but I'll bypass both towns by using country roads. It may be a rough ride.'

'Rough ride?' Paula repeated. 'So what was that we've just experienced?'

'Calouste's HQ is high up in the Ardennes. Château les Rochers, an ancient castle perched on the border of Belgium and the toy state of Luxembourg. So he can say he's resident in either country, whichever suits him at any particular time.'

'This country we're driving through is like a flat desert,' Paula commented. 'It's like a moonscape, and rocky.'

'I turned off the main route across country without your realizing it. We might just elude those police cars.'

Moonscape? As he gazed out, Tweed thought Paula's description was perfect. The Land Rover had started to wobble from side to side. The flat so-called plain was desolate. Its surface was littered with small rocks, shale and pebbles.

'This whole area is unstable,' Philip remarked casually. Paula glanced once at him and realized he was looking grim. He was wondering how to get them out of this. She had never before seen him looking so serious. Her reaction steeled her nerve. She twisted round in her seat, pressed her binoculars to her eyes, focused on the three police cars. She could hear a distant whine. The fools still had their sirens shrieking out here in this totally deserted region. And their blue lights were still flashing. Idiots. Paula focused on the lead car. A policeman was standing, head and shoulders poked through the open roof.

'A slim man,' she said, 'in full uniform with gold braid and wide shoulders. Mouth open as though he's shouting.'

'That will be Benlier himself,' Philip told her, 'shouting *en advance*.'

'Must think he's Napoleon at Austerlitz,' Tweed commented drily.

Quite suddenly the gradient changed. They were climbing a steep slope, up and up. Paula focused her binoculars on their destination.

'There's a ridge above us,' she reported. 'Perched on its edge a line of big boulders, one of them enormous.'

'They weren't there when I came here on a recce three days ago. There's been a landslide . . .'

'Head for that gap between them,' Paula urged. 'Just to the left of that huge chap. Your Land Rover will pass through easily.'

'You think so?' Philip queried.

'Do as she suggested,' Tweed ordered. 'She has some plan and so often she's right.'

'Will do,' Philip agreed with a grin.

'Newman and Harry are close behind us,' Paula reported as she glanced back.

'So are the police cars,' Philip remarked.

'This is better,' Paula said as she lowered her window a few inches and breathed in ice-cold air.

Her brain was now working at full power.

'Better than what?' Tweed chaffed her.

'Being indoors. The manor was giving me the creeps. Wasn't much better in The Forest. Claustrophobic atmosphere.'

'Which may have been an element,' Tweed observed, 'in the murders.'

'Don't miss the gap,' Paula shouted at Philip, who was just turning his wheel, heading for the opening, followed by Newman's and Harry's vehicles.

'That's better,' Paula added. 'You'll just scrape through.'

'I'll just glide through,' he said with another grin. 'And I think I've spotted your strategy . . .'

'Better late than never.'

The Land Rover had at least a foot's spare space as he passed through behind the rampart line of boulders. Paula stared at the treacherous ground scattered with a slither of shale.

'Park the vehicle pointing up the hill,' she suggested. 'We may have to leave quickly if everything starts to give way.'

'I had thought of that,' Philip replied amiably. 'It's like quicksand.'

The other two vehicles had arrived after passing through the gap. They had followed Philip's example, pointing uphill for a quick getaway. There was a crackle of gunfire even though the pursuing police cars, coming up fast, were still a quarter of a mile below them.

'Prepare to meet the enemy, as they said a hundred years ago,' Tweed ordered.

35

They divided up naturally into couples. Tweed and Paula were cautiously testing the stability of the enormous boulder. He gently leaned against it and the massive rock trembled. On the other end Paula's effort to move it failed. It remained rigid.

'It will take both of us to shift it when the time comes,' Tweed called out to Paula. 'At this end I can see through the gap when they're coming. When I shout "Now!" heave with all your strength.'

Beyond the gap Newman and Marler had tested two boulders very close together. They were positioned behind the smaller boulder, which still looked like a killer.

Beyond them Harry, with his partner Nield, also stood behind two boulders almost touching each other. Paula could see what had caused the boulders to pause where they had. Behind the rampart was quite a wide area of flat ground, before the surface again climbed steeply to another distant ridge. The flat area had slowed their momentum to almost nothing and the slight ridge they were perched against now had brought them to a halt. For the moment.

It was quiet now under the glow of the moon. Benlier must have ordered his men to silence their sirens so they could hear his commands. The three police cars had stopped moving for the moment and the only sound was the purr of their distance engines. There was no more crackle of futile gunfire and a heavy silence had settled over the Ardennes.

'Calm before the storm,' Paula said to herself.

Like the rest of the team she had donned her heavy motoring gloves. Bare hands pushing at the sharp-edged rocks would have ended up cut to ribbons and bleeding profusely. She stamped her booted legs on a flat rock to keep her circulation going. Then she walked over to where Tweed was peering round their giant boulder.

'Go back to your post,' he said quietly. 'When they come I'll shout "Now!" You push with all your strength. But be very careful you don't go with the boulder.'

'Understood.'

Their own three Land Rovers had been parked pointing uphill. The purr of their engines was lost with the engine sound of the police cars revving up.

'Won't be long now,' Tweed warned.

'Sooner the better,' Paula replied.

She was worried that her own weight added to Tweed's might not be enough to shift the massive boulder. She would have liked to have taken deep breaths but realized that wasn't a good idea. At this height the air was like liquid ice.

Peering round the end Tweed saw Benlier, motionless. He was wearing white gloves, which looked ridiculous. He was deliberately delaying to heighten the tension. To break their nerves.

Then his hands rose in the air, made a forward movement. He shouted a command which Tweed couldn't catch. The police cars accelerated upward, Benlier's in the lead, his two supporting cars behind him.

'Now!' shouted Tweed.

Paula put every ounce of strength into her push. No movement. Then the boulder was surging forward and down. She nearly went with it. Remembering Tweed's warning she dug her feet into the ridge, regained her balance, stared at the spectacle. An avalanche of boulders was speeding down the slope and now she could see the enemy.

With half his body exposed up through the open car's roof Benlier gazed in horror. 'Swerve!' he screamed at his driver, who never heard the order. Benlier was paralysed with fright. The world had gone. The moon had gone. The massive height of the boulder loomed over him. He tried to get back down inside his car but seconds had become years. The immense weight and size of the boulder hit the car, crushed it flat. Benlier's broken body was somewhere amid the smashed metal. Hardly pausing, the boulder trundled at increasing speed down the slope and soon, to Tweed and Paula, watching, it was no more than a large pebble a long way down.

Marler and Newman had got both their boulders moving. One police car swerved, avoided by inches the first boulder and was then flattened by the second boulder.

Further along the rampart Harry and Pete had both boulders moving together. Paula saw the panic-stricken driver swing to avoid them. He was broadside when both boulders hit him, turning the vehicle over as they crushed it.

The sudden silence over the Ardennes was a shock. Tweed focused his night-vision glasses, called out in a quiet voice.

'No sign of life. They're all dead.'

'Weapons,' Philip called back.

He darted downhill towards the carnage. Paula fled after him before Tweed could stop her. She caught up with Philip, who stopped to speak to her.

'This will be grisly.'

'No more than what I've seen in Professor Saafeld's lab,' she snapped back.

They reached the remnants of Benlier's car first. Protruding from an open door was half the body of a policeman who had tried futilely to escape. Taking off a glove, Paula bent down and grasped a telescopic truncheon from his belt. She wiped blood off the other end on his uniform. Philip had hauled out another truncheon from Heaven knew where. Then he gave a grunt of delight. From the belt of the same body he eased out a .32 automatic. He checked the weapon. It was fully loaded and uncontaminated with blood.

'Paula,' he said, standing up and grinning, 'a present for you.'

He handed her the automatic and she grasped it with pleasure. First, she double-checked the mechanism, noted it was fully loaded. Then she lifted up her fur coat, slid the weapon inside her left boot, which served as the leg holster she was not wearing.

Philip ran across the slope to the police car which had ended up broadside on, pulverized by the boulder sent down by Pete and Harry. He could hardly believe what he saw strewn across the ground. Four more telescopic truncheons.

He knew the Belgian police kept spares stacked on a shelf above the seats. The violent impact must have hurled them out of the window. With great satisfaction he gathered up his find. Newman with Marler and Pete with Harry arrived to see what was happening. He handed each of them a truncheon.

'Might I ask what is going on?' Tweed's stern voice called to them as he hurried down the slope.

'Weapons,' Philip said. He handed his own to Tweed.

'And why do we need these now that the police unit has been dealt with?'

'Because there are four guards at the Château les Rochers.'

'Never known how those things work,' Paula commented.

Tweed gripped the handle, then whipped it sideways quickly. The extension shot out and he was holding a truncheon at least half as long again. He handed it back to Philip after retracting the extension.

'You'll be more skilled with this that I am. So what's the next move, Philip?'

'We race to the top of the Ardennes. Then we launch our assault on the Château.'

Paula had expected the Château les Rochers to have a fairy-tale appearance. As they crawled over the last ridge she saw how wrong she had been. It was more like a medieval fortress with tiny turrets at the corners. In the centre of a flat roof reared a tall wide turret festooned with a system of wires and tall aerials. Tweed grunted as they paused.

'There's his communications centre perched even higher than the trees behind it. From here he controls his banking empire. I hope he's at home.'

*

Calouste *was* at home.

It was a mania with him to remain the Invisible Man. So he had had constructed at his different HQs a series of rooms underground – as at Shooter's Lodge. The same method had been organized at the Château. He was now working in a large, luxuriously furnished cellar under the Château.

There were two entrances. One was a large trap-door, now open from a ground-floor corridor which led down via half a dozen steps into his sanctum. The second entrance was above the desk where he was sitting. A flight of steps led up to a platform with a heavy iron door open. By the side of the door was a control system built into the wall with buttons numbered from one to twenty-four. On its own was a brown button which locked the less secure trapdoor.

Calouste was dressed in a velvet jacket, velvet trousers and tennis shoes. The room was dimly lit except for the powerful desk lamp by which he worked. He wore his tinted, gold-rimmed glasses through which he could see clearly. Above his spade-shaped jaw his mouth was moving rapidly as he issued instructions to various of his banks on his phone, linked to the sophisticated communications system on the top of the Château.

He had heard nothing of the commotion on the lower slopes of the Ardennes. Orion, his informant at Hengistbury, had warned him Tweed and his whole team had left the manor. His intuition had told him they were coming to Belgium. That was no problem. Inspector Benlier and his special unit would kill every member of that team. He was especially anxious to hear that Tweed was dead.

A coloured servant appeared on the platform above him. He was carrying a tray with a glass and a bottle of the finest cognac. Calouste poured a full glass from the bottle, then placed the bottle next to a Glock pistol. Calouste always bolstered his guards with his own weapon. It made him feel so safe. He drank to the end of Tweed, the major obstacle to his plans for the Main Chance Bank.

36

Skirting well clear of the grim fortress-like building with its tall communications turret, Tweed, with Paula by his side in the Land Rover, followed Philip's vehicle. Parked at the summit, he pointed as the others joined them.

Close to the rear fortress walls was a huge lake with a big dam at one end. Attached to the wall of the lake near the Château was a sizeable box with a thick coiled hose on top.

'What's the plan?' Tweed asked.

'Harry and I will lower the dam and a vast amount of water fed by natural springs on the top of that knoll will pour into the lake. Prior to that I'll have attached that hose to the inlet into the air-conditioning system. The other end of the hose I'll drop into the lake. On a recent recce I looked into a number of windows in the Château. All the rooms have a large air-conditioning grille let into the wall.'

'Will it work?' Paula wondered.

'You've forgotten Philip was a top engineer before he joined us.'

'And,' Harry remarked, 'the walls of the Château look shaky to me.'

'And Harry was once in the building trade,' Tweed added.

They watched as Harry dug inside a deep pocket in his windcheater, produced a chisel. Paula was amused. Harry would not go anywhere without his tool kit, now hidden in his spacious pockets. They watched as he bent close to the wall of the Château, hammered quietly at the mortar, which fell out. Brick-shaped stones above started to slide down.

'Whole miserable chute could collapse. No maintenance,' he said when he returned.

Philip waved to Harry to accompany him. First he hurried to the large aluminium chamber controlling the air-conditioning. Unscrewing a round plate with *Feu* stamped on it, he then forced one end of the thick rubber pipe inside the hole. The other end was dropped into the lake.

'I think that plate he removed,' Tweed said, 'is in case the air-conditioning system ever catches fire. The whole Château would be enveloped in flames. Unless huge quantities of water poured into it.'

'If you say so,' Paula replied dubiously.

Philip and Harry had now taken up positions at

either end of the dam behind huge wheels they began turning. Paula gazed in fascination as the top of the dam, smeared with green slime, began to sink rapidly. A wave of water penned up on the far side poured into the lake, then became a great flood as Philip and Harry continued turning their wheels.

'That's enough,' Philip said as he ran back with Harry.

Tweed felt in his overcoat pocket, pulled out something he'd forgotten was there. It was the crinkled-face mask worn by the thug he'd hurled over the chalk pit near Gladworth. He gave it to Philip.

'A peculiar object . . .'

'Made in Paris,' Philip told him, 'by the most expert mask maker in the world. Costs a fortune – it's so flexible. I think I'll wear this. Might gain us entry through the main door without a fuss.'

Arriving at the door, he hammered the heavy iron knocker. A man's face appeared when a Judas window was opened. The face looked startled.

'Oh, Mr Calouste. I thought you were in your office.'

Harry stood out of sight to one side of the door, truncheon in his hand. Turning of three keys, removal of several chains. Philip walked in, flipped his truncheon, smashed it on the man's head. He collapsed. Another man with a dagger appeared, raised it to strike Philip. Harry's truncheon struck his elbow. He gasped with pain, dropped the dagger as

Harry broke the other arm with his truncheon. A hard tap on the forehead and he collapsed on top of his fellow guard.

'That corridor ahead is straight and level,' Philip remarked. 'The one to our left slopes downward. Calouste is a mole. We'll find him somewhere along here underground . . .'

Paula slipped ahead of him, turned a corner, still going down, stopped. She pointed. Vague lighting showed a trapdoor, the lid raised vertically. Followed by the rest of the team she descended six steps after crossing a platform. The cellar-level room was large, dim except for a desk lamp at the far end. A figure was hunched over a desk with its back to her.

Harry paused, used a blurred torch to check the edges of the opening. Electrically operated. He took a small tube from his pocket, squirted a small amount of gunge between two of the electrodes. The gunge hardened immediately.

With their thick-rubber-soled boots they made no sound as they all descended to the platform. Beyond six stone steps led down into the weird room. Paula crept down to the floor.

Blinding lights flashed on. Calouste had crept up onto the platform above his desk. The team's eyes blinked in the glare. Calouste held a Glock pistol in his hand, aimed point-blank at Paula. Tweed, now at floor level, glanced anxiously at her as she stood with her back to the wall. Calouste spoke sneeringly in public-school English.

'All present and correct. If anyone moves an inch I will shoot Miss Grey in the chest.'

The team froze.

Paula glanced along the wall. Close to Calouste's platform an air-conditioning grille of some size was dribbling water. Calouste, in his velvet suit, was speaking again, theatrically.

'None of you will leave the Château alive.' His tone became sadistic. 'Your bodies will be eaten by crows, which round here are vicious. Not vegetarians.'

He chuckled. Not a pleasant sound. His eyes were as dead as his soul. Paula noticed the floor sloped down from where they stood. She fainted, sliding down the wall. Calouste was amused.

'She is scared to death. Quite rightly so. This is what is coming to her . . .'

The air-conditioning grille near Calouste was hurled across the room under the pressure of the water which had built up. A great flood rushed into the room as the second grille gave way. Calouste was momentarily distracted. Paula aimed her Browning, shot him in the left kneecap. Screaming with agony, Calouste dropped his Glock pistol, used both hands to clap his knee, still screaming. He lost his balance, fell off the platform into more than a foot of water.

The entire lake seemed to be entering the room.

Water surged towards where Tweed was standing. It was now at least three feet deep. He ran up the steps, ordering a general evacuation. When they had all reached the corridor the water below was six feet deep. Calouste was desperately trying to swim to their steps, with an odd dog-paddle of a movement. He reached the steps, clawed his way up to the platform as water slid across it. His face was now a picture of terror as he looked up, waving a clawlike hand.

'Please save me,' he screeched. 'Save me. I will give you millions!'

Harry stared down at him. He used one hand to lever the heavy trapdoor shut. Paula was sure she heard the crunch of skullbone. They were hurrying along the corridor when Harry pointed at water seeping through the walls, mortar coming loose.

'Let's get the hell out of here – the whole place is coming down.'

From near the summit of the knoll, where they had parked the cars, they watched the dramatic scene below. The Château was coming apart. The tall turret in the middle of the roof, with the fabulously expensive communications equipment, was tilting slowly towards the front wall. Its tempo of disintegration increased. It fell towards the wall facing the Ardennes slope, split into several sections and hammered a huge hole in the wall.

'Time we got moving,' Philip said.

'We're going to run the Brussels gauntlet again,' suggested Paula.

'No. We're driving down through the tiny state of Luxembourg. Heading for the airport outside the city. A late plane will leave for Heathrow. You've all got reserved seats. Here are your tickets. We must leave now.'

Philip's Land Rover led the way south. Tweed was seated next to him. Paula travelled in the rear seat. They quickly descended from the heights into narrow roads through defiles. On either side massive limestone cliffs hemmed them in with an occasional clump of trees by the roadside. Paula felt relieved to look at different scenery.

As a golden dawn glowed in the east they approached the airport, which was very quiet. A single plane waited some way out on the tarmac. Before passing easily through the formalities Tweed used Paula's mobile to call Monica and instruct her to use staff from Communications. His second call was to Jim Corcoran, Chief of Security at Heathrow, who said a bus would meet their plane. Finally, Tweed turned to Philip, shook him by the hand and thanked him warmly.

'Isn't Philip coming with us?' Paula asked.

'Not this time,' Philip said with a grin. 'My work is here in Europe. I'll be travelling a long way east . . .'

It was broad daylight when their plane took off. Paula looked at Tweed, asked him what he was thinking about.

'Who killed Bella, then Mrs Carlyle.'

37

Jim Corcoran, Chief of Security at Heathrow and close friend of Tweed's, met the plane with a small bus as soon as they landed.

'We're bypassing all security,' he told Tweed when they were all aboard. 'Explained you were SIS and pursuing a lead re. Terrorists. They phoned your Director, Howard, who confirmed it. Your transport is waiting in the parking lot.'

Tweed was soon behind the wheel of the Audi with Paula beside him. As they left the airport with the rest of the team in two Land Rovers he explained.

'I've spoken to Newman. Being a top newspaper writer he knew where to go. I need urgently to check November and December 1912 issues of the *Clarion*. Newman said Peg-Leg Pete was the answer. Peg-Leg is an eccentric. Collects old copies for a song and charges outrageously for you to see them on his rotating screen. Bob phoned him to have the issues ready.'

It had been broad daylight, sun blazing, when they landed at Heathrow. From there Paula navigated and eventually they reached Watersend Lane, at the wrong end of the East End. In the quiet cobbled street they saw a dirty window with the name *Peg-Leg Pete's* just visible in fading gold lettering.

They followed Newman inside while the rest of the team took up guard outside. A short burly individual appeared, with a wooden leg which tapped as he walked with the aid of a stick.

'Two hundred nicker,' he growled, hand held out. He glared at Tweed. 'Two 'undred pounds to your educated friend before you use the machine. *Clarion*s you want to see all ready for viewing.'

'No you don't, Peg-Leg,' Newman said roughly. 'Back into your office while my friend checks that he has what he needs.'

Taking Peg-Leg gently by one arm Newman guided him inside a small room, shut the door. Tweed had seated himself in a chair before a large microfilm reader. He turned a lever, scanned the page, used the lever again, then once more.

'Got it,' he said. He pointed to a paragraph with a headline.

MURDEROUS BANK ROBBERY

'Five copies of the whole paragraph, please.'

He waited while Paula used her non-flash camera. Then he put a finger on the date. Wednesday 7 November 1912.

When she had taken her photographs of the whole page he used the lever again. He found nothing until December issues appeared. Then he put his finger on another paragraph with a large headline. When she had her copies, automatically ejected from the camera, she knew what else he needed. She photographed the whole page with the date Thursday 12 December 1912.

'That's more than two 'undred nicker,' Peg-Leg shouted after he emerged again from his office, stick and leg tapping madly. Newman produced an envelope with two hundred pounds in banknotes, shoved it into the top pocket of Peg-Leg's well-worn woollen jacket.

'That's the fee you agreed, you old thief. So shut up. We're off.'

'I don't understand,' Paula said after they had left London and the three-vehicle convoy was heading south.

'You will,' Tweed assured her. 'Now it's full speed to the manor at Hengistbury and the solution of two horrible murders.'

'I hope that's all that faces you,' Paula mused who had on many occasions shown a deadly intuition.

38

Driving through the tunnel created by the mighty firs which closed above them Paula again had the same eerie feeling she had experienced when they first arrived. Relieved when they reached the entrance, they only had to wait seconds before the tall wrought-iron gates swung open.

'It's such a lovely day,' she remarked as Tweed drove to the foot of the steps, a remark she wished within minutes she'd never made. Behind them the other two vehicles drove round the back to park.

They ran up the steps and the left-hand door opened. Crystal was waiting to greet them instead of Lavinia. Like her half-sister she wore a white polo-necked sweater and a pleated white skirt. She stood very still, hands clasped in front of her.

'Welcome back,' she greeted them with the shadow of a smile. 'I have grim news for you. I'm determined not to give way to my volatile temperament.' She paused. 'Leo has been murdered.'

'We'll go into the library so you can sit down,' Tweed said, gently grasping her arm.

'Not necessary. But thank you.'

Tweed was shocked but concealed it. Paula watched Crystal closely but there was no sign of her breaking down. She had a stronger character than Paula had realized. As they entered the hall Chief Inspector Hammer came forward, his tone surprisingly sympathetic as he spoke to Crystal.

'I've kept my word. Let you tell Tweed what has happened. Now please, if you will, have a rest in the library while I have a private word with Mr Tweed.'

Crystal walked slowly away and into the library. She left the door open. Paula realized she was going to listen to make sure Hammer got it right.

'All the details, please,' Tweed requested.

'Killed the same way the others were. One of those unpleasant – I mean horrible – collars slipped over his head and neck from behind him in his apartment. He was sitting in a chair. Throat ripped out. I called Buchanan, who called Professor Saafeld. The Professor came straight down in the middle of the night in his Rolls with a team of medics. Until the autopsy, he calculates the murder took place between midnight and 2 a.m. this morning, subject to the usual et ceteras. I've interviewed everyone and they were all, so they say, asleep alone in their apartments. No alibis again.'

'Where is Lavinia?' Tweed asked. 'She usually opens the gates.'

Crystal came walking steadily out of the library. Paula marvelled at her self-control. She spoke firmly.

'I'm worried about Lavinia.'

'Why?' Tweed asked. 'Where is she?'

'Just after breakfast Marshal said he was going down to Seacove. He pressed Lavinia to come with him.'

'*Pressed*?' Tweed queried.

'She didn't seem too pleased at the idea. She accompanied him to the car dressed in that large overcoat because it was cold at that hour. He leaned over from the driving seat, caught hold of her by the arm and she agreed when he said he needed some company. She got in and Marshal drove off.'

'How long ago was this?' Tweed asked anxiously.

'About an hour ago. Oh, there was something else peculiar. I went out to Snape's cabin and found the gun cupboard had been broken into. Someone has stolen the Winchester shotgun.'

'Hammer,' Tweed said speaking rapidly, 'I'm leaving you in charge again. We have to rush off.'

'Where to?' asked Paula as they ran down the steps.

'To Seacove,' he replied as he jumped behind the wheel.

'Why?' she asked as she settled beside him.

'I just hope we're in time – to prevent a fourth murder.'

Paula would never forget the long drive to Seacove. Tweed swung round steep bends like a driver at Le Mans, always just inside the speed limit. He avoided the motorway often a short distance above them. He had chosen the country road the motorway had replaced.

'Too much traffic,' he replied when Paula referred to the motorway. 'Heavy trucks delivering to the West Country. That Rolls is an hour ahead of us.'

'What had disturbed you?' she asked.

'The missing Winchester shotgun.'

'You want to get there as fast as we can?'

'That's the idea.'

'Then call in at the first garage we come to.'

'Can't waste the time.'

'So how do we make it on no petrol? Look at the fuel gauge.'

Tweed glanced down. The needle was close to zero. How much longer before the engine simply stopped? He glanced at Paula.

'Good job somebody aboard has brains.'

'Don't worry.' She touched his arm. 'We're bound to find a petrol station soon.'

But are we? He wondered. This was a lonely country road. No car had passed them in the opposite direction for miles. We could be sitting out here in the middle of nowhere for ages, he thought. He kept the anxiety to himself.

The sun blazed down on beautiful countryside. Purple and gold crocuses in clumps flared on the verge, backed by masses of yellow daffodils. Rolling green hills swept up on either side. Spring had at last flourished. Tweed forced himself not to check the position of the needle on the gauge. They were in Dorset now and Paula revelled in the freshness of the world.

They rounded a bend and a hundred yards ahead several pumps were spaced in front of a small petrol station. Paula dug him in the ribs.

'See?' Paula called out to him. 'I'll get out to fill up.'

For Tweed the process seemed to take forever. Then it seemed to take an age for her to pay inside the station. He realized his fingers were rapping quietly on the wheel. He stopped. A tapping on the window on the passenger side. It was Paula. She pointed at the gauge. A full tank. He gave her a great big smile. She came back, sank into her seat.

'The Audi Express is rolling again. Would Leo have let *anyone* into his apartment at that early morning hour?'

'He was surrounded by family, people he lived with. Could have been anyone. Let's hope the weather lasts.'

'Any theory as to why he was killed?' she persisted.

'At a pure guess he may have overheard the

unknown spy phoning Calouste to tell him we were all leaving the manor. Now will you please keep quiet. I don't like conversation when I am concentrating on driving at this speed.'

Paula kept very quiet. She knew Tweed was thinking about Leo's brutal murder. In her mind she listed the people who were in the manor that night. Marshal, Lavinia, Warner, Crystal and Mrs Grandy who, so far, had not figured prominently at all in the events at Hengistbury.

She suddenly leaned forward. They were crossing the border into Cornwall. Instead of rolling green hills there were now bleak limestone ridges inland looming towards the sea, which had made its first appearance to their left.

Worse still, the sun had vanished. Drifting in rapidly from the west, menacing black storm clouds filled the sky. So dense, so low there were like mobile mountains. Tweed switched on his headlights. Heavy mist vapours were sliding over the ridges, blotting them out. A wind was rising, smearing the windscreen with the mist. Tweed started his wipers. The atmosphere was abruptly warm and cloying.

'Let's hope they haven't taken out that so-called wonder yacht, as Marshal once called it, in these conditions,' Tweed said aloud to himself.

They crested a ridge, saw ahead the long steeply sloping road and Seacove. In the distance below them they saw the white cottages, bunched together with a gap where the *Sea Sprite*'s ramp plunged down to the edge of the pebble beach. No sign of anyone. Paula gave a little gasp.

'What is it?' Tweed asked.

'Look out to the south. That fool Marshal is taking out the yacht across Oyster Bay. And he's heading straight for the gap between the capes. He's steering the vessel out into the ocean. The waves out there are storm-high.'

'Maybe we are too late,' Tweed said quietly.

39

Arriving at the beach they parked the Audi. Paula rushed out and ran through the open door into Marshal's cottage. She was only inside a short time and ran out to where Tweed was standing about ten feet away from the ramp.

'Lavinia's not in the cottage,' she said breathlessly. 'The crazy Marshal has taken her aboard.'

'Not completely crazy,' Tweed assured her. 'He's coming back in. Didn't like the look of what he saw.'

No wonder, Paula thought as she stared out at Oyster Bay and what lay outside. A fresh storm was churning the sea into mountainous waves which collided with each other, hurling up massive clouds of spray.

The yacht was racing towards the shore as oceanic waves came into the bay as though pursuing the craft. Paula watched its progress, praying the vessel would make it to the ramp.

'It does look very like a miniature cruise liner,' she remarked. Her voice changed, she gripped Tweed's arm. 'Oh my Lord – he's going off course, must have been gripped by that underwater current.'

Tweed stared. For a few minutes it was very quiet. Paula had the impression she'd heard another engine, then realized that Marshal had adjusted the throttle in a desperate attempt to change course. He failed to do so. The yacht was heading at speed for Pindle Rock. They stood close together in silence as the forward part of the vessel smashed into Pindle with a breaking sound they clearly heard. The forward section seemed to climb up the craggy rocks, then slowly sink back. They were stunned by the next development.

The rear section split away, became a separate craft as doors opened at what became the prow. At the rear an emergency wheelhouse, enclosed with glass, stood above the forward deck with a rudder projecting from the new stern.

'My God!' Paula exclaimed. 'It works.'

'Never thought it would,' Tweed agreed.

He focused his binoculars on the elevated wheelhouse. He saw Marshal with his flamboyant blue peaked cap operating the wheel. He saw the amateur skipper slip into a yellow oilskin, pulling the hood down. To see clearly, the skipper had lowered his front window and was being splashed by the wild sea.

'He might just make the ramp,' Paula shouted now the wind had risen.

'It's possible.'

'Be more optimistic,' she snapped.

'There's a giant of a wave coming up behind him.'

'It might just help him to make the shore. Do be positive,' Paula chided.

'There's blood on Pindle Rock,' Tweed warned.

'He must have been injured. It was one hell of a crash when the ship hit.'

'Possibly.'

'You have to be so downbeat?'

'I have to be so realistic,' he shot back at her.

'I don't see any blood,' she argued, scanning the rock with her binoculars.

'Not now. A burst of spray just washed it clean.'

'You imagined it,' she snapped.

'You're tense,' he told her. 'Take a deep breath, slow down.'

'I'm never tense,' she snapped again.

'I'm ordering you to take a really deep breath. Now!'

She was almost leaning against him. She took a really deep breath, held it, let it go. Salty air filled her lungs. She felt the tension ease out of her. Tweed had been right.

'Here it comes,' Tweed said cheerfully.

The strange vessel was being hurled in on the crest of a huge wave, skilfully steered to reach the ramp. The engine was switched off to slow it down. It cruised up the ramp close to them, stopped opposite to where they stood. Paula heaved a sigh of relief.

The skipper climbed down steps from the wheel-house, stomped stiff-legged across the deck, within ten feet of where they stood, staying on the other side of the hull. With a swift movement of oilskin hood and coat were removed, thrown on the deck. Long black hair draped down to the neck. From under the cast-off oilskin coat the Winchester shotgun appeared, pointed point blank at both of them.

'Stay close. Any move and I'll send you both to hell with one blast,' said Lavinia.

40

'Lavinia! What are you doing?'

Paula's voice was full of shock and disbelief. She stared at the hard chin, the white face, the shotgun held so steady in her strong hands.

'Having already murdered Bella, Mrs Carlyle and Leo,' Tweed said in the calm voice he always used in a crisis, 'she now proposes to murder both of us. How, Lavinia, if I may ask, how do you propose to get rid of our bodies?'

'Good question, Mr Tweed. Dump you aboard the deck behind me. Then send the ship out across the bay into the Atlantic. OK with you?' she asked with a sneering smile.

Paula was appalled by the sheer callousness of Lavinia's reply. Her brain was spinning with shock. Lavinia's next words didn't help.

'You've lost count, Mr Tweed. Look at the far side of the deck. Recognize the corpse curled against the hull?'

'Marshal,' he replied promptly. 'With a necklace which has ripped out his throat. Patricide, the murder of one's father, is regarded as the most contemptible of all crimes.'

'*My father?*' Lavinia's voice was venomous. 'I hated him, my pseudo-father. I was conceived when he played with Mrs Mandy Carlyle, the tramp who charged so much a night. *She* was my pseudo-mother. May she rot in hell. My own mother couldn't have a child, desperately wanted one. Marshal had the idea when Mandy Carlyle became pregnant by him to admit what had happened to my real mother. She agreed to go with the Carlyle bag to a dubious expensive nursing home well away from Hengistbury. My real mother had pretended to be pregnant. When I was born my real mother took me back to Hengistbury as her own child. The clinic where it happened faked papers to cover up the impersonation.' Her voice became grimmer. 'Can you visualize how I came to hate my pseudo-father?'

'Yes, I can,' Tweed said quietly. 'How did you find out?'

'You know that.'

Keep her talking, he said to himself. He had seen the safety catch on the shotgun was released. Lavinia had only to press the trigger and both of them would be dead.

'I'd like you to tell me, please.'

'I found Marshal's secret chequebook. Large sums

paid out to the Carlyle bitch. Blackmail. I guessed why.'

'Why did you murder Bella?'

'Obvious. She stood in my way for my ultimate succession as the bank's owner.' Lavinia's lip curled in the same sneering smile. 'She was eighty-four. She'd had her time.'

Paula was again appalled at the same sheer callousness.

'Logical,' Tweed agreed, his face devoid of expression. 'So why murder Mrs Carlyle?'

'Obvious again. I loathed the woman. And she could become dangerous, resuming the blackmailing of Marshal.'

'What happened when you arrived at Dodd's End?'

'I told her who I was. She sneered, said it was pleasant to meet her only daughter. She was drunk, and hardly got out of her chair.'

'So what happened next?'

'Her remark incensed me. I had a collar inside a carrier. I said I needed a drink, went behind her towards the drinks cupboard. It was so easy. I slid the collar down over her filthy head.' She grinned. 'I've never used more strength than when I tightened the collar. I nearly took her head off her shoulders.'

'Understandable,' said Tweed, forcing himself to play up to her. 'But how did you know her address?'

'Marshal, the idiot, had scribbled it down at the end of one of the secret cheque-books.'

'Why had Leo to be removed?'

'Oh, Leo.' She grinned, a sadistic grin. 'He overheard a call I made to Calouste warning him you'd all left the manor. I knew he'd gabble so he had to go.'

'Again logical,' Tweed agreed in the same quiet voice. 'And now Marshal?'

'Again obvious. He inherited the bank. He was standing in the way of my taking it over. Bella has left a final will naming me as owner if Marshal and Warner are no longer alive.'

'You know that because you took the will Bella handed to you, sealed when I first visited her.'

'Really?' She tossed her head. 'Solicitors are not allowed to reveal such documents. So how do you know that?' she asked, her curiosity aroused.

'You pretended to have a long lunch at the Pike's Peak Hotel in Gladworth. Actually, you were busy seducing the solicitor so he'd show you the will and then put it in a legal envelope and re-seal it. How do I know that? I took the trouble to phone the hotel proprietor and ask him if you had lunch there that day. He told me no one had had lunch there that day. I began to wonder what you had been up to.'

'Clever Mr Tweed.'

'And Calouste Doubenkian is dead. Drowned when his chateau was flooded.'

'Really?' She raised her eyebrows. 'Then I can sell to the Sultan. They crave gold in the Far East.'

'Gold?' He gazed into the deep-blue pools of her eyes. He could read her now. A hint of pure evil in the blank eyes.

'You'd have made a very first-rate detective, Mr Tweed,' she observed as she levelled the shotgun.

There was a loud explosion which echoed in the brief silence.

41

Marler had landed his plane earlier, risking flying down through the mist, parking it on the small private airfield hidden behind the cottages.

For some time he had lain full length on the sloping roof on the inland side of Marshal's cottage. He had summed up the critical situation and for some time his Armalite had rested, out of sight on the rooftop.

He had heard every word in the oppressive silence hanging over the beach. His crosshairs had had Lavinia's profile for the whole period. He had realized Tweed was extracting as much confirmation from Lavinia as he could, that he was desperately but skilfully keeping her talking.

When he heard her last remark, saw her level the shotgun, he pressed the trigger. He was using an explosive bullet.

42

The bullet had removed half Lavinia's head. Blood streamed out of her. She was so close to the hull she fell backwards, legs in the air as she collapsed heavily on the far side of the hull, her body pressing heavily on the starting lever.

The engine burst into full power. She had pressed the lever fully down, to top speed. The shotgun had fallen with her onto the deck. Marler joined them and Paula flung her arms round him.

'You always turn up in the nick of time, Marler,' Tweed said. 'Thank you.'

He was watching the progress of the vessel with both bodies aboard. It had raced down the ramp, just in time to catch the crest of a monster wave. It carried the vessel across Oyster Bay, a rolling leviathan.

'It does appear to be headed for the exit from the bay,' Marler remarked.

Paula stared at the sea beyond the two capes

enclosing the bay. A fresh and very violent storm had arrived. Immense waves were colliding with each other, hurling up tons of water. Nothing could survive in that maelstrom.

The remnants of the yacht were still perched on the crest of the wave moving at extraordinary speed. It carried the yacht exactly between the capes and entered the Atlantic. Tweed was using his binoculars.

'Both bodies are still on board. They appear to be trapped amid a huge coil of rope anchored to the deck.'

The craft was hurled from the crest of its wave into the churning sea. Through his binoculars Tweed saw it tossed from one wave to another, amazingly still upright with the corpses entangled in the ropes. Then at great speed, it plunged downwards, deep, deep, deep. It did not reappear.

'The bodies are still aboard,' reported Marler, who had been using his own binoculars. 'The Coastguard will never find anything.'

'And,' Tweed said, 'the remnants of the forward section which hit Pindle have already been carried into the Atlantic.'

'It's over,' said Paula, who suddenly realized her hands had remained clenched fists inside her windcheater pockets.

'*No!*' Tweed warned. 'It's not quite over yet. Back to Hengistbury now.'

*

Marler flew back to the private airfield he had found near Leaminster. It was the second time he had watched over his friends during their two visits to Seacove.

Later, her mind full of the traumatic events she had witnessed, Paula could never remember the long drive back. Crystal, who had opened the gates, met them at the entrance to the hall. She stood very erect and managed a smile of welcome.

'I need to see your father urgently,' Tweed told her.

'He's working in his apartment.'

Warner Chance was seated at his desk, a pile of accounts on the wide surface. Tweed immediately gave him a censored version of what had happened – how Marshal had taken Lavinia out in the yacht, how they were in the Atlantic when a storm of great violence had blown up and sunk the yacht. No survivors. Entering the apartment, Tweed had noticed a crumpled handkerchief on the desk. He could learn the truth later.

'Now, Mr Chance . . .' Tweed began

'Please call me Warner.'

'Now, Warner – the gold.'

'Gold?'

'Paula,' Tweed continued, 'show Warner those newspaper clippings we obtained from Peg-Leg Pete.'

She arranged them in sequence on the desk in front of Warner.

MURDEROUS BANK ROBBERY

> Last night three men were murdered when raiders attacked Klempner's, a subsidiary of the great Kreditanstalt in Vienna. The Director and his two assistants, still on the premises at midnight, were shot dead by two masked men. £800,000 of gold bullion was then loaded onto waiting lorries which then vanished. The police have as yet no clue as to the identity of the murderers.

Paula next produced a photograph of the complete sheet from which the report had been extracted.

'Note the date,' Tweed said, '6 November 1912.'

Paula then produced the second extract from the *Clarion*.

THE MAIN CHANCE BANK ESTABLISHED TODAY

> Ezra Main and Pitt Chance have founded a new powerful and important bank, the Main Chance. The Banking Authority has confirmed this new addition has more than adequate resources to conduct national and international business.

'Now look at the date,' Tweed demanded as Paula spread the second sheet. '12 December 1912. Just about a month after the bullion raid. The "adequate assets".'

'I didn't know.' Warner held his head in his hands. 'And I'm sure Bella never knew.'

'Earlier,' Tweed drummed on, 'on my instructions Paula went to the Land Registry in Gladworth. She obtained a copy of the plans of Hengistbury, different from the ones we were shown for searching the manor. The ones she obtained show a vast labyrinth of cellars under the manor. May we visit them now? It's the brown button, so-called for emergencies, in the lift, I suspect . . .'

The three of them were inside the lift when Warner pressed the brown button. They descended. When the doors opened again they walked out into a complex of stone-walled cellars. Warner stopped before a massive steel door, consulted a small black notebook he had discovered inside one of Bella's secret drawers. Operating the combination, he stood back as the door swung open.

They walked inside a large steel chamber with strong shelves. They had entered an Aladdin's cave. All around them gold bars were piled up to the ceiling. A strong wheeled trolley stood at the far end.

'What the hell am I going to do with all this?' Warner asked wearily. 'I don't want it. The bank is, incredibly, solvent on the cash deposits alone.'

'Klempner's was a subsidiary of the Kreditanstalt in Vienna,' Tweed said as though talking to himself.

'When it – the Kreditanstalt – crashed, bankrupt, few people know that was what triggered Wall Street's Black Monday, followed by the slump. So this gold no longer belongs to anyone. Surely it could be sold, a few bars at a time to bullion collectors. That's not advice. If necessary, I'll deny I ever said it. I'm sure that the bank will flourish in your hands.'

'Now Lavinia is gone,' Warner said, 'I'm appointing Crystal as Chief Accountant. Maybe it's the shock of Leo's death, but she has suddenly grown up.'

'And she'll be a great ally for you,' said Paula.

'We must be off now,' announced Tweed.

Epilogue

At Park Crescent the whole team, which had assembled earlier, had rushed off home to put on evening dress. Except for Paula.

Tweed had told them he was taking them to dinner at Mungano's, the most expensive restaurant in town. Paula opened a clothes cupboard.

'I've got a new outfit, protectively covered, in here. They will appreciate your gesture.'

'It's what all of you deserve.'

'You're sitting there like a statue looking so incredibly thoughtful. Why?'

'I'm really wondering whether I got this case right.'

'What? I don't understand.'

'A phrase someone uttered keeps singing through my mind.'

'What phrase?' she asked, perching on his desk.

'You remember they were playing roulette in the library? And Marshal got furious, lifted the wheel off the table, threw it out onto the terrace.'

'Yes.'

'Do you recall what Warner Chance then said?'

'No, I don't. What did he say?'

'"*Winner takes all.*"'

Don't miss these other
Colin Forbes titles!

POCKET
BOOKS

The Cell

COLIN FORBES

Is Al-Qa'eda about to attack London? Tweed, reverting to his one-time role as shrewd detective, is convinced of this. Aided by Paula Grey and Bob Newman, he skillfully eludes Government security services who believe that he is wrong.

The village of Carpford, hidden high in the North Downs, catches Tweed's attention. With its strange assortment of inhabitants – Victor Warner, arrogant Minister of Security; fascinating but duplicitous Eva Brand; Margesson, fanatical preacher – could it be a staging post for the terrorists? Key informants start to disappear overnight.

Time has run out. This Tweed does know. But what is the target and when will the attack be launched? And *where*?

Could it happen here, as it did in America?

ISBN 0 7434 6138 X
PRICE £6.99

POCKET
BOOKS

The Vorpal Blade

COLIN FORBES

An investigation into a number of horrific and apparently disconnected murders sweeps Tweed across the world.

The Vorpal Blade advances into gripping new territory. Tweed has reverted to his one-time role of Homicide Superintendent at the Yard. He also retains his position as Deputy Director of the SIS. Paula Grey and Bob Newman still assist him.

Tweed has suspicions about the strange Arbogast banking family. Roman, the bank's owner; his niece, the brilliant Marienetta; his daughter, the volatile Sophie. Wherever they go, the American Vice President follows. Why?

Tweed realizes enormous power lies behind the five murders. But it is shrewd, stubborn Paula Grey, risking her life, who eventually tracks down the wielder of the blade. By herself, underground in a remote mountainous zone.

ISBN 0 7434 4035 8
PRICE £6.99

POCKET
BOOKS

No Mercy

COLIN FORBES

A man is found by Chief Superintendent Buchanan sitting on the steps of Whitehall. The man has apparently lost his memory. He utters only three words: *I witnessed murder* … Buchanan calls him Michael, hands him over to a reluctant Tweed, ex-Scotland Yard star detective, now Deputy Director of the SIS. Events lead Tweed with his assistant, Paula Grey, to desolate Dartmoor, accompanied by Michael. There they discover two skeletons. Later, two more – one in London, the fourth on a Sussex canal boat.

The wealthy Volkanian family, from Armenia, have a mansion on Dartmoor. Are they involved? Key characters are Lucinda Voyles and Anne Barton. There is a new development. A strange freighter, cargo holds empty, is spotted heading from the Mediterranean towards the Cornish coast. Tweed suspects the vessel is linked to the four horrific murders.

The relentless pace of Tweed's investigation accelerates. Can he break the case before a sinister deadline? He fights ruthlessly to do so – in a riveting double climax.

ISBN 0 7434 9001 0
PRICE £6.99